JAMES AXLER

DEATH LANDS®

Ground Zero

A GOLD EAGLE BOOK FROM

WORLDWIDE®

TORONTO • NEW YORK • LONDON
AMSTERDAM • PARIS • SYDNEY • HAMBURG
STOCKHOLM • ATHENS • TOKYO • MILAN
MADRID • WARSAW • BUDAPEST • AUCKLAND

You can argue about a lot of things, but there's not much
dispute about who is the finest character actor ever. It's
Harry Dean Stanton. This book is dedicated to him as a
small thanks for the countless fine films that he has
decorated with his presence. And if you see him,
tell him that from me.

First edition July 1995

ISBN 0-373-62527-8

GROUND ZERO

Printed in U.S.A.

The White House, the Lincoln Memorial, the parks and fountains of the most beautiful city of the United States. It fills me with hope and pride to know that whatever might happen to this dusty old planet of ours, these things will never, ever vanish from Washington.

> —From: "A Thousand Ages in Thy Sight—An Informed Comment on the Permanence of the U.S.A.," by Angus Beauregard Wells, pub Cresta Press of Ontario, January 13, 2001 (Seven days before skydark and the end of Washington, D.C.—and the U.S.A.)

Prologue

Ryan Cawdor looked back one last time. The gusting wind suddenly tugged back the white fog, like a curtain across a huge window, revealing the shore.

There were the jumbled rocks.

Trader and Abe, standing side by side, faced away from the ocean. Surrounding them was a menacing circle of men, looking, as far as Ryan could make out, like a mix of brushwood survivors and some capering scabbies.

And at the front, leading them, was the unmistakable figure of Straub.

There wasn't a thing that could be done.

As the raft bobbed on the current, Ryan whispered, "No, Trader, nothing's forever."

Chapter One

The fog was growing ever thicker, swirling around the waterlogged raft. The currents were so fast and treacherous that Ryan's big worry was trying to steer a course out to the island that hid the redoubt.

The crossing wasn't far off three-quarters of a mile. If they missed the island, then they could easily find themselves plowing remorselessly out into the Cific Ocean. With the offshore drift and a vicious undertow, it could mean the end for all of them.

"More left!" called J. B. Dix, working hard at the broken piece of wood that was his paddle.

The clumsy craft lurched from side to side, sometimes seeming as though it might have gone through a complete circle. Ryan had a highly developed sense of direction, but even he was becoming confused.

He was also finding it difficult to concentrate on reaching safety, part of his mind retaining that last, solitary image of Trader and Abe, together, surrounded by what had looked in the mist-veiled glimpse like fifteen or twenty enemies, including the dangerous and murderous stranger called Straub.

Ryan had been reminded of a place that he'd visited with Trader and the war wags about fifteen years earlier, up in Montana, not far from a ville called Billings.

It had been the site of an old battlefield, on slopes of sun-browned grass, above a winding river that the locals called the Little Bighorn. There had been a ruined building with a tumbled sign proclaiming that it had once been a Visitor's Center.

Inside there'd been a damp-stained diorama of the climax of the fight, a blond man with long hair and beard, standing alone in a field of dead blue-coat soldiers, firing his revolver at circling hostile Native Americans.

That was the image that kept returning to Ryan, burning into his brain with every stroke of his paddle.

His eleven-year-old son, Dean, was at his side, constantly turning to look behind them. "Think they'll be all right, Dad? Trader and Abe?"

"'Course. Trader could fall into a live volcano and come out complaining he was cold."

"But I thought I saw—"

Ryan turned his one good eye toward his son, warning him with an angry glance. "Shut it, son. Just work on getting safely to that island."

The boy bit his lip and did what his father had told him.

J.B. paused for a moment, fighting for breath. "Dark night! The stink from those sulfur springs makes it hard going." He looked at Ryan. "Thought I heard an Armalite three or four minutes ago, and a big hand blaster. Sounded to me like Abe's .357 Colt Python. But the noise was flattened and distorted by the mist."

Ryan stopped paddling. "Tell you about it when we reach the island," he panted.

Krysty Wroth was kneeling waist-deep in the cold gray water on his other side. Her bright red hair was dulled, coiled tight around her nape. She rubbed at her hands, peering down at incipient blisters, managing a smile at Ryan, her deep emerald eyes the brightest thing to be seen.

"Felt trouble. Soon as Trader pushed off and wouldn't join us on the raft. Figures, good old Abe going with him."

"Feel anything now? Living or dying?"

"No. You saw them?"

"Yeah. And some brushwooders and scabbies."

She whistled. "Bad news."

"Worse to come. Straub was there. Spotted his shaved head. Think they might've bought the farm back there."

"Nothing we could've done, lover."

"I know that. My head tells me that. My heart tells me about the debt I owed Trader." He wiped salt spray from his face. "Those years me and J.B. rode with him."

"The tide had the last word." Krysty readied herself to start paddling again. "I got the feeling we're not far from the redoubt now."

"Then let's go for it."

Resuming paddling caused him a lot of serious pain. He had been wounded with an arrow through the lower back. The shaft had been withdrawn, but there'd been no time to rest, and he was aware that he'd lost a fair drop of blood.

He looked at J.B., who'd taken a musket ball through the fleshy part of his upper left arm in the same firefight. The skinny figure was doing sterling work, working his paddle right-handed. He'd taken off his glasses to protect them from the ceaseless spray, putting them safely in one of his capacious pockets. His battered fedora was pulled down over his forehead.

Jak Lauren had also been wounded, his right calf being peppered with jagged splinters of rock from a near miss. But the albino teenager was as blank-faced as ever, sitting astride one of the longer logs that made up the raft, his stark white hair pasted flat to his angular skull, his red eyes smoldering like backlit rubies. Every now and again Jak would stop working at rowing, looking carefully around him for any sign of hostile life beneath the heaving waters.

The other two people battling the ocean sat close together near what was, notionally, the bow of the raft.

One was a stockily built black woman in her middle thirties, working away at her paddle with an inexorable sense of purpose, the beads in her plaited hair rattling at every stroke. Dr. Mildred Wyeth had been born a week before Christmas in 1964. On December 28, in the year 2000, she was in hospital in her hometown of Lincoln, Nebraska, to undergo a surgical procedure for a suspected minor abdominal problem.

Things had gone wrong, and she had been taken unconscious from the operating room to be medically frozen—cryogenics, ironically her own particular speciality.

She had slept on, untouched, during the horrific nuclear holocaust that had wiped out ninety-nine hundredths of the world's population, strike and counterstrike from both sides of the political walls, beginning only three weeks after she had been hermetically sealed into her capsule.

Nearly one hundred years passed before Ryan and his companions had come along and revived her.

Mildred's story was truly amazing.

But the life of the tall gray-haired man paddling hard next to her, his antiquated frock coat blackened with seawater, was even more astounding.

Dr. Theophilus Algernon Tanner, answering most commonly to plain old Doc, had earned a science degree from Harvard, then the doctorate of philosophy from Oxford University in England.

Doc had been born in the beautiful hamlet of South Strafford, Vermont, on a cold and snowy Saint Valentine's Day in 1868, which by one way of counting, made him somewhere around two hundred years and a few decades old.

He'd married Emily Chandler in June of 1891. There'd been two children, Rachel and little Jolyon, and five and a half years of transcendental happiness for the family, with a future as bright as a newly minted silver dollar. But a time trawling experiment wrenched him from everything near and dear, a victim of Operation Chronos, devised by men of science with no thought for consequences.

"Rocks ahead," Jak called. "Hear them. Bit right."
He pointed with his bleached, long-fingered hand.

Those on the left of the raft paddled a little harder, while the other rested, feeling the tangled bulk of ill-matched wood swing ponderously in the right direction.

Now Ryan could hear the whispering of waves. He risked standing, and saw a jagged crest of rock a couple of hundred feet above the low-lying fog. On an impulse he glanced behind him, but all he could see was a solid wall of gray-white fog, the stink of sulfur filling his nostrils.

There was no going back.

THEY HIT A SHELVING BANK of granite, grinding onto it, in the middle of a bank of glittering brown weed.

"Watch out for crabs," Dean said, remembering their departure from the island.

But they saw no sort of marine life as they all scrambled wetly and safely into eighteen inches of water, and walked up onto dry rock. Above them, black-headed gulls dived and shrieked at the seven invaders.

"Might as well get straight to the redoubt," Ryan stated. "No point waiting around here getting colder."

"How about Trader and Abe?" J.B. asked. "We going back for them?"

Ryan quickly told everyone what he'd seen.

When he'd finished, J.B. nodded. "Right. Current's against us. Lucky to make it here with the raft breaking up under us. Trader'll find his own path."

Mildred shook her head. "Christ, I sometimes get so tired of you tough, brave, taciturn men!"

"What's wrong?" Ryan asked. "We can't get back there. His choice."

"It isn't that. God only knows, I didn't care much for Trader, though I could see the strengths that made him what he was. And the weaknesses that prevented him ever changing. Now he and Abe are almost certainly dead back there, and you and John just button up the grief and pretend like it somehow hasn't happened. Don't you care?"

J.B. answered her, laying a hand gently on her shoulder. "'Course we care. You add up the number of friends that Ryan and me have lost in Deathlands in the last fifteen or twenty years, and you'll still be counting this time next month."

Ryan nodded. "Caring for the passing of a friend is a luxury.... The price is too high, Mildred."

"Bullshit! Posturing macho bullshit!"

"No, it's not," Ryan pointed an accusing finger at her. "Think I don't know about grieving? We all do here. Every one of us. We've all lost friends, fathers, brothers, mothers, sisters, loved ones...."

"Children," Doc added quietly.

Ryan went on. "All of us, Mildred. I read an old book once when we were with Trader. Holed up in a library... That the right word for a predark place where they kept a bunch of books? Right. It was called *A Time To Mourn*. Still remember its name. Said that if you didn't take a couple of weeks to mourn when you'd lost someone you loved, then it sort of twisted inward. We don't have two weeks for everyone who died. It isn't macho bullshit to say that. We'd be grieving all our lives, Mildred."

For a long moment the black woman glowered at the one-eyed man, the tension between them almost visible.

Finally she broke the stillness. "Every man pays his price to live with himself on the terms that he wills," she said. "My Uncle Josh told me that."

"Kipling, my dear madam." Doc smiled, showing his strangely perfect set of teeth. "I believe that is from the works of the English poet, Rudyard Kipling. My father met him. I rather think that they were both members of a masonic order."

"Dad?"

"What is it, Dean?"

"Getting double cold, Dad."

"Right. You're right, son. Let's go inside."

THE OLD BLACKTOP up to the entrance level was a tough climb, and everyone was out of breath by the time they reached the massive sec doors.

It was particularly hard going for the injured Jak, and he ended up hanging on to Krysty's and Mildred's shoulders, his wounded right leg off the ground.

They set him down, where he sat against a large wind-washed boulder, the streaks of quartz in it matching his complexion. Krysty joined Ryan.

"Needs a rest, lover," she said. "Probably you and J.B. do as well, only you're too manly to admit it."

Ryan had been aware during the climb up the ruined highway that there was fresh blood trickling yet again over his thighs from the arrow wound.

"Could be. Dean?"

"Yeah?"

"Open her up. Remember the code?"

"'Course. Three and five and two."

"Do it."

"All the way, Dad?"

"Sure."

Almost instantly Ryan heard the familiar high-pitched whining of the hydraulic gears, then the deep-buried grinding of the powerful motor as it struggled to lift the immense weight of the vanadium-steel doors.

"We should get some rain," Krysty commented. "Skies darkening over to the east. Can't even see the tops of the Sierras now."

Ryan looked, seeing a great squat mass of black cloud, winging toward them. The faint lacing of purple-silver lightning warned of a severe chem storm.

"Be inside and safe," he said.

Jak was on his feet, hopping toward the redoubt entrance, shrugging off an offer of help from Dean. Doc followed him, with Mildred and J.B. at his heels. The boy stood by the internal set of controls, waiting impatiently for Krysty and his father to join them.

Thunder rumbled. Ryan glanced around for a last look at this particular bleak section of Deathlands. The clouds seemed almost on top of them, and he actually felt the first heavy drops of rain, acid on his skin.

It wouldn't have been good to get caught out in it.

"Close her up again," he said, as he and Krysty entered the shadowy passages of the redoubt.

"Two and five and three," the boy muttered, triggering the buttons on the control that closed the sec doors. As they dropped down, everyone could see the rain already bouncing off the blacktop.

The moment they reached floor level, with the faintest metallic whisper, all outside sounds vanished. There could have been the worst chem storm in history raging outside, but inside the redoubt it was tomb silent.

Ryan shrugged, brushing a few stray spots of the corrosive rain from his sleeve. He saw that J.B. was wiping the lenses of his spectacles clean, holding them awkwardly in the left hand of his disabled arm.

Jak was just behind the Armorer, leaning against the dusty concrete wall by the side of the sec doors, breathing heavily, his face drawn, eyes closed.

Dean squatted on the floor, with Doc at his side, tapping the ferrule of his silver-headed sword stick on the stone. The old man was struggling for a chipper manner, but Ryan knew him well enough to see that the ghastly crossing on the raft, followed by the grinding ascent to the redoubt, had really taken it out of the old man.

There wasn't really much choice.

Apart from anything else, they were all soaking wet. If they jumped in the next few minutes, there was no knowing whether they might immediately encounter a hostile combat situation.

Ryan coughed to attract everyone's attention. "Seems to me it makes sense that we hole up here for a couple of days. Anyone disagree?" There was the briefest pause. "Right."

Chapter Two

As soon as they left the entrance area, J.B. went hunting with Mildred and scoured the small living quarters, coming up with a somewhat depleted first-aid kit on the top shelf in the pantry.

"Mercy be," she said, sighing. "I can do something for all of you with this. Antiseptic cream and fresh gauze and bandages. Clean up all three of the injuries and set all of you on the road back to recovery." She smiled at her partner. "Might take a day or so longer than Ryan's guestimate. I'd put it closer to four days than two, to make sure all of you are really healing."

"Four days in here, with hot showers and adequate food and clean beds," J.B. said. "I guess I could live with that. Dark night! I know I can live with that."

"All we need is the loaf of bread and the jug of wine," she replied, kissing him gently on the cheek. "We've already got each other."

MILDRED TOOK each of the wounded men, one at a time, even before their clothes had dried, into the bath facility and did what she could to patch them up properly. Jak, as the most incapacitated, went first.

The black woman bent over his bone-white calf, peering at it carefully, using a spatula wrapped in pink gauze to wipe away the crust of blood, wrinkling her nose at the slight odor of decay that filtered from the peppered skin.

"Couldn't either see it or smell it properly back at Weyman's ville," she said. "Some of these stone splinters seem to be still in there."

"Had worse."

She straightened, her dark brown eyes staring into the smoldering embers of his crimson eyes. "Nobody loves a smart-ass, Jak," she said quietly. "Fine to be brave. Not so good if you're also stupe about it."

He nodded. "Hurts like bastard. When move ankle."

"Ligament damage, possibly," she guessed. "Waggle your toes for me, Jak. Mmm, that seems all right. Rotate the foot. Now the other way."

She had been watching him out of the corner of her eye, seeing the spasm of pain, the tightening of the bloodless lips, the whitening of the knuckles.

"Bad," he admitted.

"No," she said. "Not actually that bad. Now that I know what's wrong I can do something about it. There's a couple of scalpels and probes in this box, as well as some loc-an cream. It'll take four or five minutes to track down the bits of stone, now that I know roughly where they are." She smiled and patted the sixteen-year-old on the cheek. "This'll hurt you more than it hurts me, Jak."

BY THE THIRD DAY he was walking much better, able to take all of his weight on the injured right leg.

J.B. was healing fastest. It was just a question of giving the musket-ball wound a thorough clean then sprinkling in some antibiotic powder and tying on a fresh bandage.

Ryan lay on his stomach on the tiled floor, while Mildred knelt beside him, poking with a finger at the double arrow wound, ignoring him when he winced.

"This should be healing better, Ryan." She sat back on her heels. "The rest here will make all the difference. Been doing too much running around, keeping both the entrance and exit wounds open and bleeding."

"Sorry, ma'am. Sure will try to keep myself quiet while we're inside the redoubt."

Krysty came in, leaning against the doorframe. "Not making him holler enough, Mildred," she said, smiling at Ryan to take the sting from her words.

"Just finishing bandaging the invalid."

Krysty nodded, her fiery hair tumbling around her perfect face, her green eyes glinting at her friends. "You been telling him he should rest more?"

Mildred tied the last neat knot and stood up, patting Ryan on the shoulder. "There. All done. If we move on the day after tomorrow, I can bandage it one more time before the jump. Not doing too badly, though."

Ryan pulled on his shirt and tucked it in. "Thanks a lot, Mildred."

"Welcome, kind sir." She bobbed him a curtsy.

"Jak and J.B. getting along well?" Krysty asked. "Boy seemed to be moving easier."

"Definitely. But dear John Dix isn't used to being still in one place for three long days. Getting to him. Fieldstripped the Uzi thirty-seven times and the Smith & Wesson scattergun sixty-eight times." She laughed. "No, I'm exaggerating." A measured pause passed. "But not much."

BY NOON OF THE FOURTH DAY, everyone was ready to move. They'd all had enough of the claustrophobic concrete walls of the small redoubt, and the pleasure of hot baths and reasonable food was beginning to wear thin.

"Getting cabin fever, Ryan," Jak said.

"Yeah. Know what you mean. If I see another rad-blasted can of Aunt Abbie's All-American Avocado and Artichoke Dip, I swear I'll scream."

They'd just finished eating breakfast and were all sitting around one of the Formica-topped tables in the brightly lighted refectory.

The greasy plates were all neatly stacked at one end, and the seven plastic mugs, holding the dregs of the coffee sub, were piled with them.

"I can't stand any more of Rik'n Mik's Lemon Meringue Pie mix," J.B. added.

"I bemoan the lack of a decent Lafitte in the candlelit cellars. Or a halfway drinkable Mouton Cadet." Doc shook his leonine head sadly. "Or even a bottle of anything that remotely resembled wine."

"How about you, Dean?" his father asked. "I haven't seen you turn your nose up at anything here."

The boy considered the question, picking his teeth with a long fingernail and investigating what he'd excavated. "What do I hate most about the food?"

"Yeah."

"Feroze's Frozen Grits." He pulled a face, quoting from the label. "So good you can't stop comin' back for more." He shook his head. "Yuck!"

"Least we got plenty of hot water for washing up," Mildred said, yawning. "And I believe that today's rota has Doc and Jak on that particular duty."

"Makes fingers wrinkle," the albino protested. "Not man's work."

"How wrong you are, young fellow," Mildred said briskly. "And standing on that bad leg can help to give it some gentle exercise." She whirled. "And just where in the blue blazes do you think you're creeping off to, old-timer?"

Doc stopped in midstride, halfway to the door, his face flushing at being caught. "I swear that you are my personal nemesis, Dr. Wyeth, sent from the idle godlings of Olympus to persecute me."

"Just collect up the dishes and get out in the sluice room, Doc."

"I believe that you are a reincarnation of Torquemada, cruel leader of the Inquisition. I swear that no moral woman could be so cruel."

"Watch my lips, Doc. Do... the... dishes!"

Doc looked at his hands. "Ah, me. I shall never play the viola da gamba again."

Mildred laughed delightedly. "But you can't play it anyway, Doc!"

Jak limped to join the old man, tugging at his sleeve. "Might as well make river flow uphill, Doc," he said.

THEY STARTED toward the gateway first thing next morning, all of them glad to be moving on again. The only obstacle in their way out of the redoubt was the small elevator.

Ryan was uneasy about taking the metal cage down to the lower level. There had been some triple-bad experiences in elevators in the past couple of years. In Deathlands you always aimed to avoid putting yourself into any sort of trap.

Or potential trap.

And there were few more potentially hazardous traps than elevators.

The cage was still waiting patiently for them, the neon strip light above the entrance buzzing faintly. Its door hissed open as Dean pressed the button.

Ryan eased his finger off the trigger of the SIG-Sauer, seeing that the rectangular metal box was completely empty. "Let's go," he said.

It was a squeeze for all of them to get in, and it crossed Ryan's mind that it must have been substantially more crowded on the way up, with Trader and Abe along. All of that already seemed oddly far away.

The journey to the bottom of the shaft should only have taken a few seconds, though he estimated the drop as being close to two hundred feet.

The elevator shuddered three-quarters of the way down, hesitating a moment, seeming to hang poised between heaven and earth. The powerful winding gear groaned in protest, and everyone froze, conversation dying.

After a couple of seconds' delay the cage started to descend smoothly again.

Mildred whistled between her teeth. "Sure hate it when something like that happens. Tends toward making me a nominee for what we kids used to call the Hershey squirts award."

Doc tutted. "I do not wish to know that, madam. Kindly leave the elevator."

She grinned at the old man. "Soon as we reach bottom, we can all leave."

EVERYONE EXCEPT RYAN had taken their places inside the armaglass walls of the actual mat-trans chamber. The dense material was brown, flecked with white, allowing very little light to filter through.

There was a gap between Dean and Krysty, where Ryan would soon take his place. It was now a familiar scene—Doc's ebony sword stick lying by his side; J.B. carefully folding up his precious spectacles and placing them in one of his top pockets; Mildred holding his left hand, leaning back, the plaited beads in her hair rattling softly against the wall; Jak's mane of stark white hair spread across his narrow shoulders liked a cascade of purest Sierra ice.

"Ready?" Ryan asked. Everyone nodded, and he stepped into the chamber and closed the door firmly behind him.

Chapter Three

"Didn't work, Dad."

Ryan was already aware of that. There hadn't been the usual click as the door closed that indicated the mat-trans mechanism had been triggered. He opened it and pulled it firmly shut again. Still nothing.

J.B. blinked owlishly up at him. "Problem?"

"No. I'm standing here opening and shutting the rad-blasted door for my health." Ryan felt the pulse of anger throbbing at his temple. "'Course there's a problem."

Everyone started to shift, most of them standing, moving toward him. The armorer had fished out his glasses and was perching them on his bony nose. Only Doc remained sitting on the floor of the chamber.

"Leave it," Ryan snapped, thoroughly put out by the failure of the mechanism.

If it couldn't somehow be made to function properly—and none of them had much predark technical skill—then they were in deep trouble. They would have to go back up in the untrustworthy elevator and out onto the bleak, windswept island, try to build a new raft and make it across the treacherous narrows to the sulfurous mainland with all of its perils.

Ryan closed and opened the door several times, while the others crowded around him, offering a variety of advice.

He was so distracted by the confusion and noise that he hardly noticed that the lock had given an audible click on the seventh attempt at slamming the heavy door.

Before he even realized what was happening, Ryan had opened the armaglass door an eighth time.

It was Doc's voice, rising above all the others, like a chain saw hacking through plate glass, that gave him the warning. "It's working, Ryan! By the Three Kennedys, but I swear that the jump is beginning."

There was an instant, heart-stopping silence.

"Dark night!" J.B. breathed. "He's right. I can feel it in my head."

"Close the door, Ryan, quickly!" Krysty urged. "Gaia! Quickly!"

"It won't..." Ryan panted with the effort and could feel his heart racing, the breath dying in his throat.

The door seemed to have jammed, open by about eight inches, immovable either way.

And Doc was right. The jump had begun.

Ryan could feel it—fingers ghosting into his brain, probing inside the moist pink-gray tissues, bringing the usual deep-seated nausea.

The circular silvery metal plates set into the floor and ceiling of the hexagonal chamber were already beginning to glow, and the usual tendrils of fragile white mist were appearing near the top of the gateway.

"Everyone sit down and hang on to each other."

It was the best he could come up with. But Ryan wasn't sure if the others heard him. His voice was frail, echoing, the words jumbled and distorted.

The anteroom and the control area beyond were blurring, as if he were looking through a heat haze. Ryan closed his eye and opened it again, using the last of his failing strength to try one more time to close the door.

But it was too late.

Ryan felt himself slipping to his knees, one arm falling near the gap, sliding onto his face, sensing all the colors of darkness.

"Cold," he said.

IT WAS A TANGLED, confused mixture of half memory and new experience.

There was the vague thought that the original incident might have happened somewhere on the southern edge of the Darks. Or out on the Idaho panhandle?

The war wags had come rumbling into the township, expecting to find it a bustling frontier ville. But the stores were all boarded up, the drinkers closed, the gaudies deserted. Tumbleweed piled against the picket fences.

Trader had asked Ryan to go outside and look around. "Single man recce's the best for this," he said. "I can't smell danger."

As soon as the main rear armasteel hatch opened up on War Wag One, Ryan guessed that his chief was right. There was no smell of danger.

But there *was* the sweet, sour, prickling scent of death.

The breath came feathering whitely from his open mouth as he stepped down onto the weed-laden tarmac, looking from side to side. He wore a Browning A-500 12-gauge scattergun slung across one shoulder, the walnut stock of the Belgian-made blaster nudging at the small of his back. There was a double-action revolver—the Llama Super Comanche II, taking a big .38 round tucked in its holster on the right side of his hip.

Ryan almost knew the name of the pesthole ville. Almost, but not quite.

It kept slithering from the back of his brain, reaching the tip of his tongue, then whispering back into the darkness.

All he could remember was that it had been the center of two violently opposed religious factions.

Now, looking around the small town plaza, he could see the graffiti, bringing it all back home—Albigensians drink Satan's piss, Reformed Pentecostals will burn forever, Dung-devouring heretics, Speaking with tongues is speaking to the devil.

The electric-glowing colors flared so brightly it made Ryan screw up his good right eye against the drizzle.

His hand dropped to the butt of the revolver as he sensed movement behind him. He spun and looked to the side of the main drag, seeing a scrawny, piebald mongrel go scampering clumsily across the mouth of a narrow alley, gripping a severed human arm in its stained jaws, the stiff fingers scraping through the frosted pebbles.

Beyond the main plaza was a small square surrounded by buildings, with the twin churches on opposing sides, the squat concrete buildings glowering at each other.

Though Ryan still couldn't remember where the town was, or its name, he could visualize the open space, with an iron-railed fence along two sides and a tumbledown cupola where brass bands might have played on those long-gone, sunny predark Sunday afternoons.

He rubbed his hands together. "Cold," he whispered.

The sun was a watery blur of sickly yellow, dipping behind the range of snow-topped peaks to the west.

Shadows were lengthening across the silent settlement. Somewhere Ryan could just catch the faint sound of a screen door banging on its hinges.

Once he reached the corner of the plaza, he'd be able to see into the square.

The bitter taste of decay lay flat on his tongue, and Ryan hawked and spit in the dust, trying to clear it away. The sharp noise startled half a dozen vultures, which rose heavily into the afternoon sky, from the square, leathery wings flapping, hooked beaks open, shreds of some sort of meat dangling from their jaws.

"Bastards!" Ryan breathed, drawing the blaster, cocking the hammer with a dry click.

Three more steps and he would be able to see into the square of the little town.

Two more.

One.

"Fireblast!"

There was death.

At a first glance Ryan saw something like a hundred corpses. Or what remained of them after the carrion birds and coyotes had taken their fill.

His experience told him that they had probably been lying there on the smeared flagstones for two to three weeks. In such cold weather, they had kept better than they would have done in a Texas summer.

They had become partly mummified, the flesh shrinking from the puckered, leathery skin, leaving the long dark bones and the taut sinews exposed. Some of them resembled piles of discarded sticks, cloaked in a few tattered rags.

The soft tissues had gone first, leaving eyeless sockets and lipless, grinning mouths.

If Ryan hadn't already seen better than his fair share of corpses, he might have assumed that all of the dead were Afro-Americans, from the ebony hue. But he knew that the darkening of the tight skin was a typical sign of all bodily decay.

He walked a few steps, among the bodies, looking more carefully at them. Ryan had holstered the revolver, knowing that there was nothing left here that could possibly do him any harm.

He realized immediately that he was stepping through the aftermath of a massacre. Many of the dead showed signs of having been hacked to death by axes or machetes. Some, notably the full-grown males, had been shot. There were no cartridge cases on the ground, which pointed toward smoothbore muskets.

Most of the dead were men, with about a third of them female and a smaller proportion children.

The wind was rising as dusk began to draw its soft gray cloak across the scene of butchery, fluttering the clothes of the corpses.

Ryan hunched his shoulders. "Bastard cold," he muttered.

He wondered what final catastrophic religious schism had led to the slaughter. It seemed as though every man, woman and child in the little ville had come together to fight to the bitter end. Discarded knives, spears and axes lay everywhere, with a few bows and a scattering of arrows, tipped with black crow feathers. But the survivors of the conflict had carefully taken away all of the firearms.

As Ryan turned, his boot caught in some rags of a woollen shawl that had been wrapped around a little baby. The movement jerked at the tiny body, rolling it out on its back, sockets of windwashed bone staring at the darkening sky. The throat of the infant had been cut so savagely that the whiteness of the spine gleamed among the black threads of desiccated flesh.

Ryan turned away, fighting back an attack of nausea that threatened his breakfast, looking beyond the plaza, up to the snow-covered mountains. There was an area of rutted land, dotted with elegant cottonwoods that tilted toward a narrow river. Ryan's eye was caught by millions of tiny ice crystals, falling from the cloudy sky, glittering like a mist of diamonds.

"Enough," he said, his voice unnaturally loud in the open space.

He started to walk slowly back toward the main street and the warmth and security of the war wags, when his combat-tuned hearing caught a faint rustling sound, like a gentle summer breeze through a grove of aspens, coming from all around him.

Ryan felt the short hair bristling at his nape as he looked around at the square of the dead.

The dried-out bodies were moving.

Some of them had been lying stretched out, while others seemed to have died curled up into a fetal position, knees huddled to bony chests.

Now, everywhere he looked, there was a restless shifting, fingers creaking open from clenched fists, feet scratching in the frosty dust, teeth clacking in leering jaws, skulls turning blindly from side to side.

Ryan drew his blaster, thumbing back the hammer. His senses screamed for him to run from the charnel sight, but his feet felt nailed to the dirt.

Something touched his ankle and he looked down, seeing that the tiny, shrunken hands of the baby with the slit throat were plucking at his ankle.

Ryan opened his mouth and started to scream.

Chapter Four

As the mist thickened, making it impossible to see what was happening in the mat-trans unit, the partly open door was the center of a swirling vortex of gray air, peculiarly thick, like gruel. Ryan lay unconscious, face close to the opening, one arm jammed against the door.

The process continued.

The side effects of the malfunctioning jump struck at everybody, but Ryan was nearest to the nodal point of the matter-transfer dischronicity and was, as a consequence, much the worst affected.

His living nightmare was horrific, but the others all shared bizarre sense sensations.

DEAN WAS WANDERING across a bleak and featureless moor, with every up slope coated thick in snow.

The air was so cold that it burned his mouth and throat like living fire, and the inside of his nose was coated with sharp crystals of ice.

He was feeling very tired, overwhelmed with the simple desire to lie down and rest for a while. The boy hadn't eaten for the better part of a week, and he could feel his backbone rubbing on his belly. The sun was nearly done, throwing his long shadow ahead of him as he staggered weakly eastward.

A tiny bird, like a sparrow, suddenly fell from the sky, landing with the softest of thumps in the snow at his feet, stricken dead by the cold.

Dean dropped to his knees alongside the tiny corpse, picking it up in cupped hands, staring at the dark, sightless eyes. He could just feel the warmth on the feathered body.

Closing his own eyes, the boy lifted the dead bird toward his mouth.

THE BOWL OF RICE PUDDING was rich and creamy, dotted with plump raisins and carrying the scent of honey and cinnamon. It stood on the floor of the wooden shack, steaming in the bitter cold.

J.B. sat cross-legged, looking at it, wondering which of the guards had placed it there while he was sleeping. The irons around his ankles were frozen, scorching his flesh wherever they touched it.

He could hear whispering outside the warped planks. Dimly, against the stark whiteness of the snow that lay thick upon the rocky plateau, he could make out the silhouettes of some of his guards, waiting to snigger at him when he tried to reach the tantalizing dish of food, because they knew that the chain around his throat, secured to a heavy ringbolt in the wall, would leave him short, inches away from the bowl.

J.B. knew that, as well, and he sat very still, unable to take his eyes off the creamy pudding.

THE WALKING DEAD WERE all around Ryan, every empty eye socket turned blankly toward him. The wind blew at the tattered clothing, whistling through the shrunken holes in the dried flesh. Step by slow, unsteady step, the corpses were coming closer.

He leveled the Llama Comanche at the nearest of the shambling horrors.

MILDRED HAD BEEN on vacation with some of the other members of the Olympic pistol team, staying in a newly built block of apartments near Pagosa Springs.

The nearest shooting range was at South Fork, the far side of Wolf Creek Pass, nearly eleven thousand feet high, but this afternoon Mildred had gone off on a trek of her own, borrowing a Jeep to take the twisting, narrow trail into the San Juan Mountains, up toward Cimarron.

There had been no forecast of the snow that suddenly came swirling around her, closing visibility to twenty feet, rushing at the windshield so that it was like driving into an endless white tunnel.

It was as if the heavens had opened and dumped six months' snowfall on her, all in one storm.

The radio had been giving sports news when it died.

As she reached down to try to adjust it, the heavy-duty tires of the Jeep struck a tumbled log, jarring the wheel from her numbed fingers. The vehicle lurched to one side, off the ice-slick trail, and started to roll.

Mildred grabbed at the door handle, but the biting cold had slowed her reflexes and she was way too late. The Jeep was already tumbling, over and over, bouncing and jolting. She heard a grinding crash of torn metal and then something struck her across the back of the head, above and behind her right ear, and the darkness opened its cloak and took her in.

When she came around there was an eerie stillness, broken only by the howling of the wind. Mildred opened her eyes, wincing at the savage stab of pain that ran through her skull. She reached up and touched her face, feeling the cool stickiness of congealing blood across her cheek.

Her careful probing made her fairly sure that there was no terminal damage done by the crash.

There was a large duck-egg swelling where something had come loose from the back of the Jeep in the accident and clouted her across the head.

"Could be worse, girl," she said, hoping that her own voice might lift her spirits. But it simply made her feel that much more alone.

It was when Mildred tried to move out of the wrecked Jeep that she began to realize the seriousness of her dilemma. The seat belt was tight across her ribs and shoulders, holding her suspended in the inverted vehicle. A sharp branch of a broken pine had smashed through the driver's window, pinning her against the back of the seat. Though she wriggled experimentally, the beads in her plaited hair chattering softly, nothing much happened.

She was completely trapped.

Snow was blowing in on her face. From the position she was in, it was impossible to reach the release on the seat belt, though she tried hard.

"Gas?" she said, wrinkling her nose, aware suddenly of cold liquid trickling across her chest.

That was when she started to yell for help.

JAK HAD BEEN HUNTING the big mutie cougar for three days and two nights.

He and his wife, Christina, had been losing stock from their New Mexico spread since late October. Now Christmas was only a few days off, and every dawning brought a fresh trail of bright blood, ruby on the ermine of the snow, and the raggled remains of one of their sheep.

He had a satin-finish Colt Python holstered on his hip, and several of his beloved throwing knives concealed about him. But they weren't the right weapon for a cougar whose spoor showed he was close to twenty feet from nose to tail.

The Winchester 70A bolt-action rifle was a good reliable hunting rifle, with its chrome molybdenum steel action and narrow serrated trigger. It had a hooded-ramp front sight with a white diamond-leaf rear sight for quick adjustment.

Jak was carrying it at the high port, ready for action, his white fingers gripping the dark walnut stock with its high-comb Monte Carlo undercut cheek piece.

The pack on his back, containing survival provisions, was weighing perilously light.

The animal had led him up into a maze of meandering canyons, all coated in snow, each one indistinguishable from the one before or the one to come. Jak had a wonderful sense of direction, but the swirling blizzard was robbing him of that and he was no longer certain which way was home.

His streaming mane of white hair was coated with crystals of powdery snow and ice, making it stiff and heavy, tinkling faintly as he turned his head.

He squeezed between a large, rounded boulder and the sheer wall of rock that lined the arroyo on his right. His boots rattled into a cache of old cans and bottles, rotting away and biodegrading with an infinite slowness since the distant years of predark.

The snow had stopped falling about an hour earlier, and the covering was untouched and virginal.

Jak continued to pick his way after the cougar, pausing when he saw tracks ahead marring the perfect blanket of unsullied whiteness. He glanced behind him, feeling a momentary discomfort, then stooped to examine the trail.

They were both human and animal, combat boots and mountain lion.

His own boots.

And the mutie cougar.

Jak realized that he had been walking in a blind circle through the canyons.

He also realized with a chill of fear that the tracks of the cougar overlaid his own boot-marks, meaning that the animal was following him.

Jak started to swing around, finger on the trigger of the Winchester, knowing in his heart that it was going to be far too late.

KRYSTY LAY ON THE BUNK in the dark cabin, under the two threadbare blankets.

The oil lamp had given out so long ago that she couldn't remember, and the wood for the fire had been exhausted about three days earlier.

When Ryan hadn't come back from his trading trip to the ville across the big river, and the snows had closed in on their little home, Krysty had begun to ration the food that remained, gradually cutting down what she ate each day.

Her ribs had begun to protrude through the skin, and she could see the sharp planes of her face changing in the broken square of mirror that hung above the sink in the kitchen. The bright sentient hair was dull, clinging miserably to her head.

There was a thumbnail of dried cheese left and a handful of oats.

Nothing else.

She was deeply aware of her own weakness, and certain now that Ryan wasn't coming back, leaving her with two choices: to lie still and starve and slip away in the bitter cold, painless and easy, or to get up on her feet, pull on a coat and her dark blue Western boots, open the cabin door and try to make it to the ville.

Uncle Tyas McCann had once told her of an exploration to the farthest reaches of the Antarctic. An Englishman who hadn't wanted to slow down his companions with his frostbitten feet had walked out of their tent, saying that he was going outside and he might be some time.

Krysty had always remembered that.

Her fingers shook as she buttoned the coat, and she had hardly enough strength to pull on the boots embroidered with the pretty silver falcon wings.

She noticed that the skin around her nails had gone dark blue, almost black. Last time she'd looked at her feet, the toes had been in even worse shape.

A coughing fit racked her, making her double over the bed, eyes weeping, the pain tearing at her chest. The one small window in the cabin was coated so thickly with ice that it was impossible to see out.

She wondered what had happened to Ryan. There had been a strange vision, oddly blurred and unreliable, of him walking through a plaza in a small frontier ville, past heaps of decayed corpses. Krysty had glimpsed movement among the bodies, but then lost her hold on the seeing.

The coughing passed and she straightened, taking a few faltering steps to the door of the hut, laying a hand on the ice-cold metal of the latch.

"I'm going outside," she whispered. "And I might be gone some time."

DOC'S IMAGINING FOUND HIM sitting in front of a roaring log fire, hands cupping a tankard of mulled claret spiced with cloves and honey.

It was late in the evening of the last night before the birthday of Jesus the Christ.

The house was still and quiet, yet making the occasional small creakings of an old building. The toasting heat of the parlor contrasted with the bitter frost and driving snow outside the shuttered windows.

Emily had gone up the stairs a few minutes ago, kissing him on the cheek, whispering her affection into his ear, blushingly promising him a special early Christmas present once he joined her in their cozy bedroom, where the copper warming pans were already in place.

The children were fast asleep, two small angels in their beds, curly heads on the goose-feather pillows. Jolyon was still too young to appreciate the magic of the season, but Rachel had been becoming more and more excited over the past few nights, her little face alight with the thrill of Santa's visit.

Doc had sat them both on his lap and whispered to them of the jolly old white-bearded gentleman with the red suit who would bring gifts to all good children, telling them that they *might* just possibly catch the sound of his sleigh bells and the clicking of his reindeers' hooves on their shingled roof.

He drained the glass, sighed and stood.

The two boxes filled with brightly wrapped presents stood waiting in the large closet on the landing, ready to be put in place, one at the foot of each bed.

Doc caught a glimpse of himself in the gilt-framed oval mirror above the hearth and smiled at his image, revealing his perfect teeth.

"By the Three Kennedys, but it's time to get to business," he said, "then up to pleasure dearest Emily."

His face frowned for a moment, wondering why he'd mentioned three Kennedys. He knew nobody of that name.

The maid would see to safely damping the fire. He reached for the clock key on his silver fob chain and wound the Westminster chiming timepiece on the mantel, taking great care not to overwind it and damage the mechanism.

The stairs creaked under his knee boots, the polished mahogany banister warm to the touch.

He paused a moment on the half landing, peering out at the blizzard. The snow still beat against the house like the silent wings of tiny birds, carried on the breath of a cold blue norther that had been raging now for six days.

Doc carried on, reaching the dark at the top of the stairs, deciding to look in on his darling cherubs before bringing in the presents.

Their room was the last one to his left, and he tiptoed along, over the delicate Persian runner, until he stood outside the bedroom door.

He hesitated a moment, head to one side, straining his hearing. He could have sworn that he'd just heard the distant tinkling of golden bells and a muffled noise of animals, high up near the gable end of the roof.

"I think that my imagination is getting the better of me," he said, smiling.

He put out his hand, turned the chased brass knob and walked into his children's room, stopping, stricken.

Despite the glowing embers of a fire in the grate, the chamber was absolutely freezing. The curtains were drawn, and a small oil lamp gave a gentle glow to the room. Doc put his hand to his chest, his breath frosting out in front of his face.

The children lay sleeping in their beds, but they weren't alone in the room.

A bulky figure stood between the beds, his back turned to Doc. All he could make out was that it was a man, and he was wearing a scarlet jacket and pants, and a cap in the same color.

"I beg your pardon, but might I ask who you are, and what precisely your business is?"

The man began to turn very slowly. "I'm Santa from the wintry north, ho, ho, ho. And I've come to collect your good, good children, Dr. Tanner."

The voice was like a file being drawn over ice, implacably cold, each word grating its solitary way into the silence of the nursery. Despite the harsh attempt at merriment, it was the least humorous voice that Doc had ever heard.

"Face me, damn your impudence! I'll give you a good thrashing for your—"

The words died in his throat as the figure turned fully around, now visible in the mellow light of the oil lamp.

It was like the devil's walking parody of Father Christmas.

He was red-suited, with a thick white beard, but Doc saw that the beard was made from crystals of ice, matted together in an obscene simulacrum of the original.

The eyes were empty ivory sockets, filled with blue-tinted chips of ice, that sparkled with an evil and unnatural life that sent a chill to Doc's heart.

"Suffer little children, ho, ho, ho. Oh, yes, little children will suffer, Dr. Tanner."

The mouth opened, and Doc saw that the teeth were needle-tipped ice, as clear as glass. One hand reached out over each bed, the fingers of clicking bone tipped with daggers of razored ice, slicing down toward the pitifully exposed throats of Rachel and Jolyon.

Doc found that he couldn't move and he began to weep, the tears freezing on his cheeks.

RYAN BACKED AWAY, the twisted, dried-out corpses remorselessly following him into a corner. He aimed the revolver at the nearest horror and squeezed the trigger.

Instead of a powerful explosion, the weapon barely sighed, releasing a trickle of powdery snow over Ryan's feet.

The one-eyed man dropped the useless blaster and began to scream.

Chapter Five

The voices were familiar, but they were coming from an infinite distance away. Blurred, rising and falling, seeming to echo around the inner walls of Ryan's skull.

"He was nearest the door."

"But we all shared the same kind of dreadful nightmare, with cold at its heart."

The first voice had been a man, someone that Ryan had known many years ago, someone that he thought he still knew. And the second speaker was the black woman.

"Mildred," he tried to say, feeling his dry lips move, but not hearing any sound.

"Lie still, Ryan. It's not time to try to move around too much. Not yet."

"Sure thing, Mildred."

The last thing that he wanted to do was move. Even the thought of opening his eye was impossibly repugnant to him.

He shifted a little, trying to establish how he was lying. On his back, head turned to the left, he decided. Mildred's doing again, making sure he didn't choke on his own vomit.

"Missing," he said.

"What is?" It was Jak's voice.

"Blaster." His hand had crept down to the empty holster on his hip.

"John Barrymore removed it for safety. Yours as well as ours, dear friend. He was the first to recover from this dreadful jump and he found you, lying by the partly open door, with your pistol in your hand."

"Why?" Ryan sighed. His brain felt like it had been dragged behind a galloping horse through a mess of cactus.

J.B. answered him, his voice sounding ragged and tired. "You were waving the SIG-Sauer around like you were surrounded by enemies. But you were trying to cock it with your thumb, like it was some big old revolver."

"It was. Llama Comanche."

"Dark night! Must be twenty years since you carried that as your side arm."

"Were you caught in some kind of fantasy that involved being cold, lover?"

Ryan finally risked opening his eye and waited patiently for it to recover some kind of focus. He saw that he was stretched out on the floor of a gateway chamber, lying on one of the circular metal disks. The armaglass walls were a beautiful shade of clear cerulean blue, like a summer sky in southern Utah.

The others were all standing around him.

The first thing that caught his eye was Krysty's fiery red hair, then the flare of magnesium white next to it that was Jak Lauren's head.

"Cold?" he finally answered. "Yes. Big nightmare. Living corpses that... Why?"

"We all did," Dean said. "Real rocky horror-show stuff, Dad."

"But we all made it through the jump." Doc, leaning against one of the chamber's walls, idly tapped on the floor with the ferrule of his ebony sword stick, his gnarled fingers gripping the silver lion's-head hilt. "The mental process was peculiarly unpleasant, possibly because of the partly open doorway. But that was then . . ."

"And this is now," Ryan completed. "Someone give me a hand so I can get up?"

Krysty and Jak responded first, each of them stooping and helping Ryan to a more comfortable position, sitting with his back against one of the sky blue walls.

"Thanks. Thought for a moment there that I was going to throw up my last meal. Whatever that was." He managed a thin smile. "Whenever that was."

"In another country," Doc said sonorously. "And besides, the wench is dead."

Ryan didn't feel like unraveling one of Doc's runic sayings right then, so he let it pass.

"Anyone done a recce at all?" he asked.

J.B. replied. "Not yet. Haven't even moved the door. Didn't want to open it or close it until you got back with us. Couldn't tell what might happen."

Ryan nodded, wincing at the smothering pain that welled up from the back of his skull at the moment. "Safer." He looked across the chamber, seeing that the heavy door still stood a few inches open. It had been a close call, and a lesson for any future jumps that they might make. If the gateway door had been left open just a little bit wider, Ryan suspected that none of them would have survived the jump.

Fighting to overcome a tsunami of nausea and vertigo, he heaved himself upright, closing his eye for a moment to check the mat-trans unit from rolling and rocking around.

"You all right, lover?" Krysty asked, her steadying hand on his arm. "Take it easy."

"Be fine."

"Want door open all way?"

Ryan nodded. "Might as well. Everyone get ready." Suddenly he realized he was still unarmed. "Can I have my blaster back, J.B.?"

The heavy SIG-Sauer felt good in his hand. The Steyr SSG-70 was on the floor of the gateway, and he stooped to pick up the bolt-action rifle, slinging it across his shoulder.

The albino teenager stood by the armaglass door, the Colt Python cocked and ready in his right hand. Left hand on the door, he waited for Ryan to give the signal.

"Yeah," the one-eyed man said.

THE ANTEROOM WAS DIRTY, with piles of plaster and dust that seemed to have fallen from the cracked ceiling. There was a dartboard on one wall, the concrete pitted all around it by near misses. Three darts were still stuck in the board.

"Twenty-six scored," Doc said quietly.

"Looks like this place took a pounding." J.B. pointed into the control room, where a third of the overhead strip lights had malfunctioned.

There were long cracks in the corners, and more of the ceiling had come down, laying a film of white dust over the flickering dials of the control consoles.

"Amazed it's still running and working." Ryan holstered his blaster, seeing that the double sec doors into the section were firmly closed.

"Buried deep." J.B. brushed a finger through the dirt. "Don't know what we're going to find up top. Could be that the rest of the redoubt's been wiped."

Doc groaned. "May all of the Saints—who from their labors rest—preserve me from having to make yet another jump out of this place."

"No hurry to decide." Mildred tapped one of the desk monitors that had been standing dull and silent. For a moment it flickered into a frenetic life, colored lights glowing and dancing, disks whirring, digital display changing faster than the eye could catch.

Then it ceased to work. It simply stopped.

"Sec cameras all dead," Jak said, pointing to the small electronic ob boxes placed in the high corners of the big room.

"You feel anything, Krysty?"

She shook her head. "Nothing of life, lover. Nothing of the living. Just see a sort of fog of ancient dust. Place has the feel of a very old tomb."

Ryan hunched his shoulders protectively, remembering the dried-out corpses in the nameless ville of his nightmare.

Dean had gone over to examine the doors, sniffing at them, like a hunting dog, trying to catch any kind of scent from beyond them. "Nothing," he said. "Just the same sort of dusty smell there is in here."

Ryan joined his son, resting his hand on his shoulder while he carried out the same test. "Agreed."

Krysty glanced across at that moment, seeing yet again how incredibly alike father and son were—the same sharp, narrow face, with the deep-set dark eyes, and the same mane of untidy, tumbling, curly black hair. Even in the eleven-year-old, there was the same air of coiled menace.

"There's gum and candy wrappers on the floor," Mildred called. "Looks like this one was hit hard and early."

"Did all get out?" Jak prowled about the underground bunker like a caged cat. "Go see?"

"Soon," Ryan called.

Doc had also been nosing around. He stopped in front of a comp screen that showed several lines of white type, set against a black background.

"Do come and take a look at this," he said quietly. "Most extraordinary."

They gathered around him, peering at the dust-filmed screen. Doc read out the message.

"String of letters and numbers to start with. 'NORDEF albase. Top Urgent. Action triple soonest.' How I hate this journalese gobbledygook that soldiers and scientists love so much. Why can they not use normal speech?"

"Rest is simple, Doc," J.B. said, leaning over the old man's shoulder.

"Right. 'Red angels in flight heading from NNE. Their ETA if not intercepted by Star Wars missiles is three hours and forty-two minutes. Personnel vectors A thru E immediate evacuation. All others seal all ex-

ternal and internal ports. Nuclear generators all acti-
vated. Prepare long closed-down wait. Action
immediate. Not a drill. Repeat, this is not a drill.'
Then it gives that string of letters and numerals once
more."

"Be a kind of authorization code, Doc," Mildred
suggested. "Let them know it was genuine and not a
gremlin somewhere in the machine."

"Very probably. I remember that the whitecoats
who ran Overproject Whisper were never happier than
when their eager little snouts were immersed in man-
uals of electronic coding."

"Read the rest, Doc," Ryan said.

"But of course. Where was I? The code. 'Repeat
orders for vectors A thru E to evacuate soonest. Rest
remain under Operation Snopak conditions.'" He
paused. "Then all it says is 'God bless you all and God
bless America.' That's it."

"Like message from grave," Jak said quietly.

Mildred looked solemn. "That isn't dated, but it
must've been just before the last war broke out. The
Russian missiles were triggered, and our retaliation
would also have been under way. All too late for anyone to stop." She shook her head. "Even if anyone
had wanted to stop."

Ryan turned back toward the massive vanadium-
steel sec door. "So, did they do like they were told?
The mat-trans section is usually buried deepest. If it's
got all these cracks and stuff, what kind of damage are
we going to find up above? Guess we'd best go see."

THEY TOOK the usual precautions.
Dean operated the green lever at the side of the

door, lifting it to set the powerful gearing system into action. There was the hiss of hydraulics and then the distant, muffled sound of the nuke-powered engine starting to raise the sec barrier.

The rest of them all stood away, blasters readied, while Ryan himself flattened on the floor, the movement tugging a little at the arrow wound in his back.

"Hold it," he said, when the bottom of the sec door was only three or four inches from the floor.

"Anything?" J.B. asked.

Ryan didn't answer for several long seconds, studying what he could see under the door, trying to decide what it was. "Up another couple of inches, Dean," he said finally, waiting for the door to lift higher. "That'll do."

"What is it, lover?"

"Couldn't be sure whether it was just some discarded rags of clothing. It isn't."

THE SIGHT OF THE BODY revived the memory of Ryan's nightmare. It was virtually certain that the man—facial hair confirmed the sex of the corpse—had died close to a hundred years earlier, probably within hours of skydark.

He was stretched out, no flesh remaining on the bones, his skin blackened by the passing of the ages. One arm was reaching toward the door, as if he'd been knocking for help. Or, perhaps, had tried to get back into the relative safety of the mat-trans unit at the last moment.

"Master sergeant," Mildred commented, looking at the golden stripes on the faded, paper-thin cloth of the uniform.

"Where there's one, there'll be others, as Trader used to say." J.B. caught Ryan's eye as he spoke, looking away again in slight embarrassment.

Ryan nodded agreement. "Be amazed if we don't find more chills as we move along."

THERE WERE A DOZEN in the first hundred yards of the passage, all in the same mummified condition.

"Don't get it, Dad."

"What, son?"

"Looks like the jump rooms were safest in the redoubt. People dying out here. How come they didn't get back inside and have a better chance of safety?"

Ryan thought about the question. "Damned if I know, Dean."

"I believe that I can answer that one, my dear Cawdor." Doc stooped over Dean, like a buzzard over a ground squirrel. "I believe that the matter-transfer section of the redoubt would have been deliberately locked against anyone, because it probably represented the only sure way out of here. The authorities—senior officers and the rest of the beribboned imbeciles—wouldn't have wanted desertion on a massive scale. Not with a war to be fought." He gave a short barking laugh. "Some war, some fight. They feared the men and women under their command might've crammed in here and fled to all points north and south. East and west. So they took the obvious precaution and barred the door."

"And they all died." Mildred sighed. "Such stupidity and such a dreadful waste."

The physical state of the redoubt got worse. They climbed four sets of wide stairs, each time discovering more damage and more bodies.

The deep cracks in the hugely thick concrete walls and vaulted ceilings were more obvious, and in two or three places whole sections of masonry had collapsed, spilling piles of dusty gray stone across the passages, exposing the rusting sections of fractured reinforcing metal.

J.B. drew Ryan's attention to the small rad counters they each wore. "Orange."

"None of the corpses show any obvious signs of being shot or wounded. Likely it was seepage from the nukes."

The Armorer thought about it, looking around. They were in an open space with several alternate routes opening off, most of them blocked by sec doors. A dozen bodies lay near them, some stretched out, some huddled in a fetal position, knees drawn up to their sagging jaws.

"Probably. But if the redoubt had been sealed, some of them might simply have gotten trapped in a closed section and starved to death."

"Way the place has been pounded makes me wonder about what kind of hardware the Russkies used. Doesn't look much like neutron bombing."

The neutron missiles had been developed in the latter part of the twentieth century to take out all forms of life but leave buildings standing. The idea being that the winners could move in and take over the defeated country with as little logistical trouble as possible.

The drawback that none of the master tacticians in the Kremlin and the Pentagon had considered was that there wasn't a simple comp-programmed winner and loser, like there'd been in their billion-dollar war games.

There were only losers.

THE REDOUBT WAS a bleakly depressing place, brimming with hopeless, pointless death.

All the evidence pointed to an evacuation that had gone wrong and an attempt to safely seal the whole complex that had been a virtual failure.

The only part of the whole rambling military base that had survived more or less unscathed was the mat-trans unit.

Krysty was walking with Ryan as they approached yet another closed set of sec doors, the green control lever in the down position.

"If these poor devils were trapped down here, why didn't they just open the doors to get out? If we can do it, then why couldn't they?"

Ryan paused, turning to face her. "I wondered. Then I figured it out. When they were trying to seal the base, they must've used some master control to override the manual controls. Part of the main comp system must've been took out."

"Taken out, lover."

"Yeah. When the lines went down, the doors were set free. Might've taken a couple of weeks, but I think that's the most likely story."

"Can I open this one, Dad?"

"Sure. On red, people."

"Are these precautions really essential, my dear fellow? Surely this charnel house contains nothing that could possibly threaten us? It is as safe as any pre-dark catafalque."

"Mebbe, Doc. Mebbe not. Blasters out, everyone."

Dean stood by the green lever, waiting for the nod from his father, who was crouching on the dusty, rubble-coated floor, ready to peer under the sec door for any sign of danger.

"Six inches, son."

The control had become very stiff, and the boy had to use all of his strength to shift it. But they eventually heard the usual grinding sound and the sec door shuddered, beginning to move slowly upward.

"Stop it!" Ryan's voice held the crack of command. "And lower it. Quick!"

Chapter Six

The boy reacted quickly, reversing the lever, allowing the sec steel door to drop back to floor level with the faintest sound and a tiny puff of dust.

"What is it?" J.B. asked, holding the heavy scattergun at the ready. "Someone out there?"

"Something out there?" Krysty added. "What?"

"Stone," Ryan replied. "Bottom of what looked like a seriously big pile of stones."

"Blocking way out?"

"Looks like it, Jak. Danger of lifting the door, and it'll all come pouring in here on top of us."

"Detour?" Mildred suggested. "I was just looking forward to getting out of here into the fresh air and sunlight and— Hey, wait a minute. There was good clean air coming out under the door for the moment or two it was open."

Ryan straightened, brushing dust from his pants, wincing at the tugging of the arrow wound. "That's true. There is. Was. Must mean the top layers of the redoubt were totally driven in and collapsed in the nuking."

Jak was staring at the floor, near where Dean had been standing. "Tracks," he said.

"Where? Those are mine." Dean couched. "Real small. Like someone my age or size. But not my boots."

"Not any of ours," Ryan agreed. "Jak, can you follow them back inside? I haven't seen them anywhere else."

"I thought I saw them near the gateway," J.B. said quietly. "But the dust wasn't so thick as it is here, and I wasn't sure. They went away left in the opposite direction to the way we took."

"Two," Jak said, his red eyes glowing in the overhead lights. Only about one in eight of the long neon strip lights were now working, the situation deteriorating the higher up they got through the complex.

"Anything about them?"

The albino shook his head at Ryan's question, the errant hair a halo of white light. "Men not children. Tired. Feet dragging. Funny clothes."

"How's that?" Ryan asked.

"Long dust coats? Something like women's dresses. Dragging and leaving marks."

"Women, Jak?"

"Mebbe, Krysty. Can't tell."

He was following the faint marks as he spoke, working his slow way backward, cutting off toward one of the narrow side passages, cutting away from the route that they'd followed from the mat-trans unit.

Ryan called out to stop him. "No point in going any further, Jak. From what J.B. said, it looks like they somehow got out of the gateway. Came all the way up here by some different path. Must be that."

"You believe that the strangers had made use of the gateway for a jump?" Doc shook his head. "I suppose that anything in Deathlands is possible."

"And it looks like they got out through this sec door," said Dean, on his hands and knees, head low, like an eager puppy. "There's some fresh dust overlaying their trail."

"Well spotted, son." Ryan had joined the boy, nodding. "You're right."

"So, if they got out..." Mildred allowed the sentence to drift away.

"So can we." J. B. Dix finished it for her. "Worth a try. You reckon, Ryan?"

"Alternative is to wander around the redoubt for hours—mebbe days—trying to find another, better way out of here. If someone else risked this door, then so can we. Dean?"

"Yeah, Dad?"

"This time I want you to take it up no more than three or four inches at a time. Stop it. Check for the word from me. Then repeat that. Slow and careful. Understand?"

"Sure." The word was thrown over his shoulder, casual.

Ryan called him back, holding him by the shoulder, fingers digging into the boy's flesh. "This is serious, Dean. One wrong move and we could all get to be dead. Now, do you understand what you have to do?"

"Yeah, Dad," he replied, rubbing his shoulder, face flushed. "Sorry, but I *did* listen. Up three or four inches at a time. Hold it and check for the signal from you to go up a bit more."

"Good." Ryan ruffled his hair. "Just wanted to make sure you weren't getting careless."

"Want us back out of the way?" J.B. asked.

"No need for us all to take a risk. Dean should be safe enough at the side of the door. Up to me to move fast if it looks like the rocks are coming down."

For a moment Krysty opened her mouth to argue, then saw the tense expression on Ryan's face and closed it again.

Leading the way across the open space, toward the back wall, she stood in the hooded entrance to another of the side tunnels, waiting there with her Smith & Wesson 640 pistol cocked and ready in her right hand.

The rest of the group joined her, leaving father and son by the massive sec door.

"Ready?" Ryan asked, his voice softened and muffled by the dead air of the redoubt.

"Ready, Dad."

"Start taking her up. Watch my hand. When I do this—" he made a cutting gesture with the edge of his palm "—then you stop. Thumbs-up means go on again."

"Got it."

"Start."

When the door was about eighteen inches in the air, Ryan signaled to his son to drop the green lever.

"J.B., come take a look. See what you reckon."

The Armorer joined Ryan, kneeling, adjusting the spectacles on the bridge of his narrow, bony nose, and squinted under the door.

"Seem solid."

"Partly concrete and partly bedrock. Could be the remains of the old redoubt."

J.B. whistled tunelessly between his teeth. "Must have been one triple-nuke blast. Blow the top clean off. Take it up a bit farther?"

Ryan gave the signal to Dean, who eased the sec door up until the bottom was about two and a half feet from the scarred concrete of the floor.

"Hold it there." He crouched down, easing the rifle out of his way. Ryan could taste the air that Mildred had commented on, but he couldn't agree with her about it being fresh. It was damp, smelling of decay and wood smoke.

"What you reckon, lover?" Krysty called.

"Raining. I can tell you that. Running down the rockfall. Also—" he looked at his rad counter "—there's a high yellow reading out there, shading into orange. Must've been a serious hot spot in the long winters."

"Can we get out?" Dean had moved from his position by the control lever and was also staring at the tangled mass of concrete and stone.

His father straightened. "Don't see why not. The couple in front of us must've made it. No sign of crushed bodies out there. Looks like the rocks fell clear of the door."

The green lever was raised again, taking the sec door up to four and a half feet.

"That'll do," Ryan said.

"WASHINGTON," J.B. stated, squinting up into the late-afternoon drizzle, checking his tiny pocket sextant, its batteries—raided from a small techno armory years earlier—keeping it still functioning.

"State or city?" Doc asked, pulling his frock coat across his shoulders against the gray, misty rain that was falling steadily, blanking out visibility above two hundred yards.

"City."

Krysty's hair was already wet, clinging to her scalp, but she turned away and looked at the great pile of tumbled lichen-stained stone that had once been the top floors of a major redoubt. "Figure that those rocks hid the entrance to the complex, and stopped it being invaded. If this used to be Washington, then I guess there's still likely to be a few people around."

Doc shook his head. "I fear that there is likely to be but little remaining of that once great city. I have seen histories, copied from the verbal memories of the scant survivors, which claim that the nuclear holocaust actually began here in the seat of government, demiparadise.... There can be little doubt that the whole metropolis was blown away in the first treacherous salvo of the Third—and last—World War."

"True," the Armorer agreed. "All the years that Ryan and me rode with the Trader, I don't think we ever once came that close to this place. Supposed to be one big crater where the city used to be. Now they call it Washington Hole. Just shantytown gaudies and stuff like that."

A little to their left, beyond the crumbling ruins of the redoubt, there towered a rain-shrouded mountain, looking to be close to five thousand feet high. Mildred stared up at it with bemused fascination. "I have to turn to you, Doc, much as I regret it."

"How may I aid you, Dr. Wyeth?"

"I visited Washington a couple of times, for presidential receptions for the Olympic team. I saw Lincoln and the White House and the Monument. They were pulling down the old Watergate Hotel." She looked at the others, seeing only blank faces. "Before your time, I suppose. And way after your time, Doc. Anyway, point is, I don't remember there being a bastard great mountain anywhere around. Right, Doc?"

"Correct. Spot on. Ace on the line. Bull's-eye. Exactly right. Nothing much over four thousand feet, within five hundred miles of here, even all the way down the Blue Ridge west into Virginia. Mount Pleasant was just a few feet over that mark, to the north of Lynchburg."

"Volcano." Jak coughed, rubbing at the bandage around his injured right calf.

Mildred lifted a hand against the driving rain. "A *volcano!* In Washington, D.C.? My sweet Lord, but you're right. I can see the plume of steam and smoke from its top. An active volcano, here! Mercy me!"

"Changes in climate. Changes in altitude." Doc stared into the sky, hands clasped together like a preacher at a river-crossing meeting. "Changes in pulchritude. Changes in attitude. Changes in latitude. Changes in lassitude. Where is the bone that Lassie chewed? Lassitude. Get it? Got it. Bought the T-shirt.''

"Doc," Ryan said.

"Yes?"

"Shut it."

"Ah, right."

"Rotten stink, Dad."

Ryan sniffed. "Not so bad as back at our last stopping place, Dean."

"Not so farting. But still...like sitting next to someone in a drinker who hasn't changed their clothes for about five years. Know what I mean?"

Jak grinned. "Smells like home, Dean. Louisiana bayou sorta smell."

Ryan also smiled. "That's it all right. Except to see Spanish moss drooping from all of the trees. Not that I can see any trees around here."

J.B. busily wiped his glasses. "Guess that you can't just turn a million people into a kind of watery, bloody steam without something unpleasant lingering on. Even a hundred years later."

"So where's the city?" Dean put a muddy hand over his eyes in an exaggerated pose of exploration. "Or where the city used to be?"

The Armorer shook his head. "Can't tell you, Dean. First off, my sextant isn't accurate to more than a few miles. Second off, I've never been around here long enough to know the region. And thirdly, it's pissing down so hard that the city could be around the next corner and we still wouldn't know."

"Maybe we ought to go back inside the redoubt and stay dry," Mildred suggested. "Wait until the weather clears up before we explore."

"A little rain never did anyone any harm." Doc snorted. "I never mistook you for a namby-pamby indoor woman, Dr. Wyeth. Worried by a little heavenly dew."

"Heavenly dew! You silly old fool, it's coming down cats and dogs."

Ryan interrupted the budding argument. "Never been one for going back on my own trail," he said. "Have to agree with Doc. We're all wet now, anyway, so why not keep going? Look of the light, evening can't be all that far off. Let's move on some and take a look around. Find somewhere nearby to camp out and start a fire. How's that sound?"

Everyone nodded, Mildred last of all, her beads rattling damply.

ONCE THEY WERE OUT of the lee of the mountain, the wind freshened, driving away some of the light rain. It cleared visibility up to the better part of a mile, opening up the vista of what had once been the city of Washington, onetime capital of the greatest and most powerful country that the world had ever known.

The seven friends stood grouped together, staring down at the spectacle.

"Fireblast!" Ryan whispered.

Chapter Seven

From battered, rusting street signs, they discovered that they were in a suburb to the southeast of the city that had been called Forest Heights, standing just outside what had once been the city limits.

The newborn volcano wasn't the only change around Washington. There was the clearest evidence of massive quake activity, with ribboned, tilted highways and jutting chasms that furrowed the land. It was exceedingly doubtful that anyone who had lived in Forest Heights in the last blank days of civilization would have recognized the place now.

But many of the buildings remained.

Ryan had led them to a street of mainly Victorian frame houses, several of them rotted and tilted, leaning drunkenly against their neighbors. All of them lacked windows, but the companions found one house that seemed sturdy and, at least, still had most of its shingled roof intact. Dusk had come creeping in from over the Shens to the west, and they saw no sign of any human life.

A single dog skulked across their path, halting in a brief show of defiance in the center of the road and baring its teeth. Ryan started to unsling the Steyr, but the animal lost its nerve and scuttled off into the tall evergreen bushes that smothered most of the front gardens.

"Shame. Would have made good eating for to-night," Ryan said, replacing the rifle.

THEY GOT A FIRE GOING in the hearth of the stripped living room, using dry kindling that Dean scavenged from under the rear porch of the house.

Mildred found a battered pan and filled it from the brimming water butt, slicing up some of the vegetables that she discovered in the overgrown kitchen garden.

Potatoes, carrots and onions, with a few sprigs of herbs to give it flavor, simmered away.

The conversation turned naturally to what they'd seen while standing on the peak of Darien Avenue, looking down across the ravaged landscape.

"Just a big, big hole," Dean said. "That lake to the west, like the worst volcano in the world had blown its head off. Must've been ten miles across."

"Easy that," Jak agreed. "See why call it Washington Hole. Just 'Hole' for short."

It had been a gigantic crater, torn from the earth by the nuke bombs and, later, missiles, that had ripped the heart from the capital, and been the trigger for the dark nights and long winters that followed.

There had been no warning of the firestorm at ground zero that had literally blasted Washington into the cold dust of eternal space, slaughtering its inhabitants in the greatest megacull in history. There were precious few survivors after twenty-four hours. Then came the rad sickness with its poisoned claws.

Within a two-week period, the survivors of that first attack were so few that they couldn't be measured statistically.

The other extraordinary element of the sight was that the winding, warm, brown Potomac had vanished. Its bed scoured out and destroyed, it now formed a huge, lazy lake, miles wide from north to south, covering most of the blasted ruins of the city as well as virtually all of Arlington and Alexandria.

"That looked like one of the biggest shantytown camps I ever saw," J.B. said. "Around the edge of the crater. Couldn't see much for the cooking smoke, but there must've been hundreds of shacks there."

"Many of the old cities have their squat camps, don't they?" Krysty said.

Ryan leaned forward and sniffed at the vegetable stew. "Smells good. The cities? Yeah. But I've been to the ruins of Newyork, Norleans, Chicago... Point is that they were all wrecked, but all of them still had lots of buildings left, even if most were destroyed. We all remember what it was like drifting past the scrapers of Newyork. The dead streets and the ghoulies haunting the rad-blighted emptiness. You get squatters in all those places. But I never saw a town that was gone. Like it had never been. Just gone. Gone."

"Scares me." Mildred was sitting close to J.B., and she reached out and took his hand.

"Tiene el miedo muchos ojos," Doc said. "Fear has many eyes."

There was a long silence, broken only by the gentle bubbling of the water in the pan.

Jak broke the stillness. "Wonder what happened two men from redoubt?"

"Who cares?" Dean got up and peered out of one of the broken double doors that opened into the back garden. "Nearly dark. And it's raining again."

"What do you mean, 'again'?" Mildred said crossly. "I haven't noticed it stop raining ever since we left that nice dry, warm redoubt."

"Sourness in a maiden is as welcome as a persimmon in a bowl of cream," Doc stated solemnly.

"Did you just make that up?" Mildred snapped.

"Possibly. Very possibly."

"Attempted humor hangs on the lips of a senile old man as clinging shit on the ass of a dead goat," she riposted.

He applauded gently, making her grin, despite her ill-temper. "Well said, ma'am. Devilish well said."

"Meal's nearly ready," Krysty announced.

"Sounds good and smells good," Ryan said.

THE FIRE WAS DYING.

Ryan and J.B. had discussed the need for posting anyone on watch, eventually deciding that it wasn't necessary as there was no sign of any recent human habitation. The only thing they agreed was that they'd all move onto the top story for the night.

"I'll sleep out at the top of the stairs," the Armorer said. "I wake easy."

"So do I."

Jak had just joined them. "I sleep lightest," he said. "I'll sleep on the landing."

The two older men looked at each other. There was no point in arguing. They both knew that the albino teenager was telling the simple truth, and this wasn't some sort of game, where honor and pride were involved.

This was simply living and dying.

"Fine," Ryan said. "Good."

THE WIND FROM THE NORTH was stronger. Later it veered more toward the east, bringing the salt scent from Chesapeake Bay and heavier rain that thrummed on the roof, splattering through the broken glass of the bedroom windows.

The group had split up to sleep, as they often did. Jak took his chosen place at the top of the wide staircase. Doc and Dean shared the larger front room, with J.B. and Mildred in the middle. Ryan and Krysty chose the back room, much the most cramped of the available accommodation.

They bundled together, waiting until the rest of the house was quiet before beginning to make love. It was a hasty joining, less than satisfactory, and they had to move twice because of the spreading pool of rain that was inching across the floor toward them.

For about twenty minutes there was a sharp chem storm, with vivid stripes of purple-silver lightning, and thunder that seemed to shake the foundations of the old building.

Then they stopped moving as they both heard Dean picking his way barefooted across the landing, and a muttered conversation as he woke Jak.

"Must want a leak," Krysty whispered, keeping still, her stomach muscles fluttering and tightening around Ryan's powerful erection.

"Could just have done it out the window."

"Probably worried about all the splinters of broken glass. Boy doesn't want to risk doing himself a permanent injury. Think he's gone."

"Yeah, but then he'll come back."

"Want to call the whole thing off, lover?" she asked, feeling him begin to shrink inside her.

"No. Just wait."

"Then fill the time in with some kissing and touching. Starting just... down... there..."

AFTER THEY HAD BOTH finally climaxed, Ryan dozed for some time, waking against a particularly loud roll of thunder.

Krysty was lying on her back, head turned slightly to the left, snoring slightly, the errant beams of moonlight through the filtering clouds creating a glow around her mane of scarlet hair. The blanket had slipped down to just below her breasts, and Ryan lowered his head and gently touched his mouth to both erect nipples, pulling the blanket up to cover her.

"Thanks, lover," she whispered, miming a kiss through sleepy lips.

Ryan smiled in the darkness, listening to the sounds of the night. There was a dog... no, a pack of dogs, howling as they hunted their dreams together, far off, and the wind brushing through the sycamores that clustered at the back of the house. The rain seemed, temporarily, to have stopped.

The fire had guttered downstairs, but he could still catch the strong, bitter taint of its smoke. For a moment it crossed his mind to wonder how far that scent might carry on the scurrying wind, if there were any two-legged hunters on the prowl through the suburbs.

He felt the familiar swelling in his groin, lying still, trying to decide whether it meant lust, or the simple pressure of needing to take a leak.

A leak, he decided.

There was a great temptation to try to ignore it and stay warm and comfortable. But Ryan knew that he would be simply postponing the inevitable.

The wind brought another flurry of rain, tiptoeing across the roof, gurgling in the leaf-blocked gutters. The sound of running water was enough to decide Ryan that he needed to move. Biting his lip, he eased his way out of the makeshift bed, pulled on his pants, then the steel-tipped combat boots, hurriedly lacing them. The shirt was next, tangling itself awkwardly around his wrists, then the panga in its sheath.

He considered the SIG-Sauer and rejected it.

"Only going on the porch for a piss," he whispered to himself, picking his way carefully cross the creaking boards.

He had barely set foot on the landing before Jak was sitting up, his hair a blaze of brilliant white in the gloom, holding his heavy blaster.

"Should've slept downstairs, Ryan," he said quietly. "Whole world needs leak."

"Hear anything outside?" Ryan asked, as he stepped past the skinny figure of the teenager.

"The night. The sky. The trees. Dogs, far off. Thought heard shot, hour ago. Got up, checked around."

"And?"

"Nothing."

"Right. Be back in a couple of minutes."

Jak lay down again, closing his eyes, while Ryan left him and walked slowly down the stairs.

ONCE OUT THE BACK DOOR the one-eyed man blinked in the unexpectedly cold air, breathing in deeply, savoring the freshness. The fetid smell of brackish water that had been so strong once they left the hidden redoubt had gone, for the time being, washed away by the rain-bearing northeaster.

But he could still taste the last lingering tendrils of smoke from their fire.

Before unbuttoning, Ryan stepped cautiously onto the long porch, past the rusting skeleton of an ancient swing-seat, avoiding a jagged hole among the rotting timbers.

He could feel a faint prickling at his nape, which was often a warning from his highly developed combat sense of impending danger. Not always, but often enough for Ryan to take the sensation very seriously indeed.

His hand went for the SIG-Sauer, and he realized instantly that it lay alongside the sleeping Krysty. But there was still the eighteen inches of honed steel in its sheath. He drew it in a silken whisper of sound, looking out into the dense undergrowth of the garden, wondering if there was some hunting animal out there.

The air felt heavy, and he caught the intrusive smell of ozone, a sure pointer toward a severe chem storm hanging in the air close by.

Before he could move, there was a dazzling flash of lightning, blinding him, with a deafening roar of thunder riding right on top of it.

"Fireblast!" His ears felt numb, and he blinked furiously, seeing brilliant red spots on the inside of his eye, trying to see across the porch.

Ryan heard the voice before he could see anything of the speaker, a soft, gentle voice, sibilant, hissing at him from the darkness.

"Extremely sorry to perturb you, but I regret I must kill you. Please take your opportunity to try to defend yourself from my attack."

Chapter Eight

Ryan's brain was racing.

Who was the stranger who announced his deadly intentions in such a calm, almost courteously gentle manner?

Where was he?

What kind of blaster was he carrying?

Ryan furiously rubbed at his eye, trying to recover some elements of sight, head to one side, attempting to fix the location of his would-be assassin.

It crossed his mind to yell out to Jak and the others for help, but that might be just the trigger the killer needed to immediately execute him while Ryan stood there on the porch, almost as helpless as a day-old kitten.

There was something about the voice that nagged at Ryan's mind. It had a quite strong accent, though the way of speaking was accurate and educated. It was almost as if the man out there had learned English from a book as a second language.

"Time is of essence. I am extremely sorry, but if you will not defend yourself, I must take appropriate action and terminate your unworthy existence."

It was the letters *l* and *r* that gave the man some difficulty.

"Extremely" almost, but not quite, came out sounding like "extlemery."

"I can't fucking well see you," Ryan said angrily. "Lightning blinded me."

"Ah, so sorry to hear such unfortunate news. I did not know that. But..." There was a long sigh. "I fear I must carry on with expediting your passing, though it will bring me little honor. And you none at all."

Another lightning bolt hissed through the damp air, and an instantaneous rumble of thunder, that seemed to make the marrow of the bones vibrate, so close to the derelict house that the epicenter of the storm had to be within a quarter mile of where Ryan was standing.

With his eye shut, Ryan had been saved from being blinded all over again. But he had seen the vivid light through his closed lid. Now he cautiously opened his eye again, finding the shreds of high cloud away near the horizon were allowing some watery moonlight to illuminate the garden—and the man who was standing there, less than fifty feet away from Ryan, under the dark leaves of a dripping rhododendron bush.

He was below average height, barely five feet three inches tall, slenderly built. His face was sallow and his eyes almond-shaped. His mouth was partly open in a friendly smile.

He was wearing a long skirt, richly embroidered, that brushed the grass. Above it was an ornamented breastplate of steel, chased with silver dragons and flowers. He wore a magnificent helmet, that looked like bronze, and had two crescent moons on top, like twin horns.

The stranger was holding a long-bladed sword in both hands. Ryan noticed that the hilt was long and narrow, unlike any other sword he'd ever seen.

The combat stance was also unusual, slightly crouched, one small foot advanced in front of the other, the sword pointing back behind him.

There was something about the appearance of the Oriental-looking man that rang a tiny, distant bell for Ryan, a picture that J.B. had once shown him of Chinese warriors from medieval times—or, was it Japanese?—a still picture from some vid that the Armorer said was very famous.

But it slipped away from Ryan, driven by the urgency of his own position.

"You are now able to be seeing better, perhaps?" The question was solicitous, as though it were a good friend's inquiry about his health.

"A little."

"Good." The man sounded delighted. "We begin."

"Can I ask you a question?" Seeing the way the man was dressed, with the trailing skirt, it suddenly occurred to Ryan that this might be one of the pair that they'd tracked within the gateway. He also remembered that there had been rumors, increasing for some time, of a mysterious group of Oriental bandits, raiding here, there and everywhere, all across Deathlands.

"No. No point and no time for such closeness."

He shuffled toward Ryan, a halting step at a time, breath hissing between his teeth. As far as the faltering moonlight showed, the man wasn't wearing a blaster. Ryan yearned for the SIG-Sauer, knowing that he could easily have laid the Japanese on his back, staring open-eyed up into the drizzle.

For a moment he wondered if this was one of the strangers from the redoubt. If so, then where was his companion? Ryan felt a prickling between the shoulder blades, and he risked a glance behind him.

The house stood there, ghostly with its peeling paint and empty windows.

There was another rumble of thunder, a little farther away. Ryan knew that Jak would have awakened at a whispered footfall anywhere in the building, but would sleep happily through the worst chem storm.

"If I may offer a humble suggestion? It is wise not to turn away from me."

"Stab me in the back, would you?"

The man actually took a staggering step backward, eyes widening. "Is that the way barbarians think and act? We have been told to beware of such crudity of thought but..." He gathered himself. "No, we shall fight face-to-face."

"Your long sword against my little cleaver?"

Ryan was buying himself some time, watching the Oriental like a hawk, studying him, concentrating his attention on the way he held the sword. It seemed to Ryan that the only possible path of the attack would involve an overarm cutting blow, aimed at his own head and neck.

The problem would be how to get in his own blows, against someone shrouded in armor, virtually from top to toe.

"You do not have a sword?"

Ryan shook his head. "In the house. Shall I just go in and get it?" he asked, intending to shoot the man with the Steyr, from an upper window.

"Trickster! I think not. Come, we have squandered enough precious time in idle talk."

The fight lasted only a few seconds.

Ryan had guessed right.

The helmeted figure attacked with a strange, fluid, sliding movement, the sword coming over in a hissing arc of death, ready to cut Ryan open from throat to belt buckle.

But Ryan wasn't there anymore.

He had feinted left, then ducked right, using the back of the panga's blade to fend off the sword, sparks flying at the clash of steel.

Missing his blow sent the Oriental staggering off-balance, his small booted feet slithering in the muddy grass.

It opened up the right side of his body to Ryan's wicked reverse cut with the panga, aiming below the skirted armor, the edge hacking into the man's knee. It cut through the ligaments, slicing the cartilage apart, splintering the delicate bones of the joint.

The swordsman yelped and fell away, tumbling so quickly that Ryan almost had the hilt of the panga, blood-slick, jerked from his fingers.

It was a keystone of combat lore that a first successful shot or blow was useless unless you immediately followed it up and seized the advantage.

Ryan swung straight around again, aiming for the neck, but the fringe of steel links that dangled from the helmet deflected the blow, though there was enough power behind it to send the Oriental rolling on his back, dropping the long, slightly curved sword, grabbing at his ruined knee with both hands.

Ryan was amazed that his opponent wasn't screaming helplessly in terrible pain. Injuries to any of the major joints of the body—knee, elbow, shoulder— were among the most excruciating of any sort of wound, as Ryan himself knew from bitter personal experience.

But the Oriental mouth was tight-set under the painted visor, a trickle of blood running down his chin.

Ryan stooped and cut at the leather strap that held the helmet in place, slicing it in two, opening a long, shallow gash in the side of the throat. He knocked the heavy helmet away with his hand, revealing long black hair, tied back with a red-and-white scarf.

The narrow eyes looked up at him, showing virtually no emotion, though the man had to have known that he was staring up at his own death. He hissed something in a foreign language that Ryan didn't recognize.

For a moment Ryan hesitated, intensely curious about the alien-looking outlander, wondering where he could have come from, how he had managed to operate the gateway. If he was, indeed, one of the pair that they'd tracked both inside and outside the redoubt, which raised the question once again of where the second stranger was hiding.

Trader used to say that if you come to talk, then talk. But if you come to chill, then get on with the chilling.

He still hesitated, the panga hefted ready for the final crushing blow.

"To spare me would be to bring me only the deepest dishonor," the Oriental whispered, struggling to sit up.

One hand had moved from the damaged knee, crabbing toward the short dagger that was sheathed at the silken belt, a knife that had pretty braids of electric silk knotted in tassels at the ivory hilt. The sight of the bright-colored material nagged at a small memory at the back of Ryan's memory, but he couldn't quite remember what it was.

There was no point in waiting for the fingers to reach the knife.

The panga bit into the exposed neck with a wet thud, like a butcher's blade striking the flanks of a carcass. Blood gushed from the severed artery below the right ear, fountaining into the wet grass, black in the moonlight.

The man fell flat on his back. His legs kicked for a few moments, both hands opening and closing in twitching convulsions as the neuron lines went down.

Ryan bent and wiped the smeared blade on the man's baggy pants, straightening. He looked around the shadowed garden, feeling the rain becoming more heavy on his face.

There was no sign of any other living creature in the neighborhood.

He walked quietly back into the house.

The creaking of the hinges of the door had awakened Jak, who'd sat up, blaster in hand, as Ryan slowly climbed the stairs toward him.

"Trouble?" he asked.

"How did you know, Jak?"

"Smell on you. Hear fast heart."

"Yeah. Found one of those men in dresses we trailed in the redoubt."

"One?" The teenager was up on his feet, peering down into the moonlit vault of the hall below.

"Only one. Oriental with a sword. Kind of odd." He changed his mind. "Hold that. He was *triple* odd."

"Dead?"

"Dead."

EVERYONE WAS ROUSED.

J.B. suggested a recce to try to find the mysterious second man.

"Bushes and trees trickier than fleas on a dog," Ryan said. "Steady rain. Chem storm in the area. Light varies between poor and nonexistent."

"He didn't have a blaster?"

"No. Beautiful sword, and all this armor. Never seen anything like it in my life. Not here in Deathlands."

Doc cleared his throat. "From your detailed description, my dear fellow, I am forced to only one possible conclusion as to the nature of our visitors."

"Samurai," Mildred stated.

"I was about to say that," the old man said crossly. "The samurai. A class of professional warriors who flourished in old Japan for several hundred years. But they had died out, effectively, about fifteen or twenty years before my birth."

"You mean they gave up when they knew you were on your way, Doc?" Mildred teased.

"No. Not so. It was when Commodore Matthew Perry arrived with his so-called black ships in the territorial waters of Japan in, I think, about '53. He brought all the benefits of Western civilization that killed off these fighting men of honor. But it puzzles me to think what such a man could be doing here in Deathlands."

"And he spoke good English, lover?" Krysty asked. "Couldn't be some kind of time traveler? Operation Chronos from the farthest East?"

Ryan shook his head. "Don't know. How come they're using the gateways? And folks have been talking about gangs of them appearing, like wolf's-head bandits."

"Be interested to see him and all his weapons at first light." J.B. looked around. "Best keep a good watch for the rest of the night."

"Yeah." Ryan quickly allocated parts of the house around the group. One of them down in the hall, just to watch the front and back doors, another guard roaming around the silent first floor and a third sentry to cover the top floor and attics of the rambling old house.

HE WAS ASLEEP when Dean came in to wake him with the news that the first opalescent light of dawn was lighting up the Washington suburb.

"Nobody around?"

"No. But..."

"What?"

"No body."

Ryan sat up, glowering at his son. "You got something to tell me, then get on with it. We're not playing some stupe kid's game, Dean."

"Sorry, Dad. But there isn't any body out there in the garden."

Ryan still wasn't completely awake from the excitement of the previous night. "Nobody?" He sighed and felt a pulse of anger throbbing at his temple.

Dean bit his lip. "Not anybody, Dad. Not *any body.*"

"The corpse is gone."

"Right."

"Animals? Heard a pack of hunting dogs when I got up. Some way off."

"No sign of any blood or anything. Me and Jak went to take a look a couple minutes ago."

"Footmarks?"

Dean sniffed, looking down at the dew that coated his boots. "Jak says it was the other little man. Deep marks where he must've picked up the body of his friend and carried him off into the undergrowth. Couldn't follow him."

"What does 'couldn't' mean, son?"

"It means Jak said it would be double dangerous to go into thick brush. Like chasing after a wounded animal into mesquite. So he said to come tell you."

"The others up? Where's Krysty?"

"Taking a wash. Everyone else is up."

Doc appeared in the doorway of the bedroom, grinning wolfishly. "The sun has got his hat on,

Brother Cawdor, and there is likewise a wind on the heath."

Ryan recognized the quote from previous repetitions by the old man, but he couldn't remember the source. "Life is very sweet, brother. Who would wish to die?"

"Good. Very, very good, Brother Cawdor. We shall make something of you as a scholar after all. You've heard the body has gone from the secret garden below?"

"Yes."

"I shall go and reconnoiter what I may of this mysterious disappearance. Will you join me?"

"Soon as I can get my clothes on in some privacy. Like a gaudy saloon on a Saturday night in here."

THE GARDEN WAS MOIST and green and mostly in heavy shadow, the sun rising far off to the east, across the Lantic, behind the frame house.

"See impression where body lay," Jak said, sitting on the bottom step of the porch.

"Which way did they go?" J.B. asked. "Not that it matters much in the green hell out there."

Jak pointed toward a flowering wisteria that had curled itself around the trunk of a tall self-seeded sycamore. "Vanished in bushes."

"We going to take a look for the other man?" Krysty asked. "I can sort of feel him close by."

"Might have a blaster." Dean dropped his hand to the butt of his own 9 mm Browning Hi-Power.

"Best move on toward the center of Washington Hole." Ryan glanced up at the sky. "Could be a nice day."

Doc stood with his right hand holding one of the pillars of the porch, his fingers spread wide. "King George says go, we must obey, over the hills and far away." He sang the old song in a surprisingly melodious voice.

"Might as well move. See if we can pick up some breakfast on the road."

"Pity," Doc said. "You know, Ryan, I would dearly have loved to see a real-life samurai warrior. Or, even a real-dead samurai warrior. I am sure he could have offered so much arcane wisdom to us."

There was a strange thrumming noise in the bushes, and a whir of movement, a resonant thud, and an immensely long arrow, nearly five feet from honed tip to feathered end, cracked home into the wooden pillar, right by Doc, landing between his spread fingers.

Chapter Nine

"By the Three..." The words whirled out Doc's mouth, ending in a gasp as Ryan snatched at the old man and hurled him prone on the porch, behind the cover of an ornamental fence.

Everyone else hit the dirt, blasters drawn, peering through the gaps at the still and silent garden.

A little way off a pigeon, red-collared and crested, clattered noisily from the brush, flapping up to perch on a high branch of a stately elm.

"That way," J.B. said, pointing with the blunt muzzle of the Uzi.

"Thank you for saving my life, my dear Ryan, but I feel you might have been a little less violent. I am quite breathless with the sudden exertion of it all."

"Quiet, Doc." Ryan was looking up at the bizarrely long arrow, with its elegant goose-feather flights. "You seen anything like that, J.B., anywhere in Deathlands?"

"Never. What kind of a bow does it take to fire something like that?"

"Looks like would go through wall of house," Jak muttered.

"And it passed between my fingers. Brushed both of them with the force of its passing. Look..." Doc held out his hand, trembling a little. "See the scratches on them."

"Probably aimed for that," Mildred said.

"Not at all impossible," Doc replied. "I have read a little on the subject of the samurai, and their skill at arms is quite legendary."

"Can't see anyone out there," Dean said. "We going to go out after him?"

"That sounds like a triple-good way to get yourself chilled, son."

"Yeah, I suppose so. If he's got a big bow to go along with that arrow... It's more like a spear. I've seen people fishing through ice with a sort of arrow a bit like that one."

J.B. glanced back over his shoulder. "Thought just occurred to me that we might do better getting ourselves back into the house, friends. The samurai could easily have gotten himself around behind us."

It was an uncomfortable suggestion and a more uncomfortable thought.

Keeping low, they all crawled back inside, taking up defensive watching positions on every floor and on every side of the old building.

"Don't open fire if you see him," Ryan ordered. "Be good to take him alive and ask him some questions. Like if he and his friend used the gateway. Following from that, do they actually know how the system works? They could hold keys to unlock doors that could transform our lives."

"He's still around," Krysty said from the back bedroom. "I can feel him."

"What's his game?" Mildred asked. "Just going to try and keep us holed up in here?"

"Revenge would be guess." Jak was on the attic level of the house, his hair like a beacon in the gloom as he peered over the banisters.

Ryan walked slow up the stairs, SIG-Sauer in hand, into the room where Krysty was flattened against the wall, her own blaster drawn.

"Nothing," she said, squinting cautiously around the edge of the empty window frame. "Just a lot of green."

"Never got trapped by one man with a bow." Ryan moved fast across to the opposite side of the window, keeping flat against the wooden wall.

The second arrow came without any warning. Its splintering arrival, missing Krysty by less than a foot, followed a second later by the deep song of the bow, somewhere out among the overgrown garden. It pierced the outer and inner walls of the house, exploding in a burst of white plaster, burying itself at an angle in the far wall of the room, up close to the ceiling.

"Gaia!" Krysty gasped, belatedly dropping to the floor, brushing powder from her face.

"Son of a bitch!" Ryan stood for a moment in the window, daring the archer, his automatic searching the greenery for any sign of their enemy.

His eye caught a flicker of movement, deep in the shadows of a feathery palm tree, just in time to pull back into the corner as a third long shaft hissed into the bedroom, clear through the broken window, burying itself within a couple of feet of the other arrow.

There was the boom of Dean's Browning far below them, and Ryan was back at the window in time to see the leaves shaking as someone moved quickly away.

"Missed him, Dad."

"Nice try, Dean. Bastard came close to hitting us up here. Saw me speak to Krysty and worked out where she might be. Put an arrow clean through the wall."

"Think gone." The teenager was directly above them in one of the attics.

"Spot him, Jak?"

"No, Ryan. Just movement going away after Dean's shot. Good try, kid."

"Don't call me 'kid,' Jak."

The albino laughed softly.

J.B. WAS INTRIGUED by the quality of workmanship shown in the arrows. "Don't know what kind of wood they're made from," he said, handling it like a religious icon.

"Goose feathers, for the flights, I thought," Ryan offered. "Steel tip. Beautiful thing."

"Certainly not Native American. No tribe would use something of this length. Damned nearly as tall as me." He held it against his five feet eight inches. "To get this kind of power and velocity, the bow has to be..." He shook his head. "Wish we could capture this son of a bitch, Ryan. Surely wish we could."

AFTER TWO HOURS of waiting, Ryan had begun to think that the samurai warrior had departed, possibly going back to the redoubt to jump away to where he'd come from.

Doc stood at the bottom of the stairs. "I think that I can wait no longer, friend Cawdor."

"What for, Doc?"

"A personal matter." His voice tight with tension. "But one that can wait no longer. I beg you to trust me implicitly in this matter."

Krysty leaned toward Ryan, her face so close that her bright red hair brushed his cheek. "Doc means that he's bursting to take a crap," she whispered.

"Oh, yeah." Ryan raised his voice. "You want to go out into the garden, Doc?"

"Indeed I do."

Mildred had been watching the front of the house, peering between the tall, rambling trees toward the narrow side street. Now she reappeared, holding her Czech ZKR 551 target revolver. "Want me to keep him covered?"

Though Ryan had the hunting rifle with a Starlite night scope and laser image enhancer, he knew that Mildred was much the best shot of the party. And if the Oriental assassin appeared, the range wasn't going to be much above thirty yards.

"Sure," he said.

Doc hobbled off the porch, legs oddly tight together, glancing back toward the house. Seeing Mildred watching him from the rear second-floor window, he gave her a hurried, self-conscious wave and a broad, toothy grin.

"If our man's still out there, he could put an arrow clean through the old guy's skull and out the other side," J.B. said quietly.

Ryan had called everyone to the garden side of the building, making sure that they were all on the reddest alert, watching for a glimpse of the Oriental archer.

He was using the laser sight, its tiny crimson dot flickering among the leaves, peering through it and searching for any sign of life, breaking off now and again to check the birds in the trees. But none of a flock of pigeons was moving at all.

Which probably meant the garden was deserted and their enemy was gone.

Or, Ryan reminded himself, it could mean that the samurai had never left and was simply waiting patiently for his opportunity to avenge his comrade's death.

Doc had stopped just beyond the fringe of rhododendrons and dropped his pants, squatting down out of sight, the top of his silvery mane barely visible.

With the pressure of danger, Doc was quickly done, the bushes shaking as he plucked a handful of broad leaves to wipe himself clean.

Then he was up again, running both hands through his hair, offering a mocking bow to the six faces staring at him from the windows.

"Move it, Doc," Krysty called, her voice harsh. "Got a feeling that..."

The tall, frock-coated figure was striding toward them, walking far more freely than three minutes earlier, but Krysty's shout made him halt, looking behind himself at the great shifting bank of green.

Ryan had been watching carefully, but he didn't actually see the man come out of the foliage. One moment he wasn't there. Next moment he stood at the edge of the bushes, an enormously long bow drawn in his hands, an arrow notched on the string, aimed at the center of Doc's chest.

Ryan's instant reaction saved the old-timer. He hissed to Mildred, "Don't shoot the man. He'll loose and chill Doc."

The black woman didn't need the explanation, instantly altering her aim, the big six-shot revolver an extension of her right arm. Both eyes were open as she looked down the barrel, her finger tight on the trigger.

The man was an almost identical copy of the Oriental that Ryan had slain. Short and stocky, in a helmet with a bronze moon in its crown, a long sword sheathed at his waist, his armor glittering in the midmorning sunshine.

"I am Takei Yashimoto, and I am here to take a life for the life of my brother, Tokimasha. Then I will offer my own unworthy self as a hostage in combat against any of you round-eye barbarians who wish to accept my humble challenge."

"We have guns," Ryan called. "A word from me and you're dead meat."

"I value my life less than a feather," the samurai replied. The point of the arrow hadn't deviated by an inch from Doc, who was standing, frozen, a few yards away.

"Gonna shoot, Ryan," Mildred breathed.

"No. I told you—"

But there was the boom of the blaster, and the Smith & Wesson .38 round was on its inexorable way toward the armored figure.

There was a deafening crack, and the bow seemed to explode in the man's hands. The arrow flew sideways for a dozen feet, before flopping harmlessly to the grass.

The samurai staggered backward, his helmet sitting crookedly on his head, the two halves of the broken bow clutched uselessly in his hands.

"Brilliant, love!" J.B. exclaimed, slapping Mildred on the arm. "Brilliant shot. The best."

"Worst, John. I was aiming at the point of the arrow and hit the damned bow. Still..."

Below them, the frozen tableau had suddenly thawed.

Doc was fumbling for his Le Mat, yelling incoherent oaths at the bemused Japanese warrior, who threw away his shattered bow and stood staring in disbelief at the furious old man who was threatening to shoot him.

Ryan brought the Steyr to his shoulder again, but a dip in the land meant that Doc's greater height lay between him and a clear shot at the lone enemy.

"Move it, Doc!" he bellowed.

But Doc was deaf to anything, his blood racing as he finally managed to draw the big Le Mat and thumb back on the spur hammer above the scattergun round.

The armored figure half drew his sword, then seemed to realize he had no chance at all.

As quickly as he'd appeared from the undergrowth, the man vanished in a swirl of leaves, the quiver of long arrows snagging for a moment on a low branch.

Doc fired the gold-engraved Le Mat, disappearing in a great cloud of powder smoke, ripping a chunk out of the bushes. Ryan thought that he heard a sharp cry of pain, but he couldn't be absolutely certain.

"Gone," Jak said.

"Did I hit him?" Doc called, trying to shift the hammer to the revolver barrel, with its nine .44s.

"Mebbe," Ryan replied. "Come on back to the house, Doc, and we'll get moving. Leave this quiet suburb of Forest Heights. Come on."

"By the Three Kennedys! My heartfelt thanks to you, Dr. Wyeth, for some damnably pretty pistolry. If I ever set these glims on another of these Oriental demons, then I'll... Had I not just relieved myself, I fear that I might easily have soiled my best linen."

He holstered the Le Mat and stooped to pick up the spent arrow. He snapped it across his knee, then gripping the two broken pieces and breaking them again, hurled the four sections of the samurai's arrow into the bushes.

"Know the feeling, Doc," Ryan said.

Chapter Ten

As they walked slowly through the bright morning, along deserted streets of houses, which became more ravaged the nearer they came to the lip of the gigantic crater, the main topic of conversation was the encounter with the pair of Japanese samurai warriors.

"Think that last one escaped, Dad?"

"Could be. But I thought I heard a yell when Doc shot after him."

"I thought I heard it, too," Krysty agreed.

"Where the dark night do they come from?" J.B. asked, puzzled. "I figure we've been just about all over Deathlands, and I never saw nor heard a word of them."

"Until in the last few weeks." Ryan kicked the gnawed body of a rat out of his path.

Doc had been quiet, walking along, absently tapping his cane. Now he stopped and faced Ryan.

"That wasn't some young fool pretending to be a samurai, Ryan. I was as close to him as I am to you, and I would swear on the grave of my beloved Emily that he was the real article." He hesitated. "Her grave. I have never thought where she might lie. When I was first a prisoner I tried to discover something of her later life. Where she might have been interred, but they watched me. Now all records have gone. Did she marry again, I wonder? A part of me hopes she stayed a widow, true to my memory. But my disappearance...she would never know why I was taken or where I went. I would not truly have wanted my Emily to pull in single harness for all that remained of her life." He drew out his swallow's-eye kerchief and blew his nose. "I wandered, dear friends. I am so sorry. I was saying I believed the samurai was genuine."

"But there haven't been men like that for two hundred years or more, Doc," J.B. said.

"True, John Barrymore. True. First came the Totality Concept. A secret range of subdivided projects designed to insure the safety and power of the United States against all aggressors. A part of that was Overproject Whisper, which included the section known as Cerberus. Matter transfer was their main aim. But there was also Operation Chronos. The whitecoat murderers who time-trawled me here from my happy home."

"We know this, Doc," Krysty said. "What are you trying to say?"

"They spoke English. Mine did. You said that yours did as well, Ryan?"

"True."

Doc pressed the tips of his fingers against his forehead. "How did they learn it? And did they jump from some unknown other place? Too many questions to ponder and not enough answers. Almost no answers. And I don't think we even know what most of the questions are."

"Mebbe we'll never see any of them again," Dean said. "Gone forever."

"Mebbe," his father agreed. "Mebbe."

WHAT HAD SEEMED like one huge shantytown from the outer limits of the Washington Hole was revealed as several separate gatherings of tents and makeshift huts, separated by filthy polluted streams and swampy offshoots of what was once the Potomac.

The seven companions picked their way down through the shattered remnants of the suburbs.

The frame houses with their broken windows were replaced by similar streets of homes, but with roofs gone and ancient scorch marks on their white walls.

The nearer they went to what had been the center of the city's nukecaust, the worse the damage grew. More houses lacked their roofs, many of them showing signs of old fires. There was a small area of absolute devastation, with the melted stumps of a dozen gas pumps standing amid the ruins like the petrified corpses of nuclear soldiers. A row of stores was reduced to blackened concrete boxes.

As they made their way down a shallow hill, they went past the last of the recognizable buildings, entering a bleak region of utter obliteration. Roads had been turned into blackened strips of fused lava, at the heart of a part of the old city where there was no trace of green.

Even now, close to a century after the ending of the long winters, almost nothing grew there except the rankest of deformed weeds. There were sickly lilies, the color of drowned flesh, towering eight or ten feet above the fused soil. Bright red gardenias were mutated with poisonous spikes.

They encountered the first signs of shantytown life, a broken stump of a telegraph pole, with the body of a man wired to it. The corpse, head-down, had lost hands and feet, and a small fire still smoldered beneath it.

"Welcome to Washington Hole," Jak said.

THE SHANTYTOWNS that ringed the bleak heart of the gigantic crater all had different names, their origins mostly lost in the mists of the long winters.

Sweet William was the largest of them, Broken Heart another, to the north.

A surprisingly neat sign announced to Ryan and the others that they were about to enter the township of Green Hill.

"I wonder if that's the green hill far away in the old hymn?" Mildred said. "Without the city wall."

"There certainly doesn't seem to be either any hills or anything colored green around." Doc sniffed the air. "Though I can smell all manner of food cooking, both fish and flesh. Perhaps even some fowl. Enough to get the underworked taste buds quivering a little."

Stunted black chaparral dotted the dusty track that wound into the main street of the pesthole, with large red ants swarming around their roots.

"Big," J.B. said. "Looks like a hundred shacks and tents. Big for a city pesthole."

"We going to stay here at all, Dad?"

"Mebbe a night."

"My mother, Rona, always said we did well to keep away from pestholes."

"She was right," he replied, patting the boy on the shoulder. "Not places for children or women. Not places for anyone, come to that. But if we can get some food and beds for the night we could move on tomorrow."

"Stick together." Jak had tied his hair back with a red bandanna. "Best rule in place like this."

Ryan nodded. "Yeah. Everyone hear that? Jak's right. No wandering off on your own. Anyone."

IT WAS EARLY AFTERNOON as they trudged into the smoky shantytown.

In his life Ryan Cawdor had to have passed through hundreds of these stinking little frontier pestholes, with their filthy hovels and their poxed gaudies and brutally dangerous drinking bars. Green Hill didn't look any different to any of the others.

The street was trampled mud, with a couple of stores, brothels and saloons scattered along it. The rest of the place was tents and huts lining narrow alleys that did double service as thoroughfares and open sewers.

Few of them had anything that remotely approached a lawn. Most had open muddy yards, filled with all manner of filthy and noisome rubbish. Some had cords of wood, ready for the biting winters. Ryan saw a wheelless tractor, rusting away, with two or three more unrecognizable pieces of broken agricultural machinery beside it.

Smoke drifted low over the ville, carried on a fresh easterly wind off the ocean.

There were very few people around. Most of them looked ragged, shambling along with their heads shrouded in old blankets or shawls. At a distance it wasn't possible to tell their sex. A few mongrels came snarling and yapping out of one of the alleys, barking around the heels of the seven strangers, running whining when Doc caught their leader a brisk blow across the scarred muzzle with his sword stick.

The noise attracted attention, and tent flaps peeled back and faces appeared at the smeared, cobwebbed windows of the nearest saloon, peering at the outlanders.

"Try there?" J.B. said, pointing toward the building. "Sign says it's called the Lincoln Inn. And—" he peered to try to make out the faded paint "—says that it offers clean beds by the night and good food."

"One place'll be like the next." Ryan glanced around the suddenly deserted shantytown. "Let's go see what they have to offer."

TWO STORIES TALL, the Lincoln Inn was the most imposing building in the wretched ville. It was built from weathered wood, the first floor being taken up with a sprawling saloon. A staircase led to the shadowy second floor. An ill-matched assortment of tables and chairs stood around the splintered floor, occupied by half a dozen silent men, four of them playing a desultory hand of poker with a pack of greasy cards.

The man behind the bar was short and craggy, the top of his head shaved, with curling gray side-whiskers. His eyes were a bright, piercing blue, his cheekbones so prominent that it looked as if he'd swallowed a pelvis.

"Howdy there, outlanders. Belly up here and name your poison. Yes-siree."

"Man's seen way too many Roy Rogers movies," Mildred whispered. "Like he's playing a supporting part in a B-movie Saturday-morning special."

"We got a range of gut rot'll put hairs on your chests... Sorry, ladies. Nothing meant by that. Our own ladies are taking their afternoon siesta, but if any of you have a taste for some female company I can easy rouse them. Got a fine Mex girl, near virgin, weighs in close to three hundred pounds, gives any gentleman two downs for every up."

"How about rooms for a night?" Ryan asked. "Just that and food."

"We got... I know you, don't I, mister? That one eye sort of sticks in a man's mind. And you..." He pointed a bony finger at J.B. "Both rode with the Trader, didn't you?"

There wasn't any point in arguing with such a positive identification. The only question for Ryan and the others was how had this man been treated by Trader.

"Can't say I recognize you..."

"Name's Clinkerscales. Peter Clinkerscales. Hell of a mouthful, ain't it? I was barkeep in a gaudy close to Butte, in the Darks. Was having trouble with some trappers. You two were there when Trader leaned on them and cleaned them out. Made sure they never came back to bother me."

J.B. eased away the Uzi that had suddenly appeared as the man recognized him. "Sure. I remember. Dark night! Must've been at least ten years back."

"All of that. Sorry, friends, but I don't recall your names." He tapped his forehead. "Accounted to my age and white port wine. Don't seem to be able to remember things quite as well as I used to."

Ryan introduced himself first, running through the list of everyone's names. Clinkerscales insisted on enthusiastically shaking hands with all of them, grinning broadly, showing chipped, stained teeth.

"This is my gaudy," he said. "I been waiting all this time to repay that good deed of Trader. You can have rooms and free food for as long as you like. And as much drink as your stomachs can handle. How about that?"

"Never turn down a generous offer," Ryan replied. "Just three rooms—seven beds, two twos and a three—for one night'll do it. Won't turn down supper and breakfast tomorrow, before we get on our ways again. Thank you kindly."

"Sure thing. Tell me, Ryan Cawdor, whatever happened to that fine old boy, Trader? Heard he'd bought the farm against some renegade Utes up near the Sippi?"

"No. Last I heard he was somewhere out in the western islands. Give him your best next time I run into him."

"Do that, Mr. Cawdor. Please do that." He smiled and nodded like a clockwork Buddha. "Now, you turned down the ladies, I believe. Jack-free offer extends to them if any of you... No? Fair enough, friends. Let me show you to your rooms and then there's a bathhouse out back with good hot water.''

"Food?" Krysty asked.

"Of course." A slight frown crossed his eager face. "Right now only some heat-up soup and bread with refried beans. Cook's not here until six in the evening."

"Perhaps we might delay our repast until the evening," Doc suggested.

There was a general murmur of approval, though Dean sighed, rubbing his stomach meaningfully.

Clinkerscales smiled again. "How about a small drink before you go up to the rooms? We got the best range of predark rarities anywhere round Washington Hole."

"Predark drinks!" Jak stared suspiciously at the barkeep.

"Cross my heart and hope to die, friends. The center of the old ville was wiped clean away on minute one of hour one of day one of skydark. But plenty of the stores out in the suburbs were still left standing. Not many people alive for miles, so there's plenty of stuff around."

"What kind of drinks?" Mildred asked.

"Normally some of them go for a barrow-load of jack, lady. But for friends of Trader..."

"Come, jovial mine host," Doc urged, "list us your drinkables, there's a good fellow."

The arrival of Ryan and the others had silenced the cardplayers, who were all sitting, openmouthed, staring at the exotic newcomers.

"Well..." Clinkerscales began to tick off his drinks on his fingers, glancing at the row of dusty bottles behind him to refresh his memory. "Peach schnapps, cream of menthe, amaretto, Cointreau...that's a kind of fiery orange flavor. Real nice. Not sure how you pronounce that blue stuff next to it. Spelled c-u-r-a-c-a-o. Sounds kind of Mex to me."

"You got any fine drinking whiskey?" Ryan asked. "Those all look and sound too fancy."

The barman tugged at his curly side-whiskers, sniffing and wiping his beaked nose on his sleeve. "Well, I wouldn't steer you wrong, Mr. Cawdor. First things to go were the good whiskies. Corn and malts. There was a warehouse out beyond Rockville. Been buried under some nuke damage for years. Quake uncovered it eight years ago. Baron Sharpe was out that way on one of his hunting expeditions. Him and me had a sort of arrangement over my girls..." He winked at Ryan. "Know what I mean?"

"Yeah. I know what you mean. And you got first hands on the liquor."

Clinkerscales nodded. "Sure did. But these foreign drinks is all I got left. Folks say they taste real good. Why don't you try some of them?"

"I'll have a glass of the Cointreau," Mildred said.

"Same for me," Doc added quickly. "Make it a double, if you will. Most excellent. Fill the flowing bowl, landlord, and let who will be sober."

"How's that, Doctor?"

"Ignore him," Krysty said. "I'll try that green drink. Cream of something."

"Menthe. Reckon it means mint. That's what it tastes of. Kind of sweet."

"Can I have that as well, Dad?"

Ryan nodded. "Sure."

The barman was busily blowing dirt off the bottles, finding an array of glasses and wiping them round with a corner of his apron. He poured out generous measures of the clear Cointreau and the dark green mint liqueur.

"Gentlemen?" he said to Ryan, J.B. and Jak.

"Nothing for me," the Armorer replied. "Hot bath and a rest'll do for me."

"Got some Russkie vodka. Strongest proof you ever knew. Got to swallow it soon as it touches your lips. Or it strips the coating off of your teeth."

"Yeah," said Jak. "Try that."

The liquor had an oily sheen to it as Clinkerscales poured it into a shot glass.

"Mr. Cawdor?"

"I'll try the same."

There wasn't any kind of rotgut all along the frontier that hadn't been sampled by Ryan.

He took the glass and lifted it, offering a toast to the barkeep and his friends. "Here's to blasters fixed good and firm-feelin' women." Seeing Krysty opening her mouth to reproach him, he added, "Only joking. Used to be Trader's favorite toast," he explained to Clinkerscales.

"Here's to warm beds, good food and honest friends," J.B. said.

"Better." Krysty sipped at her drink. "That's good."

Ryan gulped half the contents of the shot glass into his mouth. For a moment this high-proof vodka tasted cold, so fast was it evaporating. Then the heat began to make itself felt and he quickly swallowed it. There was a half second when it didn't seem any worse than any other gaudy liquor.

"Fireblast!" he spluttered out as the fire scorched down his throat, reaching his stomach in seconds. He blinked away a tear from his good eye. "That'd strip the paint off a war wag's belly," he gasped.

He glanced sideways at the albino teenager, who had drained his glass in a single swallow. Jak grinned at him, showing no visible sign of distress. Though Ryan noticed that his eyes, usually pink, seemed nearer to crimson.

"Another," Jak said.

Ryan finished off the drink, managing to hold it down. "Yeah. Me, too," he said, his voice sounding higher and thinner than he remembered.

"Don't get into a tough man's contest, Ryan," Krysty warned. "Try this stuff."

"No. No, thanks. Stick to this vodka."

The second glass wasn't any easier, though Jak failed to muffle a cough as his drink burned its way down.

"Prime stuff, ain't it, friends?" Clinkerscales said. "They knew how to brew hooch in the old predark days."

"You won't hear any argument from me on that matter." Doc placed his glass carefully down on the bar top. "But I think one is sufficient. Mayhaps a second round of imbibing when we come down to dine.''

The barkeep grinned, showing a mouth that seemed overfilled with a jumble of teeth. "What I like to hear, Doc. What I like to hear. Now, let me show you to your rooms." He patted Ryan on the arm. "After supper, mebbe you could sit with me and tell some tales of Trader and those good old days."

"Good old days?" Ryan repeated, feeling that someone had replaced his brain with warm gruel and somehow made his tongue swell to twice its normal size. "Good old days? Trader used to tell us that they was just a bunch of people, doing the best they could. That was all the good old days was."

THE STAIRS WERE STEEP and uneven, and Ryan tripped halfway up, nearly dropping the Steyr off his shoulder. There was a burst of laughter from the locals in the saloon, quickly stifled when the one-eyed man looked angrily around.

Clinkerscales showed them to their rooms, a front double for Ryan and Krysty, identical one across the passage for J.B. and Mildred and a bigger family room for Doc, Jak and Dean at the end of the corridor, next to the bathroom.

"Best Green Hill's got to offer," the barkeep said. "See y'all later."

Chapter Eleven

Everyone took advantage of the unusually good bathing facilities, a proper bathroom, with a large tub and endless supplies of piped water, coming, Clinkerscales explained, from local hot springs.

Dean raced to be first, emerging as pink as a peeled prawn, black curly hair pasted flat to his scalp, looking much younger than his eleven years.

Doc insisted on the courtesy due to his age and claimed second place, singing romantically maudlin old parlor songs at the very top of his booming voice. Occasional lines gloated up from the first floor back of the gaudy to the rooms where all of the others were waiting.

"She was poor but she was honest, victim of a village crime..."

After Jak had gone down and knocked several times on the bathroom door, Doc had come out, rosy-cheeked, beaming from ear to ear. "Wonderful!" he exclaimed. "The jug of wine and loaf of bread can take second place to a hot bath any day of the week." He hesitated a moment. "Though I am rather looking forward to the loaf of bread and jug of wine a little later this evening."

MILDRED AND J.B. TOOK fourth and fifth places.

The Armorer, still surrounded by wisps of steam, knocked on Ryan's bedroom door. He had a towel around his middle, with the Uzi slung over his naked shoulder, his misted spectacles gripped tightly in his left hand.

"Good," he said, grinning. "Your turn."

"Thanks."

"How's the time?"

Ryan checked the chron on his left wrist. "Just after four in the afternoon."

"Think this place is safe, Ryan?"

"Guess so. I remember Clinkerscales. Nice to find someone who doesn't spit in your face at the news that you once rode the war wags with Trader."

"True enough. Heard him mention a baron in the region. Didn't catch the name."

Ryan sniffed. "You hear the name of the baron, Krysty?" he called.

"Sharpe, he said."

"Find out more about him while we eat," J.B. stated. "Better go get dressed."

The door opposite opened, and Mildred appeared, still only wearing a towel. "Hurry up, John. Come and get dry, then we can get ready for supper."

"Two hours to wait, Mildred," Ryan called as the skinny figure of the Armorer scuttled back into his room.

"I know it, Ryan. We'll just have to find something to do for a couple of hours." She giggled as she closed the door.

Krysty was close to Ryan, laying her hand on his shoulder and gently squeezing the back of his neck. "We have to find something to do to pass the time as well, lover."

"Like having a sleep?"

Her hand dropped lower, down his back, stroking his firm, muscular buttocks. He automatically tensed them at her touch. "Like rocks in a sack, lover," she whispered.

"I'll go take that bath and be back real quick."

"No, lover. You and I'll go down and take a bath and be back real slow."

THERE WAS A STOUT BOLT on the inside of the door and only a narrow, curtained slit window, insuring complete privacy for them. Ryan had the SIG-Sauer inside his towel, and Krysty was carrying her own Smith & Wesson five-shot blaster.

Krysty leaned over and turned on the large brass tap, marked with the symbol *H*, smiling with pleasure as hot water gushed out.

"Looking good, lover."

There was a bar of red carbolic soap on a shelf near the window, and a pile of fluffy towels on a bench in the corner of the bathroom.

Steam began to rise from the foaming water, and Krysty added some cold, stirring it with her hand.

"Smell the chemicals," Ryan said. "Sort of sulfur like the hot springs we saw back..." The words trailed away as his mind snatched at the memory of Trader and Abe standing together in the stinking mists.

"Why didn't you tell Clinkerscales about Trader?"

"Meaning he's dead?"

"From what you said, it's likely, lover."

Ryan bit his lip and sighed. "Guess so. I just figured that it's best to allow the legend to survive."

"Probably right." She turned off both taps. "There. Looks like enough water. Don't want it swilling all over the floor. The door bolted?"

He checked. "Yeah."

"Then let's get clean."

Krysty peeled off her clothes fastest, throwing them on a marble-topped table. "Come on," she teased.

Ryan had unlaced the steel-tipped combat boots, tucking his socks neatly inside them. He unbuttoned the heavy-duty dark blue pants and pulled them off, adding the blue denim shirt, leaving him standing in his shorts.

Krysty put her arms tight around him, her breasts pressed against his chest. She stood only three inches below his six feet two. Her fingers traced the complex network of scars that seamed Ryan's back.

"Every one of these could tell its own story, couldn't it, lover?"

He kissed her on the side of the neck, her fire-bright hair seeming to caress his face. "Guess they could," he said. "Not pretty stories."

As her fingers roamed lower, they encountered his most recent wound, from the arrow. He instinctively winced at the touch, and Krysty moved her hand.

"Sorry," she whispered. "Want me to try to kiss it better for you?"

Now her right hand had insinuated itself between their bodies, easing inside his shorts, finding him hard and ready.

"Might get to some kissing better a little later," he said hoarsely.

"Right," she breathed. His hand was between her thighs, moving them apart, touching her very gently. "Best get in the bath before the water gets cold, lover."

Ryan tugged off his shorts, taking care not to snag them on his erection, throwing them on top of his piled clothes. He stepped cautiously into the bath, finding the water was hot but not too hot. "Good," he said, sitting, then lying flat on his back, the level rising up over his thighs and over the flat, muscular wall of his stomach.

Krysty smiled, reaching down to hold him. "Looks like that thing that submarines used to have, so they could see when they were below the sea."

"Periscope?"

"That's it."

She climbed in, stepping carefully astride him, lowering herself very slowly, using her fingers to guide him deep inside her. The level of the water rose higher, coming close to the top of the bath.

"Best if I do the moving for both of us," she said. "Or we'll have us a flood."

"Sounds good."

Ryan held her as she started to rise and fall, using the soap to wash her breasts, covering the peaked nipples in foam, rubbing them with his strong fingers.

Krysty's head was thrown back, her bright emerald eyes closed, the cords taut in her throat. She gripped

Ryan's hands, pushing them harder against her body, moaning to herself.

"Gaia, that's so good, lover."

Ryan stared up at her perfect body, trying to judge how far along the road she was, controlling himself, holding back, despite the insistent pressure of Krysty's body sucking him in deeper and harder.

"Touch me," she panted, rocking back and forth as he probed at her with his index finger, helping her toward a racing climax.

When she came it almost took him by surprise, her mouth sagging open, leaning over him, her nails scratching at his chest, making him moan in a mix of pain and pleasure.

But he allowed himself his own surging release, closing his eye, whispering to his love. "Yes, yes, yes, yes..."

When they'd recovered their breath, they paid some attention to washing each other.

Ryan stood, steadying himself against the wall, while Krysty knelt in the hot water, soaping him, paying particular attention to his genitals. She rubbed up a fine lather, cupping him in both hands, lowering her mouth to bring him back to readiness. When he was a little slow for her, Krysty moved a hand between his thighs, sliding a soaped finger up inside him, making Ryan yelp in surprise as it had the desired effect on him.

She smiled up at him. "Some fingers come in the front door and some use the back door," she said.

Ryan gripped her by her nape, holding her steady as he started to thrust into her mouth.

But she pulled away.

"No. Not that way this time. Want you in me from behind." Krysty stood, careful not to slip in the soapy bath. She placed both hands against the wall, resting her head on them, stooping forward.

Ryan moved close in, sliding between her glistening buttocks. Using his right hand to set himself in the right place, he spread her thighs wider.

"There," Krysty whispered.

By the time they'd completed the bathing and the lovemaking, drying each other off with the thick towels, so much time had passed that they realized that supper would soon be ready.

They dressed quickly in the bathroom. Ryan slid back the bolt and, from force of habit, checked that the corridor outside was empty.

"Let's go," he said.

LOOKING OUT OF THEIR WINDOW, across the rutted mud of Green Hill's main street, Ryan saw the shantytown starting to come to life. The air was heavy from the smell of cooking fires, and kerosene lamps were appearing outside some of the shacks and tents.

A dog barked in a furious rage nearby, until the sharp sound of a blow silenced it. A woman called out, laughing, across the way, and a mule was letting the world know that it was feeling hungry.

"You've been in plenty of places like this one, haven't you, lover?"

He nodded, turning from the window, letting the tattered curtain fall back into place. "Hundreds. From the big snows down to the gulf. From the Cific to the

Lantic. If I had a fistful of jack for every frontier pesthole I've visited, then I'd be the richest baron in Deathlands.''

There was a knock on the door.

Ryan picked up the blaster and moved to flatten himself against the wall. "Who is it?"

"Me, Dad. Joint's jumping. Packed out. Clinkerscales says outlanders are rare and everyone's here to check us out. You coming down to eat?"

"Sure. Be right down."

"If the meal's as good as the bath, then it'll be an evening to remember," Krysty said.

Chapter Twelve

The Lincoln Inn was groaning at the seams.

As Ryan and Krysty paused at the top of the stairs, they could hardly see a free inch of floor space. All of the tables were occupied, and three separate games of poker were going on, with jack piled up among the beer glasses. The dartboard was the center of a noisy game, the flighted hand arrows thudding hard into the sectored cork.

Clinkerscales behind the bar was busier than a one-legged man in a forest fire, rushing from end to end, drawing beer and sliding shot glasses of the house whiskey through the spill puddles to the clamoring crowd.

The only women in the saloon were gaudy whores, working the room to try to get some custom, even though it was still early in the evening. As Ryan and Krysty looked down, one of the sluts was coming up the stairs, dragging a three-parts drunk breed behind her. The man seemed to have two sets of teeth, laid one inside the other, and he was grinning vacantly at the tantalizing prospect that lay ahead of him.

The whore was young and skinny, with a dreadful knife scar, barely healed, that opened up the left side of her face from hairline, past the corner of the eye, down to the angle of her jaw. The cicatrix was puckered, purple at its edges, a livid white at the center.

Before the scar, she might once have been a pretty girl. Ryan's guess put her at about fifteen years old.

A tubby man wearing a greasy derby was hammering out music at a tuneless piano by one of the front windows. At least Ryan assumed that it was music, though there was nothing that even vaguely resembled a tune, just an endless collection of bright and discordant notes.

"Where are the others?" Krysty asked, having to raise her voice and press her mouth close to Ryan's ear to be heard above the riotous noise.

"Don't know. Can't see any of them."

He had the SIG-Sauer on one side, balanced by the weight of the eighteen-inch panga on the other. The rifle rested under the bed in their locked bedroom. Krysty was wearing her own five-shot .38.

At that moment Clinkerscales looked up from his flurried work behind the bar and caught Ryan's eye, simultaneously waving one hand to him while wiping sweat from his shaved head with a checkered cloth in the other.

Then he pointed to a small doorway, directly beneath the stairs, miming putting food into his mouth.

"He means the eating place is through there," Krysty said.

"Yeah, I got that."

As they walked down, the hubbub began to fade away toward something that was almost silence. The game of darts stopped, and the poker players held their cards in their hands, frozen in mid-bet. The piano was suddenly three times as loud, hammering away at something that Ryan finally recognized as being close to an old song that he'd heard before, a soldier's song, about a girl wearing a yellow ribbon around her leg.

"Center of attraction, lover," Krysty whispered, taking Ryan's arm.

"Looks like she be one of ol' Sharpie's pets," someone shouted near the bar, triggering a bellow of laughter that ran clear around the saloon.

"Ignore it," Ryan said out of the corner of his mouth, not moving his lips. But his hand rested casual and easy, just above the ridged butt of the blaster.

They reached the bottom of the stairs, turning sharply into the lake of deep shadows, where the oil lamps didn't reach. Ryan pushed open the door, standing back to allow Krysty through first, keeping an eye open for any danger from the main room behind. But the moment of tension had passed and, once again, he could barely hear the thumping rhythm of the piano.

Clinkerscales had done them proud.

The private room was brightly lighted with two dozen tallow candles, set in sconces around the walls, and there was a reasonably clean cloth on the long table. Admittedly the candles were guttering, smoking and smelling, and one leg was missing off the table, but the man had tried. He'd even propped up the missing leg with a pile of dusty green hymnals to keep the table level.

Everyone else was there.

Doc was in state at the head of the table, in a huge chair of heavily carved oak with a high back. Dean sat next to him on one side, Jak on the other. J.B. and Mildred were opposite each other, next down the table, leaving two spaces for Ryan and Krysty.

"Hi, there." Ryan closed the door behind him, muffling the noise.

"Mebbe we'll get us some food now that you two bathbirds have arrived," J.B. said.

Ryan had barely sat, pouring himself a glass of nearly fresh cold water from a jug on the table, before Clinkerscales himself came popping through, holding a bunch of plastic-covered folders in his sweating hands.

"Here are the menus for this evening. Not a wide range, I fear, but all good and cooked in these very kitchens. I'll leave them with you for a few minutes. I have some passing red and white wines. Should I bring them in?"

"Two of each. Thanks," Ryan said.

The golden logo, blind-embossed on the outside of the large maroon menus, proclaimed that they came from the Maltese Falcon restaurant in Quince Orchard, Maryland.

Mildred looked at the front cover. "This meal's going to be the stuff that dreams are made of," she said, smiling, looking around expectantly at the others, the smile fading. "Name of a film with . . . Never mind."

The contents of the menu didn't quite live up to the magnificent exterior. Each one contained a single sheet of paper, hand-written, ill-spelled, with the name of the Lincoln Inn at the top.

"Soup. Meat flavur or not. Stew. Pig or sheep or cow. Or cowoty or dog. With vejetubls on the day. Fries. Tuna melts. Mex dish. Chicken done how you want it. Frute pie in all flavurs. Drinks to folow."

Doc laid the menu on the table, looking around as Clinkerscales appeared with four bottles of wine on a tin tray. "Interesting," he said. "Probably puts all of the old top hotels to shame."

"There's no labels on those bottles," Ryan said as the barman laid them on the table.

"Truth is, Mr. Cawdor, they was in a warehouse that gotten itself under the Potomac. Below water for forty years or so. But the corks was sealed and they've all been good. Man that said he knows about wine told me that the red's what they call a claret and the white's . . ." Clinkerscales scratched his forehead, finally saying, "And the white's *not* called a claret."

He busied himself pouring out glasses for everyone, while they studied the bill of fare.

"What's the soup?" Mildred asked.

"Ah, yes, now the soup. The soup is very . . . And made from the finest available . . . I can promise you that you'll enjoy it . . . Promise that."

"Yeah, but what flavor is it?"

The man tugged at his jaw, his cheekbones so prominent that it looked like they might burst clean through the skin of his face at any moment.

"Sort of soup flavor."

"What's the Mex dish?" Dean asked.

"Holy mackerel!" the barkeep exclaimed. "Never figured on havin' t'pass a test before I served you good folks your supper. The Mex dish is, well, there's chicken fajitas with onions and green peppers with sour cream and a taco and a burrito and an enchilada. Whole thing covered in green chili and a side order of our own salsa. Refried beans and black olives and lettuce. All with a big hunk of the finest bread baked in all of Green Hill."

Krysty clapped him. "Well, if it's as good as it sounds, I'll give it a try."

"Tuna melt?" Jak asked.

Clinkerscales drew a deep breath. "Chunk of that bread, crammed with a coupla handfuls of tuna... Well, that and some other fish. Topped off with cheese and held under the grill so it don't escape. Fries and salsa on the side." He looked at Jak. "Just a quick word of advice, son."

"What?"

"Around where Baron Sharpe has his ville, you'd do best to hide that snowy hair."

"Why?"

The man hesitated, swallowing hard. "Sharpie collects all kinds of odd animals and muties. Like a zoo."

"Animals or people?"

"Animals." After a long, long pause he added, "Animals, mostly."

Krysty leaned forward, wineglass in hand, and pointed at the barkeep, drawing his eyes to her. "You telling us that we could be in danger?"

"Anything unusual. Like you with hair like living fire and him with hair hacked clear out of the heart of the worst winter blizzard ever known."

"Not that uncommon for a Deathlands baron to show their wealth and power with some sort of collecting," Ryan said. "Last one we met liked coins. Others have old vids or predark books or clothes or blasters."

"Or women," J.B. added.

"Or wags or swords." Ryan looked at the barman. "How dangerous is this Sharpe?"

"Bad if you're unlucky. But his ville's far enough away from the shanties, so you should be safe. And you got some of the finest blasters between you all." He smiled at Ryan. "Remember how good old Trader liked blasters. Used to carry a battered Armalite, did he not? Looked like he'd used it to batter down a stone wall or stir his stew with it."

"Speaking of stew," Ryan said. "Let's finish the ordering and get some food on the table."

EVERYONE STARTED with the soup, which arrived in a beautiful dark blue tureen and turned out to be a mix of vegetables with some chunks of unidentifiable meat bobbing around in it. The flavor was highly spiced, which concealed any clue as to what it really contained.

"Not bad," Jak pronounced, wiping his mouth and then picking with the needle point of one of his throwing knives at a slab of gristle jammed between his front teeth.

The barman bustled in and collected their empty dishes, checking that there was still enough wine left. At the opening of the door there was a raging torrent of noise from the main part of the saloon.

"Busy," Ryan commented.

"You sure aren't farting 'Dixie,' Mr. Cawdor. Like I said. Word of strangers. Right. Bring in the main courses in just a moment." He spoke more rapidly than before, avoiding direct eye contact with any of the seven companions.

"What?" Ryan asked.

"Nothing. Just said I'd bring in . . ."

"Not that, Clinkerscales. I asked you what it was?"

"What?"

"Worrying you?"

"Ah, that. Couldn't ever tug the wool down over your eyes, Mr. Cawdor. Any man of Trader's would—"

Ryan stood, glaring at the barkeep. "Best you tell me what it is."

Clinkerscales looked around, making sure that he'd closed the door behind him. "Just that there's some men in the saloon tonight that I never saw before. Spit-and-sawdust talk is that they could be sec men, or scouts."

"For Sharpe?" J.B. asked.

"Could be, could be. Hard-eyed men, who laugh like the bark of a hunting wolf. If you take my meaning."

"How armed?" J.B. asked.

The man shook his head. "Two of them got holstered sawn-downs. Twelve-gauges, I reckon. Most have handblasters out on the hip. But I'm sure that I caught sight of a couple of hideaways while serving them."

"Food?" Mildred said plaintively. "We can talk about getting ourselves murdered by some loony baron's sec men *after* we've eaten. Hate the thought of going to meet my Maker on an empty, rumbling stomach."

"Right away, right away," Clinkerscales stammered, obviously eager to be out of the dining room and away from the pressure of the questioning.

THE FOOD WASN'T at all bad.

Ryan chose the mutton stew, finding it to be both rich and satisfying, served with diced carrots, leeks and fluffy new potatoes.

When Clinkerscales reappeared again, bringing the two extra bottles of wine that Doc had called for, he saw seven empty plates.

"As you can see, mine jovial host, Master Simon the Cellarer, we are all sturdy trenchermen here," Doc said, beaming broadly, while wiping ineffectually at a positive archipelago of grease spots down his frock coat. "And there's the dew-fresh flagons of the rich Médoc and the sharp chardonnay to keep the party swinging merrily along."

"And trencherwomen," Mildred added. "Don't forget there's ladies present, Doc."

"How could I ever forget it when you are always there, like a bad conscience, to remind me, Dr. Wyeth." He hesitated, shaking his head. "Trencherwomen! All in the name of that fearful ogre whom history calls the beast of political correctness. Sanctuary men, but never sanctuary women, my lord bishop.'' He looked across the table at the bewildered Clinkerscales. ''I saw some fine strawberries in your garden, as I passed by. I beg you...''

''Got strawberry pie, Doc,'' the barkeep offered. ''Ain't fresh, though. Place up north cans them for us.''

''What other kind of pie?'' Mildred asked.

''Key lime and cherry and hot fudge and peach and blueberry. All of them with cream.''

''Peach,'' Dean said, quickest to make up his mind.

''Cherry, please,'' Mildred stated.

''Did you say key lime was among the variety of options?'' Doc asked, getting a nod from Clinkerscales. ''Then that is for me. It has long, so long, been my favorite.''

Ryan and Krysty both went for the hot fudge.

Jak picked blueberry pie, but turned down the option of added cream.

After giving the matter due consideration, J.B. also chose the key-lime pie. Without cream.

''VERY, VERY GOOD,'' Krysty pronounced, pushing her dish away. Only a few crumbs and a smear of cream was left from the third portion of the hot fudge pie.

Dean had set the group record, having four helpings of dessert.

Starting with peach, he followed it up with strawberry, going on to sample the hot fudge and finishing up with a huge slice of the cherry pie, dripping with the hot sweet fruit, smothered in rich cream.

Clinkerscales had urged the boy to try for five, but Dean drew a finger across his own throat, indicating the level that the food had reached.

"Would you like to come out into the bar for a drink? Or, I figure you'd probably rather all go up to your own rooms and get early to sleep."

The note of tension was clear in the barkeep's voice, and he kept wiping his hands with the check apron.

"You mean *you*'d rather we all went up to our rooms?" J.B. said.

The man nodded, beads of sweat glistening across the top of his skull.

"Think there'll be trouble?"

"Could be, Mr. Cawdor. Can't be certain, but word's raced around Green Hill. Probably farther."

Ryan knew that Trader used to say that a man who went searching for trouble was triple sure to find it.

He looked around at his friends. "Sensible thing is to do like the man says."

"Nobody tell me run," Jak said.

"Let's go look." Mildred stood from the table. "Just a quick look."

"Why not?" Ryan said.

Chapter Thirteen

" 'My love commands, I must obey,
Over the hills and far away.
When I reach her I'll surely stay,
Over the hills and far away.' "

The singer was a young man with a sallow complexion and protruding teeth, standing on a small platform, next to the piano. He had long hair, prematurely gray, and he sang in a nasal tenor voice, with one hand clamped over his ear, as if he were having trouble sustaining pitch.

The packed saloon had quietened, everyone there listening to his fine rendition of the old song, nobody taking any notice as Ryan led the other six friends out from the dining room, into the dark at the bottom of the stairs.

There was a roar of applause as the young man finished the ballad, and the floor all around him rang as jack was thrown as a reward for his singing.

Clinkerscales appeared at the piano, revving up the clapping, beckoning for more money, then waving his hands for silence. "Thanks for Jake Stafford. He'll be back later with another set. Now the Lincoln Inn is pleased to offer you an unusual entertainment. An unusual lady.''

"Does she fuck mules?" a voice bellowed from a table near the stairs.

"Gentlemen, please," the barkeep said reproachfully. "This is not that sort of place. Go to Johnny Owen's if you want that kind of pleasuring. And if you want to get the clap, the gripe, the bloody flux, knob rot, blindness and facial cankers, then go to Johnny Owen's place. And may the Lord have mercy on you!"

"He's good at this," Krysty whispered. "Like someone controlling a pack of rabid dogs while standing in the middle of a tightrope."

Clinkerscales had his hands held high again. "Gentlemen, please let's hear it for a newcomer to Washington Hole, all the way from the Mohawk Gap up north. Emma Tyler!"

There was a ripple of applause, but the attention span of the audience in the Lincoln Inn wasn't much longer than the average mayfly. The darts game had resumed, as had the poker schools. And, Ryan noticed, one or two heads were already beginning to turn in his direction.

Emma Tyler was a small woman, looking to be in her early twenties, with a neat, trim face and her black hair cut short. She wore a black shirt and long black skirt that trailed in the spilled beer that puddled the floor of the saloon. As she took a seat alongside the piano, whose player had taken his place at the bar, she looked quickly around the packed room.

"Like a frightened mouse," Mildred whispered. "What kind of an act's she going to do that'll hold this mob? They'll crucify her."

The girl looked up, almost as if she'd heard the woman's words. Ryan pursed his lips, catching a glance from her, seeing the odd color of her eyes. Yellow would be too crude a word. Perhaps golden was right. They seemed to look at Ryan, inside him and then out the other side.

He shivered a little, as if a cold wind had just sliced across his soul.

Emma had pulled out a black silk kerchief and tied it tightly over her eyes.

"Bang! You're dead, slut!" called a fat man with a plaited beard.

The young woman turned her head toward him. "Your twin brother, Aaron, was burned to death in a fire when you were ten years old."

The man stood, pushing his chair back with a clatter. His face had gone as pale as wind-washed bone, and his jaw sagged. "Who told you that, slut?"

"Nobody. That's my act. I can see what happened to some people. Sometimes what might happen."

Her voice rang out, as clear as an Angelus bell. Once again the saloon fell silent.

"Lyin' bitch."

"You hated him. Thought your mother loved him more than you. She did. You were right. You set the fire with a pile of his wooden soldiers and..."

The man lost his nerve, turning and lumbering out of the Lincoln Inn, elbowing men aside, crashing out through the bat-wing doors.

"I can't promise it'll work for everyone. Anyone want to know anything?"

After a moment's silence, a skinny man at one of the card tables lifted a hand. Despite her blindfold, Emma Tyler immediately seemed to sense him and turned in his direction.

"No, you won't. Three sixes beats two pairs, queens over nines."

"I'll be fucked!"

"Later tonight. Slant Maggie. She'll try and lift your poke, so take care."

There was a roar of laughter and clapping of hands.

Ryan nudged Krysty. "How's she doing this? They shills she placed out there?"

Krysty shook her head, speaking slowly and quietly. "I don't think so. She's a doomie or a seer, or both. What she's doing is astounding, if it's genuine. And I think it is."

Emma turned in her chair, seeming to stare directly at the redheaded woman. She opened her mouth as if she were going to speak, then changed her mind.

"We going up to our rooms, Dad?" Dean asked.

"Soon, son, soon."

A man standing at the bar called out to the woman. "Here, doll! Traveling quack said I got a rad cancer in my guts. Not true, is it?"

There was a long pause. Finally Emma shook her head. "Sorry, mister. Like I said, I don't always see things clear. Get a feeling you'll be all right."

The man whooped out loud and banged his fist on the bar top. "Knew it. I fuckin' knew it! Come on, Clinkie! Pour us another and make it a triple!"

Ryan felt Krysty's breath on his cheek as she whispered in his ear. "She's lying. I got a wave of feeling from that poor bastard. Filled my mouth with the taste of decay. Emma knew it, as well. Know she did."

Once again the blindfolded woman half turned in her chair, head to one side, looking toward Krysty.

"Are the ruins safe to go scavengin' in? Friend got chilled by ghoulies."

The yell, from a tall man with his hair dyed half green and half blue, distracted Emma Tyler. "If you go in, they'll cut your throat before dark."

"Aw, they ain't that bad," someone else shouted.

"I'm just telling him what would happen to him if he went in. He stays out of the center of the Hole and he won't die there. Fact is, he'll live for another twenty years or more and die in a fall from a ladder in a barn-raising in Kansas."

"How do we know any of this crap's true?" The whining voice came from a sour-faced man who was propping up the bar. Or, who was relying on the bar to keep him propped up.

Emma coughed, clearing her throat. "I just say that if the last man who spoke does go into the heart of the Hole, the ghoulies are going to find him and slit his throat."

"So, tell me something?"

There was a hesitation, broken only by the thudding of darts into the board, as the men there resumed their game. But Emma Tyler still held the attention of most of the crowded saloon.

"You're sure you want me to tell you something secret? Your dusk-dark secret?"

"Sure I do."

"Even if it will cause you pain?"

He threw back his head and cackled with laughter. "Cause me pain! Go ahead, sweetie, if you can!"

"Right. You have four children?"

"Sure." A note of doubt crept into his voice, edging away the bravado. "So what?"

"You aren't the father of any of them. In fact, you've never once managed to make love to your wife, have you? But you don't have the same problem with the towheaded stable boy in the shantytown of Bow Regard, do you, Obadiah?"

The place was deathly still, every eye in the place turning to look at the man by the bar, who licked his lips, twin splashes of crimson highlighting his pale cheeks.

"You... Why, you...fuckin' bitch!" He reached for a heavy revolver that was stuck down the front of his pants. "Fuckin' kill—"

Ryan drew and fired his powerful SIG-Sauer in a single fluid action, shooting Obadiah through the center of the face. The 9 mm round tore into the top of the nose, bursting the septum, angling sideways, pushing one eye from its socket, where it dangled madly on the man's cheek. The bullet exited from the back of the skull, removing a chunk of bone the size of a saucer, matted with blood, brains and hair. The spent bullet drove on, hitting the octagonal, green-edged mirror behind the bar and destroying it in a thousand bright shards of glass.

Before the dead man had slumped to the sawdust floor, crimson blood pumping from the exit wound,

J.B. and the others were out in the open, ranged alongside Ryan, all with blasters cocked and ready.

"Nobody do anything stupid!" Ryan called loud and clear, the barrel of the P-226 SIG-Sauer weaving from side to side like the head of a cobra. "Nobody gets hurt. Just keep still and quiet. Real still, now!"

Clinkerscales had ducked behind the bar as soon as he saw Ryan draw the automatic. Now he straightened, brushing glass from his shaved head. He was holding a sawed-down double-barrel Bernardelli Italia 12-gauge, both hammers thumbed back, waving it around at the crowd. "Guy had it coming. Saw him drawing on that poor blind girl. Stranger did well."

"Hey, little lady, if you're a doomie," someone called from near the dartboard, "how come you didn't see that coming?"

"Yeah, right!" echoed a second man. And the saloon erupted with raucous nervous laughter, the brain-dead corpse still twitching among them.

Emma Tyler had stood up, ripping away the black blindfold, golden eyes roaming over the crowd.

"Death comes faster than a ghost wind through a shotgun shack," she said. "Comes like a stumbling heartbeat at midnight. Like a bat riding in from hell. Like a scythe through fresh corn." Her voice was low and gentle, spellbinding with its whispering intensity, shutting up the crowd.

Ryan gestured to the others to put away their blasters, holstering his automatic, seeing that the moment of crisis had passed.

For the time being.

"She's good," he whispered to Krysty.

"Wrong, lover. That girl is *very* good."

Emma hadn't finished, her voice caressing the hundred or more men gathered all around her, making them forget the dead man lying still by the bar.

"When he spoke I could catch the scent of death around him. But it was so close, like a galloping horse on top of him, that I couldn't believe what I was seeing. My skill isn't perfect. It's fallible. I say what I think I can see. But everyone controls their own destiny. Time can jerk aside, like a heavy drape over a picture window."

"Like my own seeing," Krysty said to Ryan. "Sometimes it works like a miracle. Sometimes it doesn't work. And there's no reason for the good or the bad."

"Yeah, I understand. Like my shooting. Nine from ten I can hit the ace on the line. Tenth time...I can't."

"Today was one of the nine from ten, Dad."

"Yeah, Dean, it was."

The young woman was wrapping it up, looking now toward Ryan and his group. "Some say that what I have is a blessing. I say it isn't. I say that it is all too often a curse. I'm real sorry the ace of spades turned up tonight."

Then she was gone, walking quickly behind the piano toward the bar, vanishing through a door at the back of a beaded curtain.

NOW THAT THEY'D MADE their presence known to the packed saloon, there was no longer any point in making a tactful withdrawal back up the stairs to their rooms.

"Drinks, anyone?"

Ryan grinned as everyone nodded at his suggestion. He led the way between the tables, where the poker games had continued again, past the dartboard, easing through the crowd to the bar, beckoning to Clinkerscales.

"Yes, Mr. Cawdor? What'll it be? And these are on the house, as well, after your pretty piece of shooting. Saved us a nasty murder, it did. And that might easy have carried on into a lynching."

"Where's the woman come from?" Krysty asked.

"She's a true mutie seer. Came in from the west a day or so ago. Showed me enough to know that she was for real. Thought it might be an attraction. Didn't figure on it ending with blood on the barroom floor."

He quickly poured out a round of drinks, mainly beers, with a Cointreau for Krysty and Dean.

Jak wandered off to watch the dart throwers, eventually insinuating himself into the next game.

The rest of them stayed at the heart of the crush around the bar, enjoying their drinks, enjoying the evening.

Chapter Fourteen

After the excitement of Emma Tyler and her interrupted act, the Lincoln Inn had quieted down. The whores circulated, some of them bare-breasted, lifting their ragged skirts to show prospective johns what they might be buying.

The card games were proceeding, with the occasional imprecation as an attempt to draw to an inside straight met its inevitable failure.

A few of the shantytown locals were interested in the group of outlanders, a couple of them fascinated by Ryan's powerful handblaster, asking if they could take a look at it.

"Sorry," Ryan said. "Nobody touches my blaster."

But there seemed to be no ill-feeling.

Everyone had a second round of drinks.

Around a quarter hour later, Clinkerscales passed by and touched Ryan gently on the shoulder. "Could be some trouble brewing," he said quietly.

"Last group that came in?"

"You spotted them?"

Ryan nodded. "Trader used to say that a man who doesn't keep his eyes open won't get to see his death coming. They came in together, nine of them. Now they've split up."

"Ones I mentioned before. Coldhearts. Heavily armed with sawn-downs as well as hideaways."

"You reckon they could be scouting for Baron Sharpe?"

Clinkerscales nodded, wiping away at a glass as he spoke. "He pays well for unusual strangers. Either to work in the ville or as part of his collection."

Ryan bit his lip. "We'd be no use to them dead?"

"Depends on who they want, Mr. Cawdor. I got a suss that they could be after that girl."

"Emma Tyler."

"And Mr. Lauren and Miss Wroth. Something a bit different about them."

The barkeep waved a hand to calls for service from farther down the room. "Be careful. I can't afford to fall out with old Sharpie. Take my meaning?"

"'Course. I'll collect everyone together and we'll go up to our rooms. Be away at first light. Thanks for everything you've done for us."

The two men shook hands.

"Good to know of Trader," the barkeep said. "There's still a few folks around here remember the man with thanks in their hearts. A woman I met, year or so ago, around the Hole, claimed she rode with him."

"What was her name?" Ryan asked, interested at the thought of meeting up with an old companion.

"Can't recall."

The fur-clad hunter at the far end of the room was banging with his fist to attract attention, and Clinkerscales gave Ryan a quick smile and went to serve him.

"Trouble?" Krysty asked, standing just behind Ryan, picking up the vibes.

"Could be. Gang that he mentioned earlier. Before we ate. Went out. Now they're back. Two over there by Jak. Rest are scattered. One's alongside Doc, watching the main poker game. Find Mildred and J.B. and we'll get out of here, upstairs. I'll collect Dean, Doc and Jak."

But the wheel was already in spin.

"Fuckin' cheatin' mutie!"

The voice soared over the background noise in the Lincoln Inn, bringing a hush. It came from near the dartboard.

"Yeah, you fuckin' cheat. You best come outside with us and we'll teach you good."

Jak was standing at the board, hand poised to pick out the trio of steel-tipped darts. "What's problem you two?" he said quietly.

"No mutie throws that good. Never fuckin' missed one, snowbird."

Everyone was watching the drama—except Ryan and J.B., who were looking around the room, trying to pick out the rest of the group. The Armorer had spotted the gang when they came in through the swinging doors, just as Ryan had.

But all the friends had their blasters drawn, all except Jak.

The slender youth, in his ragged camouflage jacket, was standing still, as though he were petrified with terror, fingers just brushing the flights of the darts.

The two men who'd called him out were both inches over six feet, broad-shouldered, in patched shirts. One had a sawed-down scattergun tucked in his belt, one hand resting casually on the stock. The other had a remake revolver, in a worn holster on his right hip.

Ryan could easily have gunned both of them down, but that wouldn't flush out the others in the gang. He had to wait and let Jak make his move.

"Didn't cheat."

"'Course you did, you shit-for-brains little runt! We both saw you."

Out of the corner of his eye, Ryan glimpsed the pale face of Emma Tyler, peering round the edge of the door at the side of the bar. Her golden eyes were open very wide, and she looked to be terrified.

"Come on," said the taller of the two bullying thugs. "Outside!"

Jak made his move, plucking the darts from the board and throwing them, one, two, three, almost too quick to follow with the human eye.

Both men cried out in pain and shock, and everyone in the saloon was witness to the albino's unique skill.

One dart had struck home in the taller man's left cheek, missing his eye by a scant inch, while the third one pierced the corner of his mouth, penetrating through the tongue, sticking in the gum.

The second of the missiles landed in the exact center of the other man's forehead, thrown with such force that it drove through the skin and the thin layer of flesh, driving into the bone at the front of the skull, standing out like the ornamented horn of a unicorn.

"Holy Mary!" breathed a young man at a table just in front of Ryan.

But Jak wasn't finished.

The darts were enough to devastate the two men, putting them totally off-balance, even though the injuries caused by the darts weren't all that serious.

There were two more blurs in the smoky air, as the teenager drew a pair of his concealed throwing knives, hurling the leaf-shaped blades with murderous force and accuracy.

One sliced into the taller man's neck as he staggered backward, his hands lifted to the darts that stuck out of his face. It opened up the artery beneath his ear, blood spraying thickly, splattering on the ceiling, dappling the torn frock of a screaming whore.

The other knife was also aimed at the throat, penetrating the front of the second man's neck, through his larynx, opening his windpipe, flooding his lungs with a drowning torrent of his own blood.

The gaudy saloon erupted into panic and dying.

Tables went over, poker chips and jack flying through the air in seeming slow motion. Virtually all of the men hit the floor, yelling, some of them struggling to draw blasters and knives as they went down. Whores flopped among them like helpless, wailing, landed fish.

Clinkerscales instantly had his sawed-down Bernardelli Italia in his hands, standing four-square behind the bar, his face streaming with sweat, jaw jutting angrily. He shouted for calm at the top of his voice, but failed to get himself heard above the yelping, shrieking panic.

It was impossible to obtain an overall picture of the heart of the fight, which was basically Ryan and his companions against the nine-strong gang, which had suddenly become a seven-strong gang.

The man that Ryan had been watching had a long-barreled pistol out and cocked, aiming it at Jak. But a burst of lead from the Armorer's Uzi converted his skull into a mist of blood, splintered bone and ragged slices of brain.

Doc had drawn his J. E. B. Stuart Commemorative gold-plated Le Mat as soon as the situation began to develop, trying to edge his way through the crowd toward Jak's side. But the crush of people made movement almost impossible. He noticed that a skinny balding man standing next to him had pulled out a small beat-up automatic pistol and was aiming it at Ryan.

"I think not," Doc said quietly, pushing the barrel of the Le Mat into the man's ribs, expecting him to immediately drop the blaster and surrender.

To his amazement, the shootist spit a florid curse at him and began to swing his own gun around, ready to put a bullet into Doc's chest.

"I am not..." Doc began, considering remonstrating with the fellow for his extreme foolishness, then he realized that this wasn't a time for talking.

It was a time for shooting.

He immediately squeezed the slender trigger on the massive handblaster, firing the .63-caliber shotgun round from the gaping barrel.

The explosion was muffled by the blaster being pressed into the man's body, but the effect was devastating.

The shot almost cut the balding killer in two, ripping through his entrails, smashing his spine, reducing liver and kidneys to tatters of bloodied pulp. He dropped at Doc's feet, blood pouring from his open mouth, the blaster clattering onto the splintered floor.

Which still left five of the gang of would-be assassins on their feet.

Ryan shot down one who'd drawn a Saturday-night special from a holster inside his long jacket, the bullet going neatly in one ear, coming out a lot less neatly through the angle of the jaw, exiting in a gusher of blood and shards of teeth.

The crimson fountain hit one of the kneeling sluts in the head, the sharp pieces of bone cutting her across the forehead, a curtain of her own blood blinding her. She erupted into thrashing hysterics, one of her ankle boots hitting a crouching trapper in the face and breaking his nose.

There was another of the gang near the bar. His left ear had been hacked away and a chunk of his cheek had vanished with it. The old scar pulled the corner of his mouth up into a fearsome grin, also tugging down his left eye into an angry snarl.

He had a derringer up each sleeve, on spring releases, and they popped into his hands. To gain a better shot at Ryan's group he began to clamber onto the bar, ignoring Clinkerscales and his sawed-down, which was the last mistake he ever got to make.

The barman didn't even have to move. He jammed the twin barrels up into the man's groin from below and pulled the twin triggers, firing both the 12-gauge rounds at point-blank range.

Much went unnoticed amid the general bedlam of noise and dying, but not this killing.

"Fireblast!" Ryan exclaimed admiringly.

"Gaia!" Krysty said, in appalled amazement.

J.B. shook his head, interested in the technical side of the two shots. "Dark night!"

The force of the double blast lifted the disfigured man off the bar, giving the momentary illusion that he was floating in space, a bizarre miracle of yogic flying.

But the illusion was marred by the blurring welter of blood and flesh that steamed out from the man's groin. The shots totally destroyed the genitals, ripping unhindered into the lower part of the abdomen, opening a gash larger than a man's fist through which loops of ragged intestine, gray and pinkish yellow, began to tumble.

In a deathly muscle spasm, he fired both the derringers, drilling two neat holes in the cracked plaster of the ceiling.

His flailing, flopping corpse landed back on the bar, almost on top of Clinkerscales, who calmly pushed the slimy mess off onto the floor and reloaded his scattergun.

Six were dead or dying, three of the gang remaining alive.

Less than eight seconds had passed since Jak had pulled the darts out of the board.

When death comes easy, it comes fast.

Mildred and Dean took out the seventh killer. He'd taken refuge behind the piano, trying to shoot at Doc. Mildred couldn't get a clean shot at him but the boy, farther round, was just able to see the man's kneeling leg.

Holding the Hi-Power in both hands he fired twice, narrowly missing the first time, putting a 9 mm full-metal jacket into the exposed ankle at the second attempt.

A scream of agony soared above the general chaos, and the man staggered sideways, giving Mildred the easiest of shots with her ZKR 551 Czech target revolver. At twenty-feet range there was no way she was going to miss, drilling the big Smith & Wesson .38 round into the center of his chest, putting him down in the bloodied sawdust.

Krysty had retreated toward the stairs, trying to take in everything that was happening. One of the last two survivors suddenly appeared. Seeing that their cause was irretrievably doomed, he pushed her aside and ran for the second floor and a chance of escape out of one of the bedrooms.

"No," Krysty said quietly. She leveled her short-barreled pistol, putting two rounds into the middle of the man's back, stopping him in his tracks, only a couple of steps from the landing. His body jerked under the impact of the .38 rounds, nearly throwing him on his face. He recovered his balance, gave a long, gasping sigh, straightened and toppled backward down the staircase, landing by Krysty's feet.

"One left," Ryan muttered, looking around the saloon and seeing only the panic of the living and the stillness of the dead. "Where is—"

Then he found out.

An arm crooked around his throat and he felt the sharp tingle of cold steel against his neck. A tiny worm of warmth trickled down across his chest.

"A move and the one-eyed bastard gets it. Him and me are walking out together."

Ryan was surprised by the stupidity of his attacker, who seemed totally oblivious to the fact that his victim was still holding a powerful automatic blaster in his right hand.

"Nobody fuckin' move or else I'll slit his throat open."

"Then you get to die slowly and painfully," J.B. called, distracting the man and giving Ryan the moment he needed.

It was a very small movement. He edged his right hand behind himself, until the muzzle was touching the body of the would-be killer. At the same time Ryan lifted his left hand a little, up toward his chest.

Synchronicity was important if he wasn't going to find he'd chilled his enemy but also lost his own life.

He squeezed the trigger and felt the blaster buck, sending a sharp pain up to the elbow, where he hadn't been able to brace the SIG-Sauer properly. Simultaneously he'd swept up his left hand, forcing the straight razor away from his throat, then stepped forward, turning and putting another round into the wounded man's chest.

"Cheatin' bastard..." The razor dropped from nerveless fingers, tinkling on the floor, where it was surrounded by a puddle of crimson from the two bullet holes.

"That's all nine," Clinkerscales called. "Everyone can get up now and go on home. We got some cleaning up to do. Open again tomorrow for business. As usual."

Ryan backed away toward the stairs, stepping over corpses, avoiding the pools of congealing blood. His blaster kept the saloon covered, drawing the other six after him, all of them watching for any sign of aggression.

But there wasn't any further threat.

Several of the whores were still hysterical. One or two of the others saw how much manly attention that got and threw themselves into screaming fits, as well.

By the time the friends reached the top of the stairs, the bar was resuming a faint resemblance of normality. Fully three-quarters of the surviving men in the place were already gone, scooting out through the batwing doors, vanishing into the darkness of the shantytown.

Clinkerscales came after the companions, still hefting the sawed-down.

"That's it," he said.

"The girl?" Jak asked.

The barkeep answered without looking at the teenager. "Gone. Soon as bullets started flying."

"Don't blame her," Krysty said. "Bad scene here."

Clinkerscales nodded, a slight nervous tic marking his head jerk to the side. "Worst I ever saw. One time Trader's men ride on by... Like they always said."

"What?" Ryan said, becoming angry.

"Where Trader set his foot the flowers died. And nothing ever grew there again. Same with you and Mr. Dix."

"You asked us to stay," the Armorer reminded him grimly. "Not our fault."

"Mebbe not... Shit, but I'm tired. All right. Shouldn't have said what I did. But the chilling was... Just go in the morning and don't come back." He turned away, then hesitated. "And take care if you ride near Baron Sharpe's ville."

Chapter Fifteen

During the night, after everyone had fieldstripped and cleaned their firearms under J.B.'s strict eye, they discussed whether to return to the redoubt or whether to explore a little farther.

"I'm interested in this Baron Sharpe," Krysty said. "Man with his own personal zoo—including two-legged animals—sounds like someone we should go visit."

Ryan shook his head. "You can't clear up every piece of dirt in Deathlands, lover. There just isn't enough time."

"Or enough bullets," Jak added. "Though did well saving young woman."

"Hope she got away safe." Mildred looked behind them at the shacks and tents of Green Hill, three-quarters of a mile back. Smoke from dawn fires smeared the land to the south. "I know she was innocent, but they'll see her as the trigger for what happened last night. Blame her for the spilled blood."

It was a cool morning, with streaks of high cloud slicing across the pink-blue sky. There had been a shower of rain during the small hours, and the ground smelled green and fresh.

The furrowed track ahead of them showed the characteristic ribbon effect of earthquakes, winding down a hillside, between the scorched ruins of a few buildings.

"Rad counter's on orange," J.B. said. "Best we get away from here in a week or so."

Ryan nodded his agreement. "Yeah. Right. I haven't seen anything yet round Washington Hole that'd make me want to stay here for too long."

THE CLOUDS HAD THICKENED and darkened, with the threat of some serious rain sweeping in from the north. They had already seen several vivid flashes of chem lightning and caught the distant sound of thunder.

"Old church ahead of us," Krysty said, pointing to a squat building in lichen-covered stone. One wall had completely fallen in, but the other end had a stubby tower with a twisted metal cross still fixed to its top.

"No real need to stop." J.B. blinked toward the gathering storm.

"Smear your glasses and get your blasters all wet, John," Mildred argued.

"True," he admitted. "From the look of the clouds, it shouldn't be much more than a sharp shower."

Krysty looked at Ryan. "We stop, lover?"

"Time doesn't mean much when you don't have things to do and places to be. I'm happy to stay awhile and sit out the rain. No objections? None? Then we'll stop here."

" "THIS FOUNDATION STONE laid by Senator Nicholas Webb on the fourteenth day of September in the year of 1999,' " Dean read haltingly. "Sort of eroded letters."

Wind blew brittle tumbleweed against the wall of the ruined church, and the first drops of rain began to patter into the gray dust. The sky was very dark, and the deep rumble of thunder had become constant in the background, the eye of the impending storm moving ever closer.

"What sort of church was it?" Mildred asked. "Nothing left to tell us what kind of a God they worshiped or how they went about it."

Doc looked at the barren wilderness that surrounded the devastated building. "See what He made of this planet, and you can start to wonder whether He exists at all. Or if He does exist, what kind of a deity he is. Not much of a Creator. A whole lot more of a Destroyer."

Mildred shook her head. "Could be you're wrong, Doc. You build a house and then you find that got rot in the joists and worm in the beams and damp in the cellar, then you pull it down and start again. Maybe that's what He did here in Deathlands. Saw there'd been a bad mistake and things had gone skewed. So He pretty well pulled it all down and now He's in the process of starting over."

Doc smiled toothily. "Then that makes us His wingless angels, I guess."

There was a flash of lightning, dazzlingly close, burning its afterimage into the retina, followed by a peal of thunder so loud that it made marrowbone quiver.

Everyone moved quickly inside through the heavy door. It was made of oak and had survived the nuke-caust practically unscathed, though it was pitted and burned on the outside and hung loosely on its hinges.

The inside had been totally stripped. The pews had all been taken, long years ago, for cooking fires. Some of the broken windows had been clumsily filled in with a sort of crude adobe, but much of it had crumbled and fallen away. The altar was missing, the floor covered in bits of rubble.

Ryan looked around as the rain began to fall in earnest, pounding on the damaged roof, starting to trickle through in a few places at the far end of the nave, beyond the transept.

"Door back there," he said.

Krysty touched him on the arm, half drawing her blaster. "Lover?" she whispered.

"What?" he asked, pulling out the SIG-Sauer, peering into the gloom at the back of the old church.

"Someone there?" Krysty hesitated. "Feel them, but there's something odd about... Like I can see them and not see them, all at the same time."

There was a movement in the stillness, and the narrow door began to ease open. By now everyone had seen it, and everyone had their blasters drawn.

"No need," said a voice from the blackness. "It's not now and it's not here."

"Emma Tyler!" Jak holstered his satin-finish Colt Python. "The doomie."

THE YOUNG WOMAN WAS COLD, her cloak still damp from getting caught in the rain the previous night when she'd fled the ville of Green Hill.

"No chance of a fire, not with this storm," J.B. said. "Have to wait."

"Being cold's better than being dead." Emma looked around the circle of friends. "Can't thank you enough for going and laying it on the line for me back there in the Lincoln Inn."

Krysty was fascinated by the doomie's powers. "If you see the future, didn't you know that you might get yourself chilled back there? Or did you see the danger and also see us riding out of the sunset to the rescue?"

Emma brushed a hand through her black hair, sitting cross-legged in the dirt. Her golden eyes looked intently at Krysty. "I knew you, too, had the seeing power. I felt it the first moment I was in the same room with you."

Krysty smiled. "I have *this* much of the power." She held her finger and thumb a couple of inches apart. "I can feel if there's danger around. But only some of the time. Not all of the time. Wish I could."

"You wouldn't wish it. It truly can be a curse rather than a blessing."

"But you didn't answer my question, Emma."

The eyes, oddly flat and incurious, turned again toward the flame-headed woman.

"Did I know there was to be all that killing? I can't answer that properly. To do that I'd have to explain what I see and how I see it. And that's impossible. It's like trying to explain the color turquoise to a blind man.''

''Or like trying to tell a stranger about rock and roll,'' Mildred said. ''Sorry. Old music reference. Shouldn't have interrupted. Go on, Emma.''

''I see reality, just like anyone else. But I sometimes see an overlay. Like what I think the old vids and teevee must've been like. Like I looked at that man and 'saw' all about his real, hidden life.''

''And the man with the blue-and-green hair,'' J.B. was as fascinated as any of them. ''If he follows your warning, he could live. If he doesn't . . .''

''He'll die with his throat slit in the Hole,'' she said. ''But it's not always that precise. I tasted death with incredible strength in the saloon. But I couldn't have foretold how it would come. I also felt a lot of power from you seven.''

Doc squatted, the cracking of his knees even louder than the pounding rain. ''It sounds a little like throwing handfuls of mud at a wall. By the nature of the beast, some will stick and some will fall out.''

''Could put it like . . .'' Her eyes opened wider. ''By water and stone! Where do you come from?'' She turned to Mildred. ''And you. There are colors to both of you like nothing I've ever seen before. Like all colors and no colors. How . . .''

Ryan smiled at her obvious distress and bewilderment. ''Time enough for that later. Once the rain stops we can move on. I'll introduce all of us and tell you a little about where we've come from.''

Emma stood, her face drained of blood. "No. Thanks for the offer of your protection, but I can see death if we travel together."

"Who for?" Dean asked.

"It's like I said. A color. Dark. So dark. If I travel with you, then death will come to one of us. But if you go on without me, then the shadow retreats from you all."

"But it can be cheated?" Ryan asked. "You said that yourself. We can cheat death. We've all done it more times than you've eaten hot soup."

She shook her head doubtfully. "The shadow is like a cloak made from the wings of ravens. You saved my life and turned the black spear from my heart. How would I feel if I caused the death of one of you?"

"Not as bad as whoever dies," Mildred said grimly.

"You don't believe I see the future and the past, do you? I can almost taste your suspicion."

"Maybe I don't want to believe it, Emma."

"Your father was burned to death in an attack by men in white sheets and hoods, in his church. A place like this. He had a younger brother, also a preacher, whose name was Josh. He called you 'Millie.' I'm right, aren't I? Though parts of your life are oddly distorted. Not like norms."

"That's enough," Mildred said, shaking her head so that the plaited beads rattled in her hair. "I believe you can see some of what's already happened. Doesn't mean you can also see the future. Nobody can. Future's like millions and millions of alternate possibilities. I might drop dead the very next breath. Or in five minutes. An hour. A day. A year. Nobody knows that, Emma. Not even you.''

''I do know that,'' she said very gently. ''It's what I'm trying to explain, but I guess I'm doing it real badly. I see some things to come. Just some of them. But I can't explain how or why I do it. Sorry.''

Her words hung in the darkened church, surrounded by the insane violence of the raging chem storm.

The noise of the thunder and the spilled water made any further conversation impossible.

It was well over an hour before the rain ceased and the thunder rolled south.

BEFORE LEAVING, Ryan formally introduced all of them to the mutie mystic, explaining a little about where Mildred and Doc came from.

''So that's it.'' The golden eyes opened wide. ''Doc, I can see things about your past life, but they're faint, like a whisper etched on water.''

''I must confess that I often feel like that about my past. Though I lived it, much of those years seem an enigma shrouded in mystery.''

''I feel that about yesterday, Doc.'' Mildred grinned. ''When I get to your age, if I live so long, I suspect that I'll forget everything up to five seconds ago.''

''Where are we going to go now?'' Emma asked.

''Don't you know?'' Dean said cheekily.

She smiled at him, the only time since they'd first seen her that Emma's stony mask had cracked. ''My brain would explode if I held a permanent visual map of everything that'll happen to everyone in the future. Even for myself.''

"Oh.'' He sounded disappointed.

Emma patted the eleven-year-old on the shoulder. "Other thing is that it tires me out. Like trying to do mental math for ten hours straight.''

Krysty nodded. "I can see a little, sometimes. But I also have the Earth power, taught to me by Mother Sonja back in Harmony ville. I can draw on myself and, briefly, have paranormal strength.''

"But it drains her so much she's good for nothing for a day or more afterward,'' Ryan added.

"That's right, lover. It sucks all my soul to do it. It frightens me a lot that I might try to use it one day and I'll simply die.''

The doomie's smile had gone, faded like the frost on a spring meadow. "Not so bad for me. But bad enough.''

"How do you see going with us?'' Jak asked. "Got any feelings about that?''

"Told you. Death, Jake. Strong feeling of death if I travel with you.''

"Live with death at shoulder every waking hour,'' the albino replied.

"All right. But what are we going to do?''

"Look around,'' Ryan said. "Look around is all.''

Chapter Sixteen

Though the center of Washington, and all of its immediate inner suburbs, had been totally vaporized in the first seconds of the skydark, the pattern of damage around the outer rim of the city was irregular.

Some of it was down to inconsistencies in the terrain. Nukeblast normally went in fairly straight lines, so land in a hollow would generally be less damaged than higher ground. And the same applied to buildings.

Ryan walked under an overcast sky into a shallow basin. The edges were clear of any sign of civilization, scoured away by the missiles' blast. But ahead of them there was a scattering of buildings, mostly roofless and windowless.

It was midafternoon.

Emma Tyler, for all of her mystic mutie skills, was no great walker. She'd hiked the long black cotton skirt up over her knees, pinning it into place. Her low-heeled sandals were badly worn and patched, and she often stumbled on the uneven trail that they were following.

"Can we take a break, Ryan?" she asked. "I got blisters on top of blisters."

"Sure. Mebbe find a little shelter ahead. You don't seem like you're much used to covering ground."

He realized at that moment that Emma had handled their earlier conversation with some skill. He had told her a lot about themselves. In exchange, the woman had told them virtually nothing about herself.

She smiled gratefully, kneeling for a moment to remove a sharp piece of crumbled dirt out of her shoe. "You always go this fast?"

"Moving target's easier missed," Jak said, sitting beside her.

She looked at him, eyes narrowed. "I don't know, Jak," she said, so quietly that Ryan was the only other person to hear her speak.

"Know what?" the white-haired teenager asked. "Didn't ask nothing."

"Not out loud. I just gave you an answer to the question you were thinking about me."

"Oh." Just for a moment, Ryan actually thought that Jak's bone-white face flushed around the cheeks. But at that moment an odd shaft of errant sunlight broke through the looming clouds over them. So it could have been that bringing a touch of rosy color to Jak's narrow face.

It could have been that.

THEY TOOK a half-hour break.

Emma fell asleep almost immediately, though it wasn't a quiet rest. Her body twitched and moved, and she kept up a constant whispering. Dean crawled close and lowered his head to try to catch what she was saying.

"Come away," Krysty whispered. "Private."

But Ryan overruled her, gesturing for Dean to stay where he was for a while longer. "Nothing's private when you take a stranger along with you."

"I suppose that Trader said that," Krysty said with a sneer.

"No, lover. I said that."

Dean moved away, his face puzzled. "Double odd, Dad."

"You hear anything of what she was saying?"

"Not much. Too quiet and quick. And some of it was like nonsense."

"You understand any of it?"

"About dying."

"Her dying?"

"Not sure, Dad. Said that her body was collapsing inside, like crumpled paper. She could hear the noise it was making, coming out of her mouth every time she opened it. Nothing would stop it. Said it frightened her."

"Not surprised," Mildred said, joining them. "Would've frightened me, too."

"What kind of building you think this was, Dad?"

Ryan hadn't given the question any thought. It was just a ruined building, like millions of others left abandoned and destroyed all over Deathlands. It was stripped as bare as charity, with not even a nail left in a wall. No doors, no glass, walls split either by the nuking or by the quakes. Part of the flat roof gone, exposing rotten beams and a few slates.

"Probably a store, or a garage," Mildred suggested. "Reckon they're old oil stains on the floor over there by the door. Entrance is wide enough for that."

Ryan looked at the front wall, where they'd come in. But most of it had been reduced to rubble, making it impossible to speculate any further on what the place might've been.

"Been a lot of things," Emma said very quietly. "It was a store for food at the end. Had been a garage." She stared up at the exposed beams. "Man hanged himself from there. Little man. Family died in the first strike. He had rad cancer."

"Jesus," Mildred whispered. "That is one very scary talent, lady."

"I BELIEVE that Jupiter Pluvius has finally relented on us poor mortals," Doc said, peering out of the building into the early-evening gloom.

"You mean it's stopped raining, then say that, Doc, instead of your damned archaic old quotes."

He bowed to Mildred, unable to hide his pleasure at having got a reaction from her. "I had forgotten that most women have small Latin and less Greek, ma'am."

Ryan broke up the pending argument, standing and putting the Steyr onto his shoulder. "Let's move it, people. Be dark in a couple of hours."

Everyone got to their feet, adjusting their baggage and their blasters. Krysty was first to the entrance when she suddenly stopped as though she'd been poleaxed. Emma was walking close at her heels, and she, too, stopped in her tracks, giving a small gasp of shock.

Krysty spun and the two women stared at each other, inches apart.

"Yes," Emma said, though Krysty hadn't said a word. "I feel them, too."

"What?" said Ryan. "Danger?"

"Stickies, I think." Krysty shook her head. "Very close. Coming this way."

The doomie closed her eyes a moment. "They were hidden. Mebbe in a building, like us. There's about a dozen of them, and they have three norms with them."

"They prisoners?" Jak was immediately at Emma's side.

"Mebbe."

"You carry a blaster, Emma?" Ryan asked.

"No."

"Best borrow one."

J.B. unslung the Uzi, offering it to Dean, much to the boy's delight. "You have this and give your Browning Hi-Power to Emma."

"Thanks, but no thanks."

"You have to carry a weapon in Deathlands."

Emma shook her head, brushing her bangs back off her eyes. "I've never found it necessary."

Ryan looked at her. "How long have you been out and about, Emma?"

"How do you mean?"

"I don't believe someone your age, looking as good as you do, can possibly have been walking loose in Deathlands for all that long. Not staying untouched. Tell me I'm wrong."

She blushed and lowered her golden eyes. "In your way, you can 'see' as good as me, Ryan. Tell you later. But now there's no time. Muties are getting closer."

"Take my gun," Dean said eagerly. "Easy to use. Point it and squeeze the trigger."

J.B. offered more advice. "But brace your wrist with your other hand. Powerful blaster and it'll kick some. Don't want you with a broken wrist or damaged tendons from being careless."

"All right. Under protest." She took the offered 9 mm blaster and tucked it into her leather belt.

"Better to have a gun..." Ryan began.

"And not need it," J.B. continued.

"Rather than need a gun..." Krysty said.

"And not have it," Jak concluded. "Favorite saying Trader."

Emma's attention had wandered, looking out into the dusk. "They've stopped," she said quietly.

"Close?" Ryan glanced at Krysty, who shrugged.

Emma replied. "I think so. That way." She pointed with a long forefinger.

"Camping for the night," J.B. suggested.

"Probably. If we're lucky we should be able to circle clear past and backtrack them. Find somewhere in the next hour to camp ourselves."

"They got prisoners!" Emma exclaimed. "Surely there are some things that a person can't just walk around?"

"Twelve or so stickies against seven—or eight—of us. In poor light. Not great odds."

J.B. agreed with Ryan. "And we don't know who the prisoners are. The first rule of all for survival in

Deathlands is to look out for yourself and your close friends. Rest of the world has to look out for itself.''

''What coldhearts you are!''

''Realists,'' Krysty said.

Then, in the distance the screaming started, high and thin, like a stallion under the gelding irons.

Ryan took a slow, deep breath, looking at Emma. ''All right.''

Chapter Seventeen

"What's the big water to our left?" Ryan whispered. "Is it Lake Potomac?"

Jak was at his side. He had tied his hair back, minimizing the startling flare of white. "Must be," he said.

"There was a warehouse or something like that in this direction. I saw it before the storm started and we took cover. Guess they're in there."

Jak had the best night vision of anyone in the party, though his pigmentation problem meant that he saw much less well in bright sunlight.

Now he stopped, steadying himself on the uneven muddy ground, peering into the dark. "Think I can make out the glow of a fire," he said.

"Sounds like stickies. Torture and a fire. Nothing makes the mutie sickos happier."

Krysty nudged him, pointing with a toss of the head toward Emma. "Lay off muties, lover."

"Oh, yeah, sure. Sorry."

The first burst of screaming hadn't been repeated, but they had caught the sound of raucous laughter.

"One's chilled," Emma said as they crept closer to the ruined building. "Can't tell how." Her neat, round face was as white as parchment.

"That is probably a merciful blessing for you," Doc said solemnly.

"Everything was blurred by his pain." She shuddered. "So many times I wish this curse could be lifted from me."

AFTER SOME CONSIDERATION, and a discussion with J.B., Ryan decided to split his small force, sending half one way around the wrecked warehouse, the rest coming in from the opposite direction.

He took Krysty and Dean, along with Jak. "Emma, go with J.B., Mildred and Doc."

"Mind if change with Doc?" Jak asked. "More equal divide."

"I don't see why..." He stopped speaking as Krysty touched him gently on the arm. "What?"

"Doesn't make much difference, lover."

He lowered his voice. "Then why?"

"Use your eye. See how Jak's been sticking closer to the woman than wasps to honey."

"Oh. Yeah."

He turned to Jak. "Sure, that's fine. You can go with Emma. With Emma, J.B. and Mildred."

"Go in together," the Armorer asked.

Ryan thought for a while. The wind was blowing toward them from the building, carrying the scent of wood smoke. And of burned meat.

"Looks like an entrance around the far side. You go for that. Give you...three minutes. At that point we'll pour it in through the broken window on this side. All right?"

J.B. nodded. "Sure. Three minutes from—" he checked his wrist chron "—now."

THE FIRE WAS BRIGHT, indicating that the muties had brought some dry wood with them. Ryan counted fourteen of them, mostly sitting around the blaze, two of them holding a struggling naked male norm between them. All of the stickies were also male, which meant a hunting or a killing party.

A corpse lay in the shadows close by the black hole of the front entrance. It wasn't possible in the gloom to see what precisely had caused its death, but the screams had told their own story.

Ryan held up two fingers to the others. But Krysty shook her head, showing three fingers, then cutting one in half with her other hand.

That meant she saw two living and one dead.

Where was the other living prisoner? Then he spotted him. The movement of the stickies near the fire had hidden him for a moment. He was a tall man with a full beard, wrists tied behind him. The flickering of the firelight showed the livid marks on his skin, left by the hundreds of tiny voracious suckers that lined the hands and fingers of stickies, the bizarre mutation that had given them their feared name.

Ryan glanced at his chron, angling it toward the light, seeing that there was still thirty-five seconds to go before their synchronized attack.

In that moment of inattention he missed the brutal slaughter of the second of the norms.

He was thrown to the ground, and a burning branch thrust into his mouth. A piece of stick had been forced between his jaws to hold them apart.

There was a soft, muffled explosion and a burst of yellow-white fire from his parted lips. The whole body writhed as though possessed of demons, while the stickies all whooped and clapped their suckered hands together.

"Holy fuck!" Dean breathed, clutching the Uzi tighter, as if it were a lucky totem against the unholy evil that he'd just witnessed.

"Oh, the horror, the horror," Doc said, his voice trembling with disgust and anger.

"Black powder poured down his throat." Ryan's finger tightened on the trigger of the SIG-Sauer. "Time to go and make Deathlands a little bit cleaner."

"I'm for that," Krysty whispered.

The hand on the chron ticked to the three-minute mark.

"Now," Ryan said.

"A MASSACREE OF THE MOST satisfactory kind," Doc boomed, his smoking Le Mat in one hand, the unsheathed rapier in the other. The ancient Civil War blaster had taken out three of the stickies with its single shotgun round. And another had gone down to the needled point of the sword.

Dean had jumped in, the automatic Uzi machinepistol braced at his hip, scattering all twenty rounds on full-auto, the 9 mm bullets toppling over the unsuspecting muties like fish in a barrel.

Ryan and Krysty had shot five between them, while J.B. and his assault party had taken out any survivors and the wounded.

Everyone had played their part—everyone except for Emma.

Now she stood shaking, Jak's arm around her shoulders, her borrowed Browning Hi-Power still tucked into the belt around the black skirt, not just unfired—undrawn.

She was trembling like an aspen in a hurricane, eyes brimming with unshed tears, fingers knotting in front of her. If Jak hadn't stepped in and put his arm around her, it seemed likely that the young woman would have fallen to the bloodied dirt.

"So much killing since we first met," she stammered. "All my fault."

"That's crap," Ryan said briskly, knowing there was little point in offering softness and sympathy to someone so close to the edge of a breakdown.

J.B. had quickly moved, light-footed, from stickie to stickie, checking that all were dead, using one of his pair of stilettos to slit open the throat of the only mutie that still showed any sign of life.

He went to kneel by the semiconscious prisoner, carefully slicing through the whipcord that bound his wrists and ankles together.

Ryan moved to join him, while the others gathered around Emma, whose golden eyes had rolled back in their sockets as she subsided into Jak's arms.

The Armorer glanced back, seeing the tableau in the bright light of the stickies' fire. "Passed out," he said. "Never fired the blaster. Can't walk without stopping all the time. What kind of a useless life did the girl have before we ran into her? Answer me that, Ryan. She's a total liability. Like riding with a hoof-split burrow.''

"I'm interested in how and where she lived," Ryan admitted, "but this isn't the time. How is he?" He pointed with the SIG-Sauer to the naked prisoner.

The bearded man blinked his eyes, wincing at the pain from the dozens of tiny, raw sores that covered his body. "You done the fuckers?"

J.B. nodded. "We did."

"All?"

"Every last one."

Ryan knelt by the man. "Just take it easy," he said. "Safe for now."

"What happened to the rest of my friends?"

"How many were there?" Ryan asked.

"Six of us to start. Sec men from the ville of Baron Sharpe. On patrol."

J.B. and Ryan exchanged glances across the top of the man's head.

The sec man coughed. "Got any water, friends?"

"Not much." J.B. offered him a sip from his own canteen. "Could do with fresh."

"I'll show you. When I'm fit. Plenty when you know where to look."

"Likely all your friends are chilled." Ryan sat back on his heels, reloading the blaster while he spoke. "There were only two more of you here when we arrived. Both done for."

"Others could have escaped," Krysty offered, joining the three men.

"No. Stickies ambushed us and..." He looked up at her, his eyes widening at the sight of her brilliantly bright hair. "Ye gods! You're a woman!" His hands covered his groin.

Krysty grinned at him. "Last time I looked I was. You hide whatever you got, mister. Doesn't bother me. Won't be anything I haven't seen before."

Ryan looked over his shoulder. "Dean!"

"What is it, Dad?"

"Find the tallest of the stickies and peel off his shirt and pants. Long as they aren't too bloody."

"Sure thing."

The man had laid back, fingers cupping his genitals. His face was long and narrow, with prominent teeth, like the skull of a horse. He looked on the ragged side of exhausted.

"Was saying... Stickies came at us when we stopped for a noon break. No warning. No word of mutics in the vicinity of the ville. Nothing."

The Armorer stood, reaching out to take the Uzi from Dean, who'd just arrived with a ragged red shirt and white pants, splattered with a ripple of crimson.

"Best I could get, Dad," Dean said.

J.B. started to reload the automatic pistol, tutting at the boy. "Full-auto, boy! You think bullets grow on trees? Twenty rounds gone in a couple seconds." The firelight danced off his glasses as he lowered his head to check the blaster. "Still, not many wasted."

One eye on Krysty, the man wriggled into the clothes, turning the cord that had bound him into a makeshift belt. "Better," he said.

"How far's the ville?" Ryan asked. "Can we make it tonight from here?"

"Not sure where 'here' is, mister. Got a blow on the head first off. Dived deep into the black pool, if you take my meaning."

"Wait for dawn," Krysty suggested. "Not a bad place to rest for the night. Roof, walls and a fire. There's some fresh wood by the entrance."

Ryan uncoiled himself, walking over to where Jak, Mildred and Doc were gathered around Emma. She was conscious, and Mildred had found a half-full canteen by the body of one of the stickies.

"Sorry," she said quietly. "I'm like a gull around your necks, aren't I?"

"Albatross, dear child," said Doc, who was fiddling with the task of reloading the Le Mat and realigning the scattergun hammer.

"How's that?" she asked.

"The bird. 'And a good south wing sprung up behind, the albatross did follow.' From 'The Rime of the Ancient Mariner.' Samuel Taylor Coleridge. The ill-fated bird was an albatross hung around the neck. Not a gull."

"Sure," the young woman said. "Tired. Sorry for letting you all down." She closed her eyes and lay back again, her head cradled in Jak's lap.

Ryan raised his voice. "We'll stay the night here, people. First job is to get all the bodies outside. Let the scavengers have them. We'll set a double watch. Might be more of the stickies around here."

Mildred had gone over to the wounded man, using some of the water and a torn length of shirt to bathe the weeping, circular sores.

"Hope they're not infected," she said.

"Have a good bath when we get to the ville tomorrow. Baron Sharpe'll be pleased and make you all welcome. But all of those dead."

"Five dead and one living's a lot better than six dead," Ryan pointed out.

"Specially when I'm the one living. Look, I'm Sec man Joshua Morgan. And I haven't thanked you yet."

Mildred looked at Ryan, addressing the sec man. "No trouble. Some things a man just doesn't ride around," she said.

Chapter Eighteen

"The interesting thing is what the dogs did during the night," Doc said.

"The dogs didn't do nothing," Dean replied, puzzled.

"Anything," Krysty corrected automatically. "The dogs didn't do anything."

"Precisely." Doc grinned, looking self-satisfied.

Mildred wagged a finger at him. "I know what you're talking about, this time, Doc. Just for once. It's a sort of quote from that detective. Sherlock Holmes."

"Oh, I had hardly anticipated anyone recognizing... I had the privilege of meeting with the author, Arthur Conan Doyle, during my visit to London. A striking and intelligent young man. I felt he would go far." Doc smiled, shaking his head reminiscently. "It was my belief that Artie modeled his greatest creation on your humble servant."

Mildred laughed. "Only person I know that might have been modeled on you was Baron Munchausen, the greatest liar in all history."

Joshua Morgan was up and about, looking pale and frail in his borrowed stickie rags. "Did you say something about dogs in the night?" he asked.

"Just a small jest, friend," Doc replied. "In point of established fact, I *did* hear the dogs in the night. Perhaps wolves or unusually large and fierce coyotes. From the munching and crunching I would doubt if there is much remaining of the bodies we dragged out into the brush."

He was right. When they all went out into bright sunshine, there was only some black, dried blood and a few gnawed and splintered bones. A track through the dense undergrowth showed where the predators had dragged away the raggled corpses to mangle them at their leisure.

"I wish we could have carried the bodies of my two colleagues back to the village," Morgan said.

"They were past caring about it." Ryan looked at the sec man. "We could have tried to bury them, then your baron night have sent out another hunting party to retrieve them and have them interred in the ville."

Morgan sniffed, his fingers brushing over the myriad small scars on his face. "No." He sighed. "My lord, the baron, isn't a man given to warmth and caring. But he is a good man for all that," he hastily added.

"For all that, and all that," Doc chanted. "He's a good man, for all that."

"You honing my blade, Doc?"

"Am I teasing you? My dear fellow, nothing was further from my mind."

"You know where we are now?" Ryan asked, pointing to the glint of water through a grove of elms.

Morgan nodded. "It must be Lake Potomac. Think so. They brought us some way south and east."

"How far to the ville?"

"Eight or nine miles is my guess."

"Then we'll get started. Everyone about ready?"

Dean tugged his father's sleeve. "Can I keep the Uzi for a while, Dad?"

Emma had given back the handblaster, to the boy's disappointment.

"No. Hi-Power's real good for you. You're used to it by now, Dean."

"Oh . . ." He shuffled his feet in the dirt.

"And don't whine."

"Sorry, Dad."

Ryan looked up at the sky. There were a few wispy clouds riding high, over toward the distant Lantic. The air was fresher and cooler than it had been.

He had told Joshua Morgan a little about themselves, falling back on the usual story that they were travelers whose wag had suffered terminal breakdown a couple of days earlier. Ryan mentioned the fracas in the Lincoln Inn, though he chose to play down their part in the mayhem. And he kept Emma's mutie gifts totally to himself.

He also managed to have a quiet word with the woman before Morgan had awakened.

"From what we learned back in Green Hill, Baron Sharpe has some sort of zoo. Mutie animals. Strong possibility also two-legged muties."

"Like me?"

"Anyone who looks or acts different. Might mean Krysty and Jak, as well. Watch our backs."

"Morgan isn't essentially a bad man," she said.

"You get any feelings about the baron yet?"

"No. Have to meet him. Then I still mightn't feel anything from him."

BARON SHARPE'S MEN found them before they reached the village, mounted patrol, on good-quality horses. There were twelve men, all in a uniform of dark green jackets and rich blue pants, all armed with identical single-shot muskets.

They reined in a hundred yards or so ahead of Ryan and the others, forming a loose skirmish line, every man bringing his blaster to the present at a single word of command.

"Efficient," J.B. said. "Good to see someone who cares about security and decent order."

Morgan nodded. "Sean Sharpe's not a man to allow sloppiness."

"Stay there, outlanders, and don't move your hands to your weapons if you wish to see another dawn."

"Sounds like Clint Eastwood writes his script," Mildred muttered. "Sorry, didn't think. Probably none of you has ever heard of him."

"We going wait?" Jak whispered. "Could be best chance take them now."

Ryan remembered, as he knew J.B. would be doing, that Trader always used to claim that the best time for successful aggression against an unknown enemy was in the first five seconds of the encounter.

"Wait," he said. "No reason to think we're in any danger here."

"How about the story he collects muties and puts them in a zoo?" Krysty asked.

She was interrupted by another shout from the leader of the sec men. "You hear me, strangers?"

Emma closed her eyes for a few moments, looking as if she were counting the beats of her own heart. She opened them again. "It's safe, for now," she said.

"Hi, there, Joaquin!" Morgan yelled. "They're friends. Saved me from stickies."

"Who the fuck're you, calling me by... Is that Morgan? Josh Morgan?"

"Yeah."

"Where's your uniform?"

"Stickies stripped me. These people chilled them all and saved me. Clothes came off of a dead stickie."

There was a gust of wind, rustling the leaves on the elms, carrying the first part of the next shout. But they all heard the ending of it. "...all the others?"

Morgan turned down both of this thumbs in the universal sign of death.

"All?"

"Yeah."

"Sure these people are ace?"

Morgan started to walk toward his colleagues, beckoning for Ryan and the others to follow him toward the line of waiting horsemen.

"Stay on red," the one-eyed man hissed, his own right hand resting on the butt of the SIG-Sauer.

But there was no problem.

The sec patrol was far more interested in the return of their lost prodigal, gathering around Morgan, firing questions at him, though Ryan noticed that some of the men's eyes kept sliding uneasily to Krysty and to Jak. But none of them were taking any notice of Emma.

Finally the sergeant, the grizzled veteran called Joaquin, slapped his gelding on the side of the neck. "Enough of this. Time for talk later." He searched out Ryan.

"Baron'll want to thank you. Thank you all. We found the scene of the ambush." He coughed into his gauntlet. "Not a lot left of the poor devils. There'd been no warning of stickies in the baron's lands. No bastard warning at all."

Ryan had removed his threatening hand from the blaster. "No man would have ridden around that," he said.

Morgan went on tiptoe to say something to Joaquin, who nodded. "'Course," he said. "Josh says there hasn't been much in the line of food for a day or so. On behalf of Baron Sean Sharpe I invite you to come with us to the ville and be our guests and enjoy both bed and board."

"Glad to," Ryan said. "Real glad to."

THE SEC SERGEANT'S generous invitation didn't extend to ordering any of his men off their mounts, offering them to the outlanders. Though he did, hesitantly, ask if Krysty, Mildred and Emma wished to ride or walk.

"Walk, thanks," said Krysty.

"Me, too. Thanks all the same. Never been that great on the back of a horse." Mildred smiled at Joaquin.

Only Emma hesitated.

"Yes, little lady?"

"By stone and water! No, you won't!" she said angrily, taking a few steps away from the mounted man.

"What?" He looked at Josh Morgan for an explanation. "She a stupe?"

Krysty answered him, speaking quickly, addressing her words more to the visibly disturbed Emma. "Had a bad time in Green Hill. Lot of men tried to rape her. Lot of chilling went on. Then, a day later, the fight with the stickies. She was very quiet seeing the way that the last of your men died."

"How was that?" His curiosity made him forget the outburst from the golden-eyed young woman.

Krysty moved closer, putting herself physically between Joaquin and the distressed Emma, seeing out of the corner of her eye that Jak had stepped in again to comfort her.

"They had him tied, his jaws forced open. Stickies tipped in black powder and set light to it. Poor devil's head practically exploded."

The sec sergeant looked at Joshua Morgan. "Who was it? Who was last?"

"Didn't know at the time. They had me stripped and tied in the shadows. I couldn't see." He swallowed hard. "It was only after, when I looked, that I recognized Harry."

"Harry Nodes?"

"Yeah."

Joaquin tugged at the reins, stopping his horse from moving sideways. "If... Woman said that his head was practically... How could you be sure?"

"Had that tattoo of two pigs fucking across his back, between the shoulders."

"Oh, yeah. Right."

The sun still shone down brightly, but there were banks of snowy clouds, fluffy-topped, gathering toward the north of the region, characteristic thunderheads with the promise of plenty more rain to come.

Joaquin suddenly recalled Emma and her strange reaction. "Lady with the yellow eyes... She doesn't want to ride double-up with me or one of the men?"

By now she'd recovered most of her self-control, even hanging out a watery smile to dry. "Thanks a lot, but I think I'll be better if I walk with the others."

"As you like. Looks as if there's a big old chem storm on the way. Best move on to the ville and report to Baron Sharpe. Never keep a baron waiting is what I always say."

He offered a hand to Joshua Morgan, who swung up onto the horse's back. He locked his hands around the sergeant's waist, giving a half wave to Ryan and the others.

The horses moved on. Ryan noticed that Joaquin sent two men ahead as scouts, confirming the professional skill they'd already noticed.

The seven friends, with Emma, strolled along the weed-strewn blacktop after the sec patrol. Ryan dropped back a little to walk alongside the doomie, who had Jak in close attendance on the other side.

"What did you see?" he asked her.

She shook her head, still keeping the smile in place. "Stupe of me. Can't get used to it. Many of them in the group wanted to bed me. The one called Joaquin most of all. He was planning to try and get me in the stables. No. I guess 'planning' isn't the right word. Too strong. More a sort of fantasy for him. But it made me feel choked and sick.''

Jak looked across at Ryan, his white hair dazzling in the sunshine, his ruby eyes screwed up against the painfully bright light.

"This good move?" he asked.

Ryan shrugged. It was a question that was nagging at him. But they needed food and shelter. And Baron Sharpe, whatever his faults, should welcome them as helpers of his sec man.

"I don't know," he said.

Emma patted Jak on the arm, looking at Ryan. "Can't feel real danger."

It didn't console Ryan all that much, remembering how often the doomie had protested that her mutie skills were often variable and unreliable.

Chapter Nineteen

The ville had once been a huge rambling country mansion, built around 1885 in the classic Victorian Gothic style—towers, turrets, winding corridors and stained glass. It seemed that there had once been a number of multistory buildings surrounding it that had taken most of the nuke impact during skydark, preserving it, though there had been some minor damage to the roof where modern repairs stood out like a sore thumb.

A number of outbuildings and barns and courtyards were set among spreading woodlands. But the high wall, set with spikes and electrified wires—powered by a big water generator—was the main defensive feature that struck Ryan's eye as they trudged the last hundred yards toward the spread.

Joaquin had reined back to walk his horse alongside the outlanders.

"Impressive, huh?"

"Can't argue with that," Ryan said. "You get a lot of trouble here?"

The sec sergeant laughed. "Josh, you tell him."

"What happened yesterday was the first serious incident we had for about a year."

Joaquin corrected him. "Closer to eighteen months. Mob of Hole ghoulies, stoned on the jolt they bought from the man with steel eyes.

"Steel eyes?" said Ryan.

"You heard of him? Called the Magus."

"Also known as the Warlock."

"And the Sorcerer," J.B. added. "Used to pick up stickies and sell them on to Gert Wolfram. Fat bastard used to use them in his traveling freak show. So the Magus is still around peddling his dirt?"

Joaquin clicked his tongue, setting spurs into his gelding's flanks, moving it on again. "Yeah. Controls most of the jolt in Deathlands."

"And this mob attacked your ville?" Ryan asked.

Morgan replied. "Came out of the night. Raving and screaming. Stormed the wall. Plenty got chilled on the wire. Until their corpses blew all of the main fuses. Few of them managed to get through and we took some losses. More than an hour to clear the scum away."

"The ghoulies tend to stick in the heart of the old ruins, do they?" Krysty asked.

Again it was Morgan who replied. "Not really ruins. I been around and seen the black canyons of Newyork. Those are what I call ruins. Washington Hole isn't much more than what the name says. Big hole. Ash and fused lava glass. Biggest crater in the world some say. High rad count. Get some triple-serious muties there, which is good news for Baron Sharpe with his—"

"Enough, Josh," Joaquin said sharply. "Don't let your tongue taste so much air."

He pushed the horse ahead at a faster walk, leaving Ryan and the others behind him.

BARON SEAN SHARPE was waiting for his returning sec men as soon as the heavy gates swung open. He stood in the main courtyard, hands locked behind his back, wearing nondescript shirt and pants of dull beige with worn knee boots.

Ryan's first glance went automatically to see how the man was armed, that being one of the most important things to check out in Deathlands.

It was a satin-finish Ruger revolver, stuck in a workmanlike holster on the left side of the belt.

"The GP-160," J.B. said at his side. "Double-action, six-round, .357 Magnum. Live rubber stocks. Handy blaster."

The man himself stood a little over six feet, broad shouldered and deep-seated, with the easy stance of someone who kept himself in top shape. Ryan's guess put Sharpe at around thirty years old. His blond hair was cropped, and his eyes were the chilling milky blue of Sierra meltwater. He was strikingly good-looking.

The horsemen reined in around him, but nobody spoke a word. Ryan led his party in a few yards behind, stopping and waiting. The silence was broken only by the shuffling of the animals, the jingle of harness and by the rising wind that carried a few spots of rain in its teeth.

Sharpe looked around, his eyes taking in everything, lingering on Jak and then on Krysty.

"Well," he finally said. "Well, I see you alone, Joshua, with marks on your face that tell me we have stickies on our lands. Best hear your initial report, Sergeant." He turned slowly to look at Joaquin.

Sitting stiffly upright in his saddle, the man gave a concise account of what had happened: the ambush and the slaughter of the other members of the first scouting party, the rescue by the outlanders that had resulted in the deaths of all of the muties and the freeing of Joshua Morgan.

The baron stood very still, listening. When Joaquin fell silent, he still didn't speak. Out of the corner of his eye, Ryan could see that Emma was trembling. It could have been exhaustion.

Could have been.

"Well. Good report, Joaquin. Thank you. Gives me the things I need to know and didn't waste words. Glad to see you back alive, Morgan. Go and have a bath and get out of those filthy, bloody rags. Then we will be very pleased to hear your dark story in your own words."

"Aye, Baron." He slipped down and walked quickly toward the main building.

"Dismiss the men, Sergeant, and then come and see me in a half hour."

Ryan and his companions moved out of the way as the horses clattered across the cobbled yard, through an archway that presumably led to the stables, leaving them waiting alone with Baron Sean Sharpe.

The moment grew longer, and the spots of rain became more insistent, but Sharpe ignored them, his eyes running back and forth along the line. Each time, Ryan noticed, he hesitated at both Krysty and Jak.

"Well, now. We will spend plenty of time while you tell me your fascinating tales. Perhaps while you lunch with us? But I would know your names and where you've come from. You," he said, pointing unerringly at Ryan, "are the leader of this group, aren't you? Introduce me."

"Sure thing. I'm Ryan Cawdor, from the Shens. My son, Dean. This is Krysty Wroth from Harmony ville. Mildred Wyeth from out of Nebraska. Emma Tyler who comes from—" he faltered for a moment and knew that Sharpe had spotted it "—Emma's from the north end of the Shens. J. B. Dix from Cripple Creek. Jak Lauren from the bayou country. And—"

But Doc took over. "I am Dr. Theophilus Algernon Tanner, Doctor of Science from Harvard and Master of Philosophy from England. Born in South Strafford, Vermont, now a resident of the open highway. Delighted to make your acquaintance, Baron Sharpe. And may we now go in and get out of this damnably miserable rain, which seeks out the flaws in my poor old body?"

"In from the rain? Yes, of course. Most welcome. My people will show you to some rooms where you can make yourselves comfortable." He turned away, then looked back at them. "And thanks for your help." He frowned. "The pity is that it was so little and so late."

For a moment Ryan stood still in the heavy downpour, watching the tall, handsome figure stride toward the main entrance to the house.

"Yeah, and fuck you, too," he said quietly.

KRYSTY BOUNCED on the double bed in the third-floor room that a silent servant had showed them. Outside the mullioned window, the rain pounded against the small panes of glass. There had been two flashes of lightning, but they had been halfhearted affairs compared to the earlier storm.

"What do you think, lover?"

"The ville, Sharp, our situation, or Emma?"

"Yes."

He grinned. "Which?"

"All of them. The ville?"

"Workmanlike is the word that kept comin' to me. Not grand and not poor. Good sec men. Defense isn't anywhere like as good as they think it is. I could get in and take it with half a dozen good men. Or women. Well organized, though."

"Sharpe?"

"You feel anything about him?"

Krysty had found a brush lying at the vanity and sat down in front of a gilt-framed mirror, working the knots out of her bright hair.

"Nothing. Tough. Harsh. His comment about our saving Josh Morgan came as a shock."

"And to me. Met a shitload of barons in my time. Sharpe's one of those that I wouldn't care to cross. My father used to have a saying that someone ran a tight ship. I guess he was thinking about a man like Sharpe."

"How about our own situation?"

Ryan stood behind her, resting his hands on her shoulders, massaging the muscles in her neck. "That's the odd thing about Sharpe. We saved one of his men.

Put a dozen of potential enemies across the black water. Says we're welcome and gives us good rooms. Invites us to stay awhile and eat with him. But there's that bitter cold to him, like his heart had been carved from a slab of Alaska ice."

"Best we don't turn our backs on him, lover." Krysty stood and put her arms around him, holding him tight.

Ryan kissed her softly on the lips. "Agreed."

"How about little Emma? What do you make of her? Something just doesn't set right, does it?"

"Yeah." He let go of Krysty and pressed his face to the cold damp glass of the windows, staring out across the streaming roofs of the ville. "Time'll come when I'm going to want to know where she's been all her life. And when she found out that she had the doomie power. She still doesn't seem able to control it, like it's something new."

"I worry she'll get herself killed with it."

"And us?"

She nodded. "Mebbe us as well."

"Jak's stricken with her. Did you notice?"

She laughed delightedly. "Does a pigeon shit on your head? 'Course I noticed. Good for the kid after all the bad times he's had. Jak's earned some happiness."

"If he finds it with Emma."

Krysty stopped smiling, catching the serious note in Ryan's voice. "You think she's bad news, lover?"

"I think she might be. That's all it is. No more than a feeling. Partly because there's far too many dark places hidden in her life."

ONCE AGAIN, the word "workmanlike" came to Ryan's mind when the food was served in a large dining room, with a vaulted roof of oak beams: a sturdy beef stew with plain baked bread, no salt or pepper or herbs or spices seemed to be allowed to desecrate the table of Baron Sharpe; a joint of roasted pork, carved thick, well-done, with a dull gravy poured over boiled potatoes and sliced carrots served with watery cabbage; and a steamed pudding, heavy on suet, with a lumpy custard sauce.

Thin beer was served from brimming glass jugs by a pair of elderly servants. And water. Krysty chose to have the water and found it to be slightly brackish, with an underlying taste of copper.

"I must compliment you on the underwhelming adequacy of your table, Baron Sharpe," Doc boomed, dabbing at his mouth with a patched napkin.

"What was that? I'm sorry, my thoughts were elsewhere on more important matters."

There it was again, the strange lack of social manners that they'd seen earlier.

"I remarked that you must surely have a descendant of the great Escoffier working in your kitchens."

"Who? I don't think we have anyone of that name as kitchen servant, do we, Joaquin?"

"Don't think so, Baron."

"Doc," Mildred whispered warningly, "don't go too far and push your luck."

But the old man was off and running, following his speeding train of thought, not too concerned to engage his brain before operating his mouth.

"Are you by any rare chance familiar with the word 'logy,' Baron?"

"You ask a lot too many bloody questions, Dr. Tanner. No, I'm not."

"Then kindly allow me to say that this has been one of the most logy meals that I have ever encountered."

"What's it mean?" Krysty whispered.

"Shan't tell you, my dear. Anyone wants to know is at liberty to look it up. My lips are sealed. Perhaps by the glue that passed for custard."

Ryan didn't understand a lot of what Doc had been saying, but he could tell by the impish gleam in his eyes that he was indulging his wit at the expense of the baron, which was never a good thing to do.

"Heard tell you collect animals, Baron," Ryan said, changing the subject.

"Where did you hear that?" Sharpe asked suspiciously.

"Around and about. I think it was probably a hunter up in Green Hill."

Sharpe nodded. "Could be. Yes, that would make sense. I collect very special animals, Cawdor."

"Special?" J.B. asked.

"I wasn't aware that you suffered from deafness, Dix. Perhaps I need to speak more loudly to allow for your disability. I said they were special."

"In what way?" The Armorer took off his glasses and polished them carefully on the cloth, refusing to allow the baron to rile him.

"I don't have the time or the energy to try to explain my collection. If you don't understand, then nothing I say would help. And if you do understand, then no explanation is needful."

"Can we go and see it? See them? Please?" It was almost the first thing that Emma had said since they'd arrived in the ville.

"Why not?"

"When?" asked Jak, who'd been sitting next to Emma.

The baron drained his tankard of beer and wiped his mouth on his sleeve. "Now." He pushed his chair back and walked quickly from the hall.

Joaquin was the only member of his staff allowed to eat with them, and he rose to follow his master, beckoning to Ryan and the others. "Come on. Baron doesn't care for late or slow."

"I can believe that," Ryan said, leading his companions after Sean Sharpe.

Chapter Twenty

Ryan noticed that Jak seemed to be limping more badly than he had earlier in the day. "Those stone splinters in your calf still giving you trouble?"

"Some. Knocked going after stickies. Loose stones. Hurt on walk here."

"Need Mildred to take a look at it later?"

The albino shook his head, the stark white of his hair seeming to illuminate the dark hall through which they were passing.

"Just wound knitting." He hesitated a moment, as though he were trying to decide whether to ask a question, finally making up his mind. "Ryan?"

"What?"

"Why does Baron keep looking me and Krysty?"

"I don't know, Jak. I noticed it, as well." There was no point in pretending to someone as acute as Jak that he was imagining things.

Emma tugged at his sleeve, delaying him until they were last in the line. "Good lie," she said quietly.

"About the baron?"

"You think he's considering Krysty and Jak for his collection, don't you?" She tried for a smile and nearly got there. "No point lying to me, is there, Ryan?"

"Guess not. Can you see Sharpe doing anything?"

"No. No, I can't." She paused. "At least, I . . . Not yet, I can't."

THEY CAME OUT a bolted door into a courtyard at the rear of the main building, having followed the baron past the kitchens and a laundry room.

Sharpe set a fast pace, not doing anything to check that his guests were following successfully. Joaquin, the sergeant, acted as a link, trying to keep his master in sight ahead of him, glancing back to make sure Ryan and his seven companions weren't getting left too far behind.

Through the next door was a formal knot garden, constructed from box and yew. Sharpe seemed to be gathering speed, vanishing through an archway on the far side of the garden before Ryan and his friends had reached the near side.

"Nearly there," Joaquin called.

Krysty's bright crimson sentient hair was curling tightly about her nape, where it had earlier been flowing freely over her shoulders. Ryan spotted it, knowing that it was often a sign of unease.

He moved closer, dropping his voice. "Trouble?"

"Not a good feel. Not exactly danger. Guess it must be the mutie animals he's supposed to have in this collection of his. Soon know."

Jak and Emma brought up the rear. The black-clothed young woman was pale, and it looked to Ryan like the teenager was supporting her. But it didn't seem a good idea to draw Sharpe's attention to her weakness.

The baron stood impatiently by a steel door with three heavy sec bolts on it.

"You say you want to see my pets, then you can't be bastard bothered to turn up on time. I think I'll cancel my invitation to you."

His voice was harsh, like a cold norther over a granite slab. The handsome mouth was curled in disdain.

Krysty stepped closer to him, smiling. "That would be a great disappointment, Baron. We hoped to pass this way, before the accident to our wag. We had heard so much throughout Deathlands of Baron Sean Sharpe and his unusual collection."

"Unusual, Miss Wroth?"

"Yes."

"Wrong. It is fucking unique." A wintry smile drifted across his lips. "However, I wouldn't have it said through this fair land that I refused the plea of a pretty woman. No, not pretty. Quite beautiful. You may see my pets."

"Thank you, Baron." Krysty came close to dropping him a curtsy.

"But I will waste no time with it. Joaquin?"

"Baron?"

"Do the honors. Make sure all is locked and safe. Any mistake and I'll have the skin off your back."

"Aye, Baron." The hesitant note of doubt was impossible to mistake.

"What is it, man?"

"He won't show us." Emma was right behind Ryan, and he just caught her whisper.

"How much should I show them, Baron?"

"Ah, yes. Well, well... Good man, good. The animals and reptiles and fishes."

"Nothing more?"

"No." The syllable was like the snapping of a steel-spring beartrap.

"Right, Baron."

Sharpe looked along the group of outlanders. "Enjoy," he said. "Meet at supper."

He turned on his heel and stalked off, back toward the main house, the heels of his boots clacking off the stone path, fading into the distance.

"I'll open up," the sec sergeant said.

Ryan stopped him. "Question, Joaquin."

"What is it?"

"Sharpe ever married?"

"No. Not that taken by women. Not in that sort of way." He continued quickly, "Nor boys, neither. Not that way at all. Once every few months he asks me to find him a good clean girl from one of the shanties."

"But if they're good they're not clean, and if they're clean they're no good," J.B. said, repeating one of the old war wag jokes.

Joaquin grinned. "Ace on the line. I get a slut in. Have her washed and looked over by a woman. Goes into the baron's room. Hour later comes out. Handful of jack. Warning about keeping her silence. And that's it."

"He changes a lot, doesn't he?" Mildred said. "Almost like he's two different people, both of them living in the same skin and sharing the same brain."

The sec man nodded his agreement. "Been like that since he had a bad fever, about a year ago. Bloody flux and black water. Life was feared for. Seems to some of us been serving him a long time that he's not quite the same man he was before. Says one thing, then says something else. Like watching a butterfly going around a flower garden.''

"He hear voices?" Mildred asked.

Joaquin shook his head. "Baron Sharpe? You kidding me? You sayin' he's a stupe, lady?"

"No, no."

"Good. Because there's nothing much wrong with him that time won't heal."

The black woman had worked in general practice before becoming a specialist in the medical science of freezing, and she knew that a good doctor listened carefully for what wasn't said as much as for what was said.

"Nothing much that time won't heal? I'm interested, Joaquin. I have medical training. Anything else that you've noticed?"

The sec man looked at her for several long, considered seconds. "Not my place to talk about the man who pays me jack and places food on my plate."

"But..."

"'Couple things. You've seen him be changeable. Times the baron seems upset by things that are going good. Other times he's amused by bad news. And he's gotten to be a whole lot more interested in his 'collection' than he used to be three or four years ago. Main thing in his life.''

"What kind of interested?" Ryan asked.

"Ville's going to rack an' fuckin' ruin, Cawdor. Me and some of the older servants, men and women, run it. He kind of walks through. Half the days he never seems to notice any of us, like a man in a dream. Only time he shows any excitement is when he hears of some new sort of mutie in the outlands that he can send off and try to get for his zoo.''

Mildred was nodding at everything Joaquin said, though she chose not to speak again.

Dean broke the slightly uncomfortable silence. ''Can we go in now?''

The sergeant grinned at him, rubbing fingers through his salt-and-pepper beard. ''Why not, young man? One thing, for all of you. No touching or knocking on cages or anything like that. Keep your hands to yourselves.''

He opened the outer door and led the way through, Dean at his heels, the others following.

Mildred waited to go last, catching Ryan's eye so that he lingered with her.

''You spotted something about the baron?'' he asked. ''Some sort of sickness?''

''My guess is that he's become schizophrenic, Ryan. Kind of split personality.''

''Like he's two different people living in the same body? That it?''

''That's it, Ryan. What we heard before we came here made me think he was someone you took care with. Now I'm even more certain. Maybe we shouldn't linger too long around his ville. What do you think?''

Ryan squeezed her shoulder. ''Good to have you along, Mildred. Things you know. Likely nobody else in all Deathlands has your knowledge.''

''We staying here?''

"A while. Supper. One night."

"Then?"

"Sleep light and walk careful."

"One of Trader's?"

Ryan nodded. "Yeah."

Dean suddenly appeared in the doorway, his face flushed with excitement. "Come on, you two. Joaquin's about to open the main doors."

IT WAS LIKE an air lock, a small room set between the double sets of doors, the outer, looking almost as if they were made of sec steel, with massive bolts and triple locks. The inside doors, where Joaquin and the others waited, weren't quite as impenetrable, but they were still solid, with steel bolts and a double sec lock.

"The place is built rather more like a fortress than a zoological collection," Doc observed.

"Right." J.B. looked around the anteroom. "Dark night! What are you trying to keep out of here, Joaquin?"

"Not trying to keep anyone out."

"Then why..." The Armorer nodded. "Yeah. I get it. Not stopping anything from coming in here. The doors are to stop anything getting out."

"Right." He pushed them open.

The first thing Ryan noticed was the smell, a bitter, acrid stench. The second thing he noticed was the noise.

Chapter Twenty-One

The smell of the baron's collection was vaguely familiar to Ryan. It was only afterward, in the calm of remembering, that it came to him.

There'd once been a time when he'd holed up on a ledge at the back of a large cave, not far from the wilderness of Canyon de Chelly, down on the Colorado Plateau. A combination of ill luck had left him ill clothed and unarmed, and he'd stayed up on the ledge for four days and nights, unable to come down for the family of mountain lions who regarded the cave as home. They couldn't quite reach the ledge, no matter how they tried.

And by the Lord, they tried!

The smell of that cavern was graven in Ryan's nose forever and a day—bitter, gripping the back of the throat, overlaid with a feral taint of fearsome hatred.

The noise wasn't like anything that he'd ever heard before, not like anything that any of them had ever heard.

"By stone and water!" Emma exclaimed her golden eyes rolling in their sockets as she stumbled. She would have fallen to the damp stones if it hadn't been for Jak's lightning reflex in catching her.

"Affects some women like that," Joaquin said. "Best take her out of here into the fresh air. It only gets worse. You need a hand, son?"

"No. Manage."

He picked the woman up in his arms as though she weighed only feathers and carried her effortlessly out through the double set of doors.

"Strong little bastard, ain't he? Can't be much over a hundred pounds, skinny-dipped," Joaquin said admiringly. "I never seen hair like his. Noticed that Baron Sharpe saw it, as well."

"Let's get on," Krysty said, wrinkling her nose at the fetid air.

"Fine. Most people see this, they don't like to talk much. Most of things in here sort of speak for themselves. Don't need labels or nothing. But if you got questions . . . ''

None of them had any.

RYAN'S MEMORY of that low, dimly lighted building was confused and blurred.

If you lived and traveled in Deathlands, then you were constantly aware of the rich variety of mutated life that the nukecaust and the long winters had left behind. But it was a bizarre and unsettling experience to see so many extreme genetic deviations all gathered in that single building.

One thing that crossed Ryan's mind was the extreme danger that had to have been endured to capture some of the more lethal examples and safely cage them.

There was the scorpion, nearly a yard long, its barbed sting as long as a man's finger. It sat crouched in a stone-filled container, lined with wired glass for security.

A colony of red ants was shown in an earth-filled cross-sectional tank, the smallest of which was two inches long.

Several snakes, the largest of them a mutie rattler, fully twelve feet in length, lay coiled in its cage, seeming asleep, the remains of several rabbits rotting near it. Krysty moved close, and it reared and struck at her with murderous ferocity, the blunt head striking the armored glass like a sledgehammer, leaving a slimy trail of milky poison eighteen inches long.

"Gaia!"

"Told you keep away," Joaquin said.

One of the odder exhibits was a seemingly normal family of beavers in a tank that had been half filled with muddy water and a few logs.

"They don't look mutie," Dean said, peering cautiously at the animals.

"Watch!" Joaquin went toward a series of metal boxes with slits in their tops. He opened one and pulled out a handful of white mice, tossing them into the beaver's tank, so that they landed on the dirt.

The nearest of the beavers, lazily preening its glossy fur, turned slowly to look at the scared rodents.

"By the Three Kennedys!" Doc exclaimed, watching the horrific transformation.

It was as if the animal had skulls within its own skull. Its nostrils curled back and its mouth opened. A second set of razored teeth moved slowly outward, with a third set of dripping fangs emerging from within those. There was a faint hissing sound from the mutie beaver, before it lunged with its hideously elongated skull, snapping up the nearest mouse and sucking it into the slimy pit of its mouth.

A second beaver moved over with a sickening, graceful speed, unlike the normal amiable waddle of the breed. The same change took place, and the mouse was gone.

Moments later the muddy water boiled as the rest of the tribe of mutie animals surged out and devoured the remainder of the mice.

Once they were devoured, the retractable jaws slid back into place, and all that sat there in the tank was a family of harmless beavers.

Ryan and the others stood still, watching them, paralyzed by the horror of it.

J.B. broke the silence. "Who collects these things for the baron?"

"Trying to get us sec men to do it, but I'm opposed to it. Don't mind patrolling around the ville and listening for word of strange new muties. But we pay jack—good jack—for outsiders to bring them in here. They get money and they take the risks. Way it goes."

"High price," Mildred said.

"Right there, lady," Joaquin agreed. "I believe those flat-tailed little boogers in that tank there took the lives of eight men before they were installed safely in here. One of the baron's very special favorites. Stands and watches them, he does, hour by hour."

Ryan was beginning to feel dizzy, the warm, moist stinking air wrapping itself around him like a noisome shroud, as was the bedlam of noise racketing about the concrete-walled building—barking, hissing, screeching, clicking and howling, all going on endlessly.

Joaquin demonstrated a monstrously bloated spider, covered in a sickly yellow fur. Larger than the biggest dinner plate, it lay still on a bed of white sand. The sec man dropped in a bright crimson finch, first breaking its wings. It fluttered helplessly to the floor of the tank, aware of the lethal menace of the spider.

"Sure it's alive?" Ryan asked. "Seems like... Fireblast!"

From some hidden orifice below its belly, the creature sent out a tiny thread of sticky silk, trapping the bird, spinning it at dazzling speed, binding it into a cocoon until only its straining head was uncovered.

Only then did the spider deign to move itself toward its prey. Its long legs articulated like crooked fingers, lifting it from the sand and carrying it slowly across the tank.

"I don't think I want to see any more of this," Mildred said. "I'll go outside and check how Emma is. Catch the rest of you later." The door clanged behind her.

The spider lowered itself, huge eyes fixed on the struggling little bird. Bringing the serrated pincers nearer, it neatly nipped the beaked head off, a tiny spray of blood dappling its prickling fur.

"Think I'll join Mildred and the others," Krysty said. "Limit to what I can watch. See you later, friends." Again came the sonorous boom of the door shutting.

For the price of two new pins, Ryan would have given it up and followed her. But Dean was still endlessly fascinated, running from cage to tank, calling out for his father to come look at some fresh aberration of Nature.

He swallowed hard, tasting the bitterness of bile at the back of his throat and followed Joaquin and the boy, J.B. and Doc trailing behind.

Amid all of that demonic collection, Ryan only noticed some of the more gross exhibits, the rest passing in a haze of horror and disgust.

There were three-headed sheep and ten-legged pigs; a furless bear, endlessly pacing up and down a tiny, cramped enclosure, banging its head against the wall, leaving a trail of blood wherever it stepped; a vulture, raw-necked and crimson-eyed, with leathery scales instead of feathers; a flock of tiny, cheeping jays, with vicious, hooked claws lining the fore edges of their wings; a boar, with the longest tusks that Ryan had ever seen. Curved and needle-tipped, they were so heavy that the poor beast could hardly lift its head from the urine-sodden straw.

Many of the mutie creatures in Sharp's zoo were in surprisingly poor condition, many of them galled and covered in scaly sores and raw ulcers.

"Why doesn't the baron bother to have them cared for?" Ryan asked.

"You fancy going in to clean them out?" Joaquin answered his own question. "'Course you wouldn't. Sharpie uses prisoners now and again for it. Offers them life if they look after the collection. Trouble is, no matter how much care they take, the odds are stacked against them. On average, they don't survive more than two or three days. Just look in that next cage, for instance.''

It was better than twenty feet across, half-filled with more of the fine white sand, its surface smooth and undisturbed. A few broken branches lay jumbled in the corner, but there was no sign of anything living.

"What is it?" Dean asked, keeping a healthy distance from the thick glass front.

"Watch." A broad grin split the sec man's face. "I'll put in a couple of fine big rabbits."

He vanished around the back and they saw a white-painted hatch slide open at the rear of the cage. Joaquin's hand appeared, holding a couple of black-and-white rabbits by their floppy ears. He dropped them in. Both the animals seemed paralyzed with terror, their fur twitching.

The sergeant came back to join the others, looking in, seeing that the rabbits hadn't moved at all, huddled together for comfort, watching the shining sand.

"Speed things up a little," he said, rapping sharply on the glass with his knuckles.

"Dark night," the Armorer whispered.

Ryan realized that his mouth was hanging open, and he closed it slowly.

Dean took a couple of steps back, hands going up in front of himself as if he feared for his life.

Doc half drew the rapier from its ebony sheath, his eyes widening in shock.

It had all been *so* quick.

The surface of the sand rippled, then, just for a fraction of a second, a funnel seemed to open below the rabbits, and they totally disappeared. Another faint disturbance of the sand, then all was completely still.

"What the fuck was that?" Ryan said.

Joaquin laughed out loud. "Truth is, we don't know what it is. Wizened old guy arrived with it in a steel barrel, about a year ago. Told us how to build the cage and fill it with the sand. Went in himself and opened up the barrel. Fed it some rabbits and Sharpie fell in love with it. It's one of his favorites. Calls it 'Rupert.' No idea why. Man took his jack and we never saw or heard of him again. Claimed he brought it all the way from Mexico, but we don't know."

"I think we've seen enough, thanks, Joaquin," Ryan said. "Come on, Dean."

"Aw, Dad, there's more."

"More of the same, son."

Joaquin didn't seem all that anxious to continue with his guided tour of the collection. The light in the long narrow building was dim, but it looked to Ryan that the sec man's face was noticeably more pale than it had been.

"I would cast my vote for departing from this seventh circle of the inferno," Doc stated. "And I would further propose that we do not hasten back here again. Not ever. May the Lord have mercy on the souls of these poor benighted creatures, cast into eternal darkness by the madness and ambition of mankind."

"Hear, hear, Doc," J.B. said.

They were standing next to a narrow glass tank that held dozens of small fish that seemed to be all jagged teeth and mouth. Ryan recognized them as being voracious piranhas.

"We'll go then," Joaquin said.

"Wait a minute."

"What is it, Cawdor?"

"This the whole of the collection?"

"What do you mean?"

"Simple question. This building. What we've seen here. Is this all there is?"

"Sure."

"What's through that other exit, down at the far end? Double-locked sec doors?"

"Mind your piss-ant business, outlander!"

"More of the collection?"

The sec man shook his head, hand dropping to the butt of an indeterminate revolver on his hip.

"Nothing for you to see," he insisted.

Ryan decided not to push it.

"All right, stay cool," he said, turning to lead the way toward the main exit.

Chapter Twenty-Two

The air outside the thick-walled building tasted like the finest nectar. J.B. hawked and spit, again and again, trying to clear his mouth and throat from the vile taste and smell.

Doc waved his hand in front of his face. "If only one could obtain such a thing as a pomander, scented with fresh cloves. But one cannot."

Ryan looked up at the sky, seeing that heavy clouds were again hanging over the ville, carried on a gentle northerly wind. Though it was still only the midpart of the afternoon, the light was dismal, fading fast.

"Could do with a drink to wash that filth out of my mouth," he said. "Water in your rooms." Joaquin locked and bolted the doors. "Supper's at six. You got chrons? Yeah, I saw them. Don't be late. Baron doesn't care for late."

Dean was the only one who didn't seem to have been at all affected by the horrors that dwelled within the baron's zoo, and he kept up a ceaseless flow of chatter, all the way back into the main house.

"That lizard with about a dozen tails, Dad! How about that? Not as good as the beavers, though. Way all those sets of teeth came sliding out like on gear wheels. That thing in the sand that chilled those rabbits. What about that, Dad? Huh?''

Ryan gave the boy back mumbled monosyllables, locked away into his own thoughts. His uneasy concern about the collection was made stronger by the sec man's refusal to allow them to see the rear part of the big building. He wondered whether it would be worth the risk to try to get into it that night, or safer to play the cards close to the chest.

Should they get away from the ville at the first opportunity?

He couldn't decide.

KRYSTY WAS WAITING for them in the corridor, looking anxiously to see if any of the sec men had kept them company.

"Trouble, lover," she whispered.

"Where?"

She beckoned them all into the end room of the corridor, which had been given to Jak, Doc and Dean.

Emma lay on the bed, as waxen as a corpse, eyes closed tight.

She was barefoot, her dress spread out over her legs. Jak sat on the bed at her side, holding her right hand in his left.

"Bad, Ryan," he said.

"What's happened? She fainted?"

Mildred had been bathing the young woman's forehead with water from the flowered china washbowl. "Not a faint. Been talking but not making sense. Could have been going close to that disgusting building and those freaks inside it."

"She's a sensitive." Krysty carefully closed the door behind them, having checked that the passage was still deserted. "Easy to lose balance."

"Oh," Jak gasped, as the fingers tightened around his, turning his flesh even whiter.

"The waxwing has been slain, brethren," she said in a piercing whisper.

"Fever?" J.B. asked.

"No, John. Pulse is slow, around forty. Temperature feels a tad low, if anything."

Her eyes flicked open, the golden light seeming to illuminate the whole room with their intensity. For a moment they weren't focused, then they sought out Ryan, settling on his face. Emma sat up, without any help from Jak.

"Feeling better?" Ryan asked.

But she ignored him. Though her eyes drilled into him, Ryan had the uncomfortable feeling that the dark-haired woman wasn't actually seeing him.

She was looking through him, past him, within him, beyond him.

When she began to speak, Emma's voice was oddly flat and strained, as though she were being forced by someone to deliver a speech that she'd barely managed to learn.

"I stand upon a beach and the mists close about me. I cannot breath for the fumes, and the noise of the sea beats in my ears. They confront me in this place of death and darkness. But I do not fear them."

"Who are you?" Krysty whispered.

"I'll be hung, quartered and dried for the crows!"

"Trader!" Ryan gasped. "How..."

Emma's face was carved from stone, and her voice didn't change. "Abe's here with me. Trusty Armalite cocked and ready at the last. Surrounded by bastard ungodly. Bald fuck with shaved head and pretty crystal."

"That's Straub," J.B. said. "She's talking about how we left Trader and Abe."

"Death on every hand. Over, under, around or through."

"One of Trader's favorite sayings." Ryan felt a cold sweat trickling down the small of his back, the hairs prickling at his nape.

"Fog gets thicker."

"What happened, Emma? Did Trader and Abe pull through after we left them?"

The woman shook her head, her black hair swaying from side to side. "Can't tell anyone what I can't see. But you must remember that today is just the tomorrow that you were so worried about yesterday."

"She's coming out of it," Jak said.

"I'm coming out of it," she agreed, blinking and rubbing her eyes with the sleeve of her black shirt. "What happened? Where was I? I could see a ragged mob encircling me on a shingled beach, among weed-covered boulders. I was old, with a nagging pain in my stomach. It seemed like it might have been my ending, but the seeing stopped before the curtain came down."

Ryan had been leaning against the window, wiping at the steamed glass, glancing out through the leaded panes. "Raining again," he said.

Emma stared at him. "There's something wrong, Ryan. Tell me what it is. Something about me." She closed her eyes, leaning her forehead in her hands. "The mutie power. When did ... You must clear this or it'll be like a high wall of raw stone topped with razor wire, between us."

He nodded, realizing that he was already taking for granted her truly remarkable powers in reading his mind. "There's questions," he agreed. "Should I ask them now?"

"I'm well enough," she said, shrugging off Jak's hand, turning to him. "Truly I'm fine. And, Jak, you mustn't . . ."

"What, Emma?"

She sighed. "Nothing, love. Just that you mustn't think too much of me."

"Why?"

The young woman touched her index finger to his lips. "Wait, Jak," she said softly. "There can be good as well as bad, if that's the way you want the bones to fall."

There was an uncomfortable silence. Somewhere lower down in the mansion they hear a door slamming and a burst of chattering from two of the women servants.

Ryan coughed. "Want this to be you and me, or all of us, Emma? We don't have secrets between ourselves."

"Then it might as well be all of us. And it might as well be now."

There was a general shuffling around as everyone tried to find a more comfortable position, without making it too obvious that this was what they were doing.

When everyone was settled, Ryan sat on the end of the bed, facing Emma.

"Ask what you want, Ryan," the woman said, running a hand through her cropped hair. "I know what bothers you about me. And you're right to be bothered. Quite right."

"Only two things."

"How long have I had the power of seeing?"

He nodded slowly. "Right. That's number one. Number two is where have you lived your life?"

"Before I discovered the power or after?"

"Both."

Her bright eyes were hooded, as though a spider had woven a fine web across them. It seemed once again that a part of her mind had moved someplace else.

"I lived for the first twenty-one years of my life in the northeast, in a small ville called Naven, a bleak and miserable place, with a long beach opening onto the Lantic. Children were told never to go down by the sea as there were tens of thousands of devil crabs there, some of them eight or ten feet across. Horned creatures with spiked tails. Nobody was safe from their ravages. Even the headman of Naven, Guido Smith, fell victim to the curse of the crabs."

"And you had the power then?" Ryan asked.

"No. There were odd times that I had a sort of... a sort of 'feeling' about things. I could help finding a lost cow or a mislaid ring. Knowing when there might be a storm on the way. Most if it I kept to myself. There were a couple of times I saw that someone taken sick would die and not get well. I was rarely wrong. But nothing compared to now.''

"Don't have to tell this if not want," Jak muttered, looking ill at ease with the interrogation.

"No," she replied, favoring the albino teenager with a brief wintry smile. "I don't mind, Jak. In a way it's a relief to be able to talk to someone about it. Someone you know you can trust." The gold eyes looked around the room. "One of the few good things about my cursed gift is that I can tell when someone can be trusted. I paid a price for learning that." She shook her head. "But I run before my horse to market."

"Did any of your family have the gift?" Krysty asked. "Because 'seeing' ran in my family, at my mother's generation. Always through the women."

"No, Krysty. Your mother must've been a most remarkable woman."

"She was. Gaia, but she was!"

Emma carried on with her story. "We often went fishing in a small boat, off the shore. Winters were cruel and iron-hard. The sea turned gray and froze, so thick you could drive a wag over it or roast an oxen on it. It was a winter past that it happened. A bitter day with a wind that would cut you to the bone. The white bears had been seen within a stone's throw of the ville."

"Polar bears?" Doc asked.

"Seen in old predark books that they called them that, Doc," J.B. said.

"We had a number of fishing holes cut, and it was the job of the younger women to keep them open, day and night. I was out on the sea, a hundred yards from

shore, when I saw a white bear approaching me from
the north. It had already come close enough to cut me
off from the ville, so there was nothing to do but stand
and fight. I screamed. 'Course I screamed. But I knew
it wouldn't chill me. *Knew* it inside. But I was still terrified. Had a spear with me. But I tried to dodge it,
hopping around the fishing holes in the ice, with the
leaden water surging and slurping beneath. You know
it turns thick, like gruel, in bitter cold.''

She paused as they all heard booted feet walking
slowly along the passage outside the room. The foot-
steps stopped for a moment and then carried on, the
sound fading into stillness.

"Yeah?" Ryan prompted. "What happened? You
fell in one of the holes?"

She nodded. "You certain sure you don't have the
gift, as well, Ryan?"

"Good guesser is all," Krysty said.

"I slipped and my feet went from me. Next I knew
I was deep under the ice." Emma's voice became
dreamy as if she were reliving the experience. "I can
see the light. Dappled like the sun through a forest.
The cold took my breath. I swam toward the light, but
the undertow had pulled me sideways and I had lost all
sense of my bearings. When I came up toward the
surface, I bumped my head on ice."

"That's triple scaring!" Dean exclaimed. "Reckon
I'd have just shit myself."

"Perhaps I did, Dean. I don't remember that. I
know I wasn't frightened by then."

"What about the bear?"

"I never knew, Dean. It must've been nearly as surprised as I was when its prey disappeared."

"Don't keep interrupting, son," Ryan said.

Emma gestured to a water pitcher and glasses by the side of the bed, and Jak quickly poured some out for her, holding it as she sipped.

"Thanks. Not much more to tell. I tried to breathe in the narrow gap of air between the sea and the bottom of the thick ice. But the movement of the water made it impossible."

Doc cleared his throat. "It was said that Harry Houdini, the famous escapologist, did that once when a trick went wrong. But my belief is that it was simply a clever piece of self-publicity on his part."

"Can't be done in the sea," the woman said. "Believe me, Doc, I know like nobody else. My lungs were bursting, and my sight went black and I passed out. Nobody was sure how long I was under, but someone had seen the bear and my fall. They came from the ville and smashed the ice all around as quickly as they could. And there I was, floating on my back, face like snow, my skirt drifting out all around me."

"Ophelia," Mildred whispered, but nobody took any notice of her.

"They got me out and bumped and pumped me. Stripped me and rushed me to a fire where they piled heaps of furs on me. I was in a coma... Is that the right word, Mildred?"

"Yeah. A coma. A long period of unconsciousness. It would figure."

"I was in that black sleep for a week. When I recovered I found I had the power."

"Did you tell people?" Ryan asked.

"Not exactly. I couldn't help saying things as they came to me. There was talk of burning me as a witch. I could see both past and future. Father helped me to escape before they came for me with their ropes and their smoking torches."

"Where did you go?" Jak took the glass from her hand and put it back on the table.

"South. To get away from the cold. I don't think they pursued me. Glad to be rid of the witch. I know they were all frightened of me." She sighed. "Wandered for a few months, toward the Shens, doing kitchen work and taking what came along."

"Where in the Shens?" Ryan asked.

"All around. Into the Smokies. Finally found myself in the ville of a baron called Paddy Clancy. I got work in his kitchen, but he saw me. Had a big appetite did Clancy. Specially for tender young females." Her voice was bitter and cold.

"Heard of him," J.B. said. "Visited him with Trader. Remember, Ryan?"

"Tall man with red hair and a pair of matched Navy Colts? That him?"

"Yeah. 'Course he was younger when we visited him. Only been baron for a few months. After his father died."

Emma nodded. "I saw the death when I was first in the baron's company. He killed his father."

"Thought the old man was trampled to death by a stallion," J.B. commented.

"Supposed to think that. I 'saw' his son with a club that had an iron horseshoe nailed to its end. Used it to batter his father to the dirt. Puddled his brains."

"You didn't let on you saw this?" Mildred said.

"No, of course not. Stupe question."

Emma was silent.

"You let baron find out you knew chilled own father?" Jak said disbelievingly. "How? Why?"

She was on the brink of tears, talking only to the albino, her golden eyes locked to his ruby eyes. "You don't understand what it's like being a mutie, Jak. I keep telling you all that I can't control it. What I see and when I see it. Comes in a flash without warning. So I can't get ready for it, ready to try to conceal my emotions at what I see."

"The murder came to you out of the blue," Krysty said. "That it?"

"Sure did. Clancy wasn't a bad baron, and I saw enough to figure his father deserved the killing. And he wasn't the sort of man to have his sec guards tie you naked to a bed while he fucks you from midnight to tomorrow."

"But?"

"There's always a 'but,' isn't there, Ryan? He said he wanted to marry me. Said it out in front of half his family. We'd ridden to a picnic, on horseback. Paddy had a fine stallion called Bluegrass Prince. When he said he wanted to marry me and be as good a husband as he'd tried to be a son, I *saw* it all."

"The killing?" Dean asked breathlessly, carried along by the bizarre tale.

Emma sounded tired. "Yeah, yeah. Paddy stood there in front of me, offering a glass of elderberry wine. Brothers and aunts and nieces and all, around him. But I saw another guest at the picnic. Another Paddy Clancy, gripping the metal-tipped club he'd made, oh, so secret. Blood on the horseshoe. Blood and brains splattered all over his white shirt and across his face and all down his arms. Matted in his red hair."

"What did you say?" Doc asked. "It must have been a thoroughly dreadful moment for you, poor child."

"It was, Doc. By stone and water, it was!"

"Go on." Ryan's mind was only half listening to the young woman's story, since he already knew how it was going to turn out. Obviously she blurted out the murderous secret, yet she must have escaped. Otherwise she wouldn't be here with them now. He was more worried that what she'd done once she might do again.

And there was the strange locked section at the rear of Baron Sharpe's mutie collection to worry about.

Emma had just explained how she'd gasped at the horrid specter, saying what she'd seen. "It was like I'd spit in everyone's face. The baron turned white as a fresh-laundered sheet and broke the glass in his fingers, the white wine tinted pink with his blood. For once, I recovered faster than any of them and broke and ran. Threw myself on the back of Bluegrass Prince and snatched loose the reins from a thunderstruck groom and was away."

"They chased you?" Jak had got up off the bed and was walking around the room, brushing his long pale fingers across the tops of the furniture.

"Nobody could catch the Prince. I rode the poor beast until he frothed and foundered, bloody-lunged, full forty miles away from the ville."

"And came wandering east." Krysty shook her head. "It'll happen again, you know, Emma."

"I know it. I try to hide it, but it's like having a dagger of ice thrust into your heart. Anyone would cry out."

"Got take triple care." Jak sat by Emma again and took her hand.

"I know. It's a horror to me. Like spending all of your life with a naked ax blade suspended above your head by a single human hair."

"Let the wrong word slip and you can get yourself chilled," Krysty said.

Ryan shook his head. "No, lover. Wrong word slips and she can get us all chilled."

Chapter Twenty-Three

Supper with Baron Sean Sharpe passed without any problem. The food, as before, was dull at its heart. A haunch of mutton, steamed with cabbage, turnips and okra, was the main course of the meal.

During a watery soup with shredded eggs and fragments of gristly bacon that preceded it, Baron Sharpe seemed to be almost asleep. He asked what they had thought of his collection that they'd visited during the afternoon, but hadn't even bothered to make the pretense of listening to their answers, cutting off Krysty in midsentence.

"Yes, I know all this. And like so much else in this wretched life, I find it ineffably boring. Joaquin showed you all the animals, did he?" He looked across at his sec chief, who shook his head in a barely perceptible movement. But Ryan noticed it and wondered at the message that lay behind it.

"Yes, he did. But I won't bore you further, Baron, with my poor thoughts on them."

"Better, yes, better. Well, well, better. That is the most amazing hair, Miss Wroth. I don't suppose it conceals any strange skills, does it?"

"What kind of skill?"

He leaned back in his carved oak chair and belched, not bothering to stifle it with his hand. "Any sort of... unusual skill, my dear."

Ryan stepped in quickly, seeing the hazardous direction that the baron's thoughts were taking. "I don't think any of us have any special skills worth mentioning. Though we're all fair hands with a blaster or with a knife, as your sec man, Joshua Morgan, can testify."

"What of the snow-headed lad?"

"What of me?" Jak asked, laying down his soup spoon. "What of me, Baron?"

Sharpe shook his hands wearily. "You outlanders are all so eager to take offense when none is intended. I still have a slight curiosity. Such pale skin and eyes that glow like the embers of a fire. Do you see in the night? That might interest me a little, if you did."

"See bad in sun, Baron," the teenager replied.

Halfway through the eating of the stolid main course, Sharpe showed a peculiar change in his personality.

He pulled a face of disgust and spit a mouthful of meat onto the floor at his side.

"This is ditch water! I can't abide food that tastes of nothing!" He yelled to the group of servants that was huddling by the doors to the ville's kitchens. "Spices, damn you! Bring peppers, salt and chilies, and be quick about it!"

Mildred was sitting next to Ryan, and she whispered the single word "Schizophrenic" to him.

Ryan watched as Sharpe stood, throwing his napkin across the table, yelling out to the room in general that the food was shit. Fit to tar a boat but not fit to serve to guests. His face turned red, and a vein pulsed with rage.

"Lot of fuss about nothing," J.B. whispered.

Doc smiled gently. "It seems rather like taking a toothpick to a mastodon," he said.

White-aproned, sweating kitchen servants ran in, carrying bowls and jars, laying them on the table in a semicircle around the enraged baron, who attacked them with an unsettling ferocity, scattering spoonfuls of powder over his platter of mutton. Yellow powder and red powder. Speckled powder, gray and green. And red and green pastes, some with tiny seeds showing in their midst.

In considerably less than a minute, the food was almost totally obscured.

"There," he said contentedly, sitting back at his place. "Now you can all help yourselves to give this dreck a passing, temporary resemblance to real food."

The condiments and spices were passed around, most of Ryan's group helping themselves to some of them, though there was a deal of suspicious sniffing and dipping of fingers to taste what was in each container.

"Cumin," Mildred said. "Tarragon." She licked her lips after trying the light green paste, freckled with seeds. "Ah, that's good hot chili. Sort I used to get sent to me by an aunt in Chimayo." There was also a plain pepper mill that she used to sprinkle the minute black grains over the unappetizing meat. "Thanks, Baron Sharpe. It surely makes a difference."

She whispered across to Dean, "Go easy on some of them, son. Specially the green chili. Make your lips and tongue feel like they've been blasted with molten glass."

Ryan had also tried the chili, and he watched in stunned admiration as Baron Sharpe tucked into the equivalent of a couple of pounds of mixed spices, including a good quarter pint of the chili.

The brutally handsome face of the blond man was quickly streaming with sweat, pouring down his cheeks and dripping from his chin and from the tip of his nose. His complexion grew so flushed that Mildred muttered to Joaquin, sitting on her far side, that some tumblers of water would be a help for everyone.

Sharpe seized the jug as it was laid on the table and drained it in a single, gasping, gulping draft. "Better, well, better," he panted. "More of it."

Everyone ate in silence, uncomfortable at the baron's unpredictable lack of mental balance.

Doc broke the munching stillness. "This proves what I always say."

"What's that?" Mildred asked.

"Food is killing the art of conversation."

IT WAS CLOSE TO ELEVEN, and most of Ryan's party had retired to their beds for the night. He and Krysty had opened the windows of their room, allowing cool damp air to blow away the mustiness. Now they were sitting together by the casement, content to be quiet in each other's company.

There had been a piercing cry from out in the night a half hour earlier, but there had been nothing to be seen. Except for lights shining in what seemed to be the rear part of the building that housed Sharpe's zoo.

The sharp knock on their door made both of them jump. Ryan stood and walked across the room, picking up the SIG-Sauer and cocking it.

"Who is it?"

"Morgan. Josh Morgan."

"Yeah?" Ryan kept the door locked and double-bolted. "What do you want?"

"Got an old woman in the infirmary, asking to see you."

"Why?"

"Can I come in, Ryan? Don't want to shout this all around the ville."

"You alone?"

"Sure."

Holding the blaster in his left hand, Ryan slowly slid back the bolts and turned the ornate brass key. He opened the door a couple of inches, keeping his foot set against the bottom of it, seeing the tall bearded sec man standing anxiously outside. The flickering lights showed that the scars on his face from the stickies were already healing.

"Come in, Morgan."

Ryan closed the door again, carefully locking it again. The sec man watched him.

"You take care, don't you, Cawdor?"

"Living is taking care. What is it?"

"We heard word from Clinkerscales at the Lincoln Inn about what happened. The young woman's a doomie, isn't she?"

There was no point in denying it. "She claims to be," Ryan replied cautiously.

"Caused a riot. Blood knee deep on the floor."

"Ankle deep," Krysty said.

Morgan nodded. "Baron doesn't know it yet. I'm the only one knows. Word doesn't get around the Hole too much. Better Sharpie doesn't know."

"Why?"

The sec man stared directly at Ryan. "I owe you my life. But the baron could take an interest in Emma if he knew she had true mutie powers."

"But why should—" Krysty started.

Morgan held up a hand. "No! I'll go so far along the road for you. No farther. But this is only a part of what I've come for. Just take it as a warning. Clinkerscales also told me about you and John Dix riding with the Trader. How he met up with you, years back, and all. I never actually saw the Trader, but I heard plenty of tales of him."

"Most men have," Ryan stated.

"The old woman in the infirmary said she used to ride with him. Wanted a word with you, Cawdor."

"And J.B.?"

"Just you. Says you'll know why."

"What's her name?"

"Won't give it. She's real triple sick, Cawdor. Best take a couple coins to lay on her eyes. Hours at most. Mebbe minutes. No time to waste on talk."

Ryan rubbed a finger down the side of his nose, considering the request, automatically looking for the possibility of a trap, rejecting it.

"Right," he said.

Ryan turned to Krysty. "Keep the door safe, lover. Go to bed if I'm more than an hour."

She kissed him on the cheek. "Take care."

MORGAN LED HIM silently through the rambling ville, past pairs of patrolling guards, all of them well trained and alert, making Ryan reconsider his original thought that it would probably be easy to take the ville.

"Nearly there, Cawdor." They were the only words that Josh Morgan said to him until they reached a half-glass door with the painted sign over it, proclaiming that it was the infirmary.

"You coming in, Morgan?" Ryan asked.

"No. This is one ball you have to carry on your own, outlander. Woman's in a private room beyond the main ward. Nobody else in there. Bell by the bed if you need to call for help."

It looked for a moment as though he were going to say something else, but he turned on his heel and walked back along the shadowed passage.

Ryan opened the door and entered the infirmary, finding himself in a silent dormitory, with five beds to a side. An occasional light glowed dimly on the walls, showing the stark folded sheets and the fluffed pillows.

The air tasted of antiseptic and sickness.

Ryan moved slowly, like a one-eyed ghost, his hand resting on the butt of the P-226 SIG-Sauer. His combat boots whispered on the polished linoleum floor.

Blinds were drawn over the windows, deepening the effect of an undersea cavern.

At the end of the ward, Ryan saw the corridor stretched ahead of him for another fifty or sixty feet, with several doors opening off on both sides. The first of them stood ajar, showing an empty office. The door opposite was locked.

A narrow strip of pale fire glittered coldly from under the next door along on the right-hand side, and Ryan paused outside it, fingers reaching for the cold brass handle and turning it.

The light was on above the single bed. The solitary window was closed, the shutter thrown back, showing only a polished blackness. The room smelled of death.

Ryan's first thought was that the mysterious woman who claimed to have known him had already slipped peacefully into the big sleep. Her eyes were closed, the toothless mouth sagging open. He had no doubt that Morgan had been misinformed. Ryan had an excellent memory for faces, and he knew immediately that this skeletal old woman, looking to be closer to ninety than eighty, had never ridden the war wags with him.

He was about to turn and walk away when the veiled eyes opened and looked at him, and a croaking, feathery voice spoke.

"Never used to walk easy away from me, Ryan."

Chapter Twenty-Four

"Oh, fireblast! Jenny? Jenny Bolam, is it you?"

Jenny Bolam had been nav officer on War Wag Two when Ryan had joined Trader. She had been no more than four or five years older than him, which would make her half the age of the animated skull lying in the bed.

"Changed a bit, have I?"

Ryan found his mouth had gone as dry as desert sand, and he cleared his throat, finding that he couldn't set his mind to any lie that would have any point.

"Some, Jenny, some."

"Silver-tongued bastard! Like always."

"Where did you hear I was around?"

"Lincoln Inn. Clinkerscales has been a good friend. Didn't know of my connection with Trader. And you. Gave me a bed to die in. Then there was the shooting, and he told me about a one-eyed son of a bitch with black curly hair and a chilling way to him. Knew it could only be one man in all Deathlands."

It was terminal rad cancer. The signs under the pitiless overhead light were unmistakable.

Jenny Bolam had been plump and blond, with eyes as bright and blue as a summer sky in Montana, full-breasted with muscular thighs and firm buttocks.

Ryan had known and loved every inch of that fabulous body, and Jenny had encouraged him, showing him things and teaching him ways that he'd never known before. Never even dreamed of. Offered herself as an instructor, making him aware that "wham, bam, thank you, ma'am," wasn't good enough, and that sex was a two-way street.

"Thinking back, are you, Ryan?" She made a feeble sound that might have been a laugh. "Times past, not worth forgetting."

"You were marrying, Jenny. Ville we traded for some mortar shells."

The head nodded slowly. The woman was almost completely bald, with just a few strands of fine silvery hair hanging limp over the ears.

"Hanging Tree, in old Tennessee. You always had a good memory, Ryan."

"What happened?"

The eyes closed and opened again. "Pour us a drink of water, will you, lad?"

Ryan went to the side of the bed, struggling to hide his revulsion at the overwhelming stink of racing decay that seeped from Jenny.

There was a thick glass tumbler and a jug of water with a circle of beaded muslin draped over it to keep away the insects. Ryan half filled the glass and offered it to Jenny, who smiled, showing the stumps of yellowed teeth between ulcerated gums. "Can't hold things steady anymore. If you could ..."

"Sure."

He leaned over the woman and put one arm behind her shoulders, feeling the frail sharpness of bone beneath the taut skin, easing her upright and holding the drink for her.

His face must have showed the shock at how unbelievably frail she had become.

After three or four sips she gestured for him to take the water away. "Lost some weight, haven't I, Ryan? Well, you always said I had a few ounces too much meat on my bones. Now that's all I am. Just bones."

"What happened?"

"Big question. I married. Good man. Made shoes and boots. We had four children. One died at birth. Another went to cholera. My husband was helping in a harvest and a tractor went over on him. Crushed his ribs and lungs, and he drowned on his own blood. Third child, sweet little Billy, was sickly. Left him a fire to keep warm while I went out to...to bring in some jack. House went like a torch. Just me and my firstborn. His name was Ryan, too. Can't think why."

She was breathing hard, the sheet across her shrunken breasts rising and falling quickly. "Don't talk, Jenny. Save your strength. We can—"

She held up a frail, clawed hand. "No shit between us, lad. Never was. Too late for it now. Ryan was stabbed to death in a gaudy brawl. Went there as a bully-minder. Fifteen, he was, but a big strong boy. Been a downhill blacktop since then, lad."

"I'm sorry, Jenny. Empty words, but I mean them. I'm truly sorry for it."

"Worked in frontier pesthole near an old hot spot. Hotter than I thought. Got the cancer that's eatin' its way through my guts to my heart, Ryan. But what of you? And what of Trader?"

"Been around. Traveled a lot with John Dix, the Armorer. You recall him?"

"Some. Married, lad? Always thought that you'd make the worst husband between Portland, Maine, and Portland, Oregon."

"No. Not spliced up. Got a woman. Good woman. Things about her remind me of you, Jenny. Got a boy. Dean. Twelve years old. No, eleven."

She nodded, her rheumy eyes narrowing. "Settle down, 'fore it's too late, Ryan. You'll be a guest of the old man with the midnight cloak for a long time. Do it."

"Been thinking on it, Jenny. One day."

"Trader? Everywhere I went, his name'd come up. Last was he'd been wiped out in a standoff up on Lakota lands."

"Ran into him not long ago. Not changed much. Him and Abe were riding together."

"Abe!" She went into a coughing fit that ended only when Ryan gave her another sip of water. "Runt o' the litter. Tell you what, though. Little Abe was about the second best at lovin' I knew. Don't have to tell who was the best, Ryan. You always was and you always will be."

"You taught me more than I'll ever forget about bedding, Jenny."

"If I didn't pain so much, I'd ask you for a final ride, lad, for old times' sake. No need to look so horrified. I'm not up to it, and I doubt you would be. Christ!'' Her hands went to her chest, gripping through the sheet. "Heart's goin' like a trip-hammer, lad. Could be..."

"Can I get someone? We have a real doctor with us. Mebbe she could..."

Though he knew that she couldn't.

Her right hand stopped him, like the claws of a small bird. "Like I said, lad, no shit between us."

"Do you want something to eat, Jenny? I could have them make some soup?"

"Get real, Ryan." A spark of the old spirit flared up for a moment. "The last train's in the station, and I'll be pulling out on it in a short while. I wanted to see you. Part to see how life's treated you." A single bright tear eased from her left eye and trickled down the furrowed cheek. "There's something else, lad. Something else to warn you about."

"What?"

"Sit on the bed, close, Ryan, so I can see you. Light's failing. That's better. Heard from Clinker-scales about your rescue. Blood knee deep."

Ryan didn't speak, watching as speech became a greater and greater effort for the dying woman.

"Part of what I did for Trader was navigate. Get cross bearings. Find the two facts that met together so we'd know where the sweet Jesus we were."

"You were terrific, Jenny. Got us out the three-day whiteout in the Darks."

"Flattery gets you most places, like Trader used to say, lad. But here's two facts for you. One is that Baron Sharpe collects mutie animals. Folks around the

Hole know it ain't just animals and birds. It's stickies and ghoulies and swampies and doomies and any poor son of a bitch that's not like norms."

"I heard this," Ryan said quietly, glancing over his shoulder to make sure they were still alone.

"Cross bearing comes from the black-haired little woman you saved. Clinkerscales said she was the most frightening out-and-out, knock-'em-down doomie he ever saw. That true?"

Ryan nodded. "Scary thing is that Emma can't understand it or control it."

"Emma?" Jenny repeated mockingly, with a momentary glimpse of the sparky young woman that Ryan had known and loved. "Suppose you've been fucking 'Emma,' have you, lad?"

"No."

"Then you're getting old, Ryan. Remember that predark song that Ches used to sing? 'Hope I die before I get old'?" Ryan nodded. "Better believe that, Ryan."

"You think that Sharpe'll try and keep Emma, if he gets to know her mutie skills?"

"Sure as eggs is eggs. Never saw a truer cross bearing in my life, lad."

"One of his sec men said as much. Only a matter of time before the baron finds out. I owe you some serious thanks for the warning, Jenny."

Jenny nodded. "Another drop of...of water... Ryan. Can't you turn...up the light and turn up... the light?"

He gave her another sip of water, but most of it dribbled from the corner of the woman's mouth, dripping into the sheet.

"Thank...lad..." Her breathing was faster and more shallow, and Ryan knew that the ending was very close. "Hold me and...and kiss...lad..."

He leaned forward and lifted her, taking the utmost care not to crush her fragile body against his. It was like holding a handful of dry, brittle bones.

She turned her face up to him and he slowly lowered his mouth, trying to hold his breath against the charnel odor that swelled and filled the room.

Jenny's lips touched his, and Ryan felt her trying to push harder against him, the hot, dry tip of her tongue pressing between his teeth.

He fought the temptation to pull away too quickly, finally easing himself back on the bed, gently laying her head onto the pillow.

"That brought..." he began, when he realized that there was no longer any need for the kindly lie.

Her eyes were still open, but they stared sightlessly up into the bright light.

Ryan stood slowly and looked down at the empty husk of the woman that he'd held and loved so many times. So many years ago. He reached up and turned off the lamp.

"So long, Jenny," he said, his voice alone in the darkness. "And thanks. For everything."

As Ryan left the infirmary and started back toward the main house, his eyes were brimming with the lost and lonely tears of memory.

Chapter Twenty-Five

Krysty was still awake, lying in bed with the lamp turned off, the window open. Cool night air filled the room, the ragged clouds filtering the moonlight.

"All right, lover?" she asked as soon as she'd opened the bolted door for him, moving quickly back to bed, allowing him only a silvered flash of her breasts, back and thighs.

"I knew her. From the war wags. She died in my arms of rad cancer."

"Oh. Did..." But no question followed.

"Two things she said. Both we partly knew or partly guessed. Emma's act is all around Washington Hole. It'll only be a matter of time before it gets back to Sharpe. And Jenny confirmed that he has human muties in the back part of that building. Collects all non-norm oddities."

"Gaia! Bad news. We go now or wait until the morning?"

Ryan was quickly getting undressed, his face turned away, surreptitiously wiping his tears on his sleeve. "Have to talk to the others before first food tomorrow."

"Sure. You all right, lover?"

"Fine." He climbed into bed alongside her, putting out a hand and finding Krysty's, holding it tight.

She felt the tension riding him. "Lover? Do you want to?"

"Yes," he whispered. "I'd like that very much."

WHEN RYAN WENT to all the other rooms, just as the first glow of dawn was lightening the eastern sky, he wasn't all that surprised to find that Emma was sharing her bed with Jak. It was the young albino who came to the door in response to the gentle knock.

The teenager wore only a shirt, his pale legs sticking out under it like white fence posts.

"Yeah?"

"Leaving."

"Why?"

"Sharpe definitely collects human muties. It's common knowledge that Emma's a triple-good doomie."

"Baron know it?"

Ryan shook his head. "No. But he could find out at any moment. Sooner we get away the better."

"I'll tell her."

"Sure."

By five-thirty, everyone was dressed, packed and armed, and assembled in Ryan and Krysty's room.

THEY PASSED a few sleepy sec men, none of whom took any notice of them, knowing that they were the legitimate guests of Baron Sean Sharpe.

The ville was only just coming awake, with maids appearing at the corners of corridors, carrying wood for fires and fresh linen for beds.

Ryan thought they were actually going to be able to get away free and unchallenged. They were moving quietly and fast on condition red, without taking the final precaution of drawing blasters, though they were all ready to draw at a word from Ryan. To walk through a baron's ville with blasters in hand would only trigger a full-out firefight.

They were passing the gloomy dining room, places already laid for breakfast, when the grizzled figure of Joaquin appeared by the main doors. His green jacket and blue pants looked as though they were fresh from the laundry and the ironing board. His hair was neatly parted, and he was holding a rebuilt percussion revolver in his right hand.

"Early to leave, outlanders," he said quietly.

"Don't want to outstay our welcome here." Ryan was trying to measure the man, seeing how far he might go to stop them from leaving the ville.

"Baron might be offended."

"Make our apologies," J.B. said.

Doc made a half bow. "Pray do us the favor of explaining to him that we suddenly discovered that we had a subsequent engagement, elsewhere."

"Could be he'll be pissed about it."

"Could be it doesn't bother us all that much." Ryan allowed his hand to move, quite openly, to rest on the butt of the powerful SIG-Sauer.

"Don't like being threatened," Joaquin said, showing no sign of concern at being massively out-gunned.

"Thought you were the one doing the threatening." Ryan took three steps closer to the sec sergeant. "We don't seek trouble with you, Joaquin. But we're leaving, like it or not. Easy or hard. Clean or bloody. We're leaving."

Joaquin looked at him, not shifting his eyes. "If we both push this, then it won't be easy and there'll be some cleaning to do afterward."

"Agreed." Ryan moved two steps closer. The revolver came up, almost imperceptibly, pointing at his groin. "You see a way around this one?"

Joaquin nodded. "Sure. Stay and eat. Tell the baron you've decided to move on. Probably he won't give a small-jack shit about it. That way it's all open."

Ryan considered the offer, trying to think all around it and see whether there was something lying coiled behind it. But he couldn't see it.

"Fine."

He turned to the others. "We eat first."

"Can't we go?" Emma's face was pinched with worry. "Please, let's go now."

Joaquin's eyes opened wider with interest. "What's the problem, little lady?"

"Nothing. I can't cope with being inside buildings for too long. Panic sort of feeling."

"Surely another hour won't fret you too much, will it? Unless there's another reason."

Jak had his arm around Emma. "Be all right," he said. "Stop eat, then go."

"Just that I have a feeling about—"

"That's enough," Ryan snapped, deliberately stern to shut her up from blabbing out something that might risk all their lives. "I'm hungry. We're all hungry. So let's cut out all the talk and sit down to it."

As they sat down, the young woman passed close behind Ryan's chair, dipping her head to mutter to him. "Stone and water, but this is a dark day."

BARON SHARPE APPEARED before the first food was brought to the long table. He was wearing a black silk shirt, unbuttoned, over a pair of ancient stone-washed jeans, tucked into low-heeled Western boots of dark maroon gator skin.

His cold, milky eyes turned first to Ryan. "Dressed for a trip outside into the Hole?"

"If it's all right with you, Baron, we figure you've been hospitable to us, and we'd like to move on."

The eyes turned to his sec man. "Have we repaid the debt we owed for their saving of that clumsy fool, Morgan? What do you say, Joaquin?"

"Done enough, Baron."

Sharpe helped himself from a black iron caldron filled almost to the brim with cooling, leathery, unsalted scrambled egg, piling some salsa on the side and taking two rashers of fatback bacon and half a dozen links of pork sausage.

"Weather'll be bad," he said, as though the subject of their leaving the ville had been settled.

"Air feels heavy," Ryan agreed.

"Real bad."

"How do you know?"

The baron paused with a forkful of egg halfway to his mouth. "Got a tank of mutie prairie dogs. Midgets. Go ape-shit when bad weather's in the way, or a quake. Visited them this morning and they were tearing each other apart. Fur and skin and blood everywhere. So it'll either be a big quake or a triple-evil storm."

Emma, trying to cover her fear, had become preoccupied with the meal, eyes never leaving her plate of grits, fried tomatoes and a pair of sunny-side eggs. But a part of her mind had been listening to what was being said.

"Tornado," she said suddenly.

Ryan's heart sank and he reached toward the SIG-Sauer, seeing that J.B., Jak and Krysty had also picked up on the flaring danger signal, seeing that Joaquin had also noticed what Emma had said. He put his knife down and stared at her.

Baron glanced across at the woman. "I'm sorry?" he said quietly.

"Said that it would be a big tornado."

"Really?"

"Sure."

"Not a quake."

Ryan stepped in, aware that he was probably too late. "Yeah, it could be a quake, couldn't it, Emma?"

The sharpness in his voice penetrated to the doomie, and she dropped her mug of coffee spilling it all over the cloth. "By stone! I wasn't thinking, Ryan. Sorry."

Now Sharpe was becoming seriously interested. "What are you sorry about, lady?"

"Spilling my coffee and making such a stupe mess."

"But you said you were sorry to Ryan, rather than to me. Were you upset by the lady ruining my cloth, Cawdor?"

Ryan for once couldn't come up with a quick answer. The light of suspicion was riding high in the baron's eyes, and he knew that this was one of those razor-edge moments.

Dean helped the tension to pass. "Your prairie dogs figure it for a big quake, Baron? That would be a hot pipe. Never been in a big shaker."

Sean Sharpe, distracted, slipped into one of his odd changes of mood. "Well, well. Quakes bore me. So do storms. If you all want to go and get yourselves torn apart by the ravening forces of Nature, then who am I to try and stop you?" He went on with his meal, then paused a moment. "Best you leave quickly, but tell Joaquin where you're going in case it becomes our turn to rescue you."

"Sure thing, Baron," Ryan said.

KRYSTY WANTED to get as close as they could to the actual center of Washington Hole, where the nukecaust had its unholy spawning.

Joaquin was insistent on knowing their plans. "You heard Baron Sharpe. The Hole's one of the toughest places in all Deathlands. Shanties and ruined suburbs of the old superville. All kinds of muties hanging around underneath the stones. And most of the norms'll slit your gizzard, soon as look at you. Whole family got butchered the other day, just because the old man was carrying a Randall knife on his belt."

Ryan nodded. "Trouble is, we don't really know what our plans are. Just take a look around."

The sec sergeant sniffed. "Not good enough. Sharpie might send me out with an armed patrol to make sure you all do like he said. He wouldn't want any of you to get hurt. No way, José!"

"We'll likely skirt the Potomac Lake. See how near we can get to the centre of the old ville of Washington—"

"Before your rad counters go screaming off the top end of the scale." Joaquin grinned. "I'd say that the heat of the crater, most of which is like rippled, jagged black glass, is probably the hottest hot spot you'll ever see."

"How long?" Ryan asked.

"Much over a half hour and you get sick. Teeth drop out and gums bleed and hair falls and... Shit, Ryan, I don't have to tell you, do I?"

"No. Guess you don't."

"So, take care out there."

Ryan turned away, then faced Joaquin again. "Baron's goin' to have us tracked anyway, isn't he?"

The grizzled veteran sec man laughed. "You might say that, outlander, but you can't expect me to comment on it, now, can you?"

RYAN LED HIS FRIENDS, and Emma, out of the ville a little after eight in the morning.

Josh Morgan shook hands with all of them, embracing Ryan in a bear hug, using the chance to whisper in his ear.

"Women in kitchen say Emma spilled her guts. Tornado, she said. Loud and clear, she's likely a doomie. Lit Sharpie's fuse, good and proper. You'll be followed at a distance by Joaquin."

"Grief?"

The beard was scratching Ryan's cheek. "Baron likes to be sure. Day passes without a tornado, then you walk safe away. Otherwise…watch your backs."

"Appreciate it," Ryan said.

"You remember it." Morgan moved back to join the other sec men on guard by the main gates to the ville complex, waving a hand as they walked away.

Ryan didn't mention what the man had told him. Time enough for that if the weather took the turn that Emma had predicted for them at breakfast.

THE WEATHER WAS an odd mix of a chill breeze and overpoweringly humid air.

The early-morning sky was a strange sulfurous color, the deep yellow overlaid with high streaks of crimson. The wind was constantly veering, coming in gusts from the north at one moment then driving in from the southeast.

Emma's mouth was twitching with nerves, but she didn't say anything until they were a good quarter mile away from the ville. "Sorry, Ryan. I'm so sorry."

He grinned and put his arm around her, feeling her trembling. "Don't worry, Emma. It'll be fine."

Chapter Twenty-Six

Joaquin stayed three hundred yards behind them, riding his stallion at a slow walk, reins trailing. He had three sec men with him.

"Getting to be like itch can't scratch," Jak moaned. "Why not call them close and use Steyr? They only got muskets. Chill easy."

Ryan shook his head. "No reason for that. Visibility's good enough. We can see them just as well as they can see us. Take the broad view, Jak."

"What?"

"Two possibilities. No tornado, they'll finally let it be and ride away."

"If there is tornado?"

Ryan looked up at the darkening sky. "Well, *if* there is, and it looks like it might just happen, then you have to ask yourself what do they plan to do."

"Ride in and take Emma away," J.B. said. "No, I don't think so."

"Nor me," Ryan agreed. "We got them outnumbered and outgunned. They can wait and watch. That's all."

THEY ENTERED A PLACE where the nuke-blasting had been less severe. From a hillside it had been possible to look out toward the center of the Washington Hole, the square miles that had been the throbbing and vibrant heart of the great capital metropolis of the United States, the center of the most powerful democratic country in all the world.

It was as people had described it.

"Wasteland," Mildred said, taking a deep breath. "Can't believe that something can be wiped away so thoroughly that it's just a huge crater of barren blackness."

Doc tapped the ground with his sword stick. "In olden days they would have pulled down every wall, stone by stone, plowed the ground and seeded it with salt so that nothing would ever grow there again."

"Rad counter's showing orange into red," J.B. warned. "Not a place to linger."

Ryan looked up at the sky, which seemed to be growing more menacing every minute. "Might start thinking about getting some cover. Could be that Emma's right."

"Can't we go back to the redoubt and jump out of here again, Dad?"

"Soon, son."

Emma looked across at the boy. "You'll be miserable through most of the long separation, Dean," she said in the flat toneless voice that indicated she was way beyond control. "But it won't last forever."

Jak tapped her on the arm. "Dean and Ryan already been separated," he said. "Seeing past, Emma."

Her eyes stared at him, struggling to focus. "No. Definitely future."

THE SUBURB of old Washington was relatively untouched. Usually such places would have been turned into the epicenter of shantytowns and pestholes. But it was immediately obvious why this place was shunned by norms.

During the quakes, rivers and streams were often diverted. Here, in outer Washington, they had run together, breaking through shattered storm drains and sewers, until the whole region was underlaid by a swamp of brackish, slow-moving sludge that filled the cellars and basements and oozed out into the first floors of many of the buildings.

The sky had become like pewter, dull gray, menacing, with banks of black clouds that swirled around as though propelled by some life of their own.

Ryan glanced behind, trying to spot Joaquin and the sec patrol, but they had vanished into the maze of tumbled ruins.

"Nothing here," Krysty said. "Why don't we cut and run, lover? Wasting time in this sinkhole."

"Not worth going in, is it?" he agreed. "There's not likely to be anything worth the looking."

"Horrible stink," Dean commented, pinching his nose and pulling a face.

Mildred smiled. "Right on, boy. I reckon you'd find just about every disease ever invented in this place, and quite a few others beside."

"Wind is rising, my friends." Doc's mane of silvery hair was blowing around his face.

"Tornado," Emma stated, her black skirt tugging at her ankles. "Getting close. No way of avoiding it now. We're in way too deep."

"Could be." Ryan blinked as dust peppered them from the wind swirling around the ravaged buildings.

"Shelter." The Armorer took Mildred by the hand. "Come on, now."

The street ahead of them looked like it had been a mix of stores and apartment houses. Many of the buildings lacked roofs, and there wasn't a single pane of glass for miles around. But walls still stood firm against the elements.

Ryan led them quickly along, avoiding pits of thick mud that looked like they could easily have been fifty feet deep. Rats, as big as dogs, scattered at their coming, some of the bolder ones stopping and going up on their back paws as if they were prepared to do battle.

Dean drew his big handblaster and started to level it at a particularly large, verminous brute with scarred flanks. But Ryan warned him to put the weapon away.

"You don't know what's living in this place," he said.

"Ghoulies?" Dean looked around in the deepening gloom. "Good place for them."

Krysty held up a hand. "Got a strong feeing about this place," she said. "Some things walking here, and they aren't walking alone. You feel them, Emma?"

The young woman shook her head. "Sorry, but I'm not getting anything right now."

Jak suddenly pointed to their left. A tall, skinny body lay sprawled, half in and half out of a doorway. It didn't look like it had been there very long. It was barefoot and shirtless, but still had on ragged pants.

They moved a little closer, everyone now with blasters drawn and ready. The chest had been ripped open, and all of the organs had been torn out. The face had been stripped of flesh, leaving only the smeared white of the skull. Something had sliced the throat open from ear to ear.

"Look at the poor bastard's hair," J.B. said. "Remember the Lincoln Inn?"

The corpse had dyed hair—half blue and half green.

"I told him," Emma said in a small sad voice. "Told him what would happen." Her words were almost drowned out by the wind that was surging to a full gale.

The roaring sounds also covered the noise of the approach of a party of a dozen ghoulies, hiding them from Ryan and the others until they were almost on top of them.

Jak was quickest, spinning and tossing one of his throwing knives straight to the throat of the nearest mutie, sending it staggering back with a gurgling cry of shock and pain.

Ryan squeezed the trigger on the 9 mm SIG-Sauer as he turned, but his foot slipped in the slimy dirt, and the bullet went wide. Next moment he was fighting for his life against two of the ghoulies. He was vaguely aware of shooting and screams and shouts, bodies jostling against one another.

But the wind had become a hurricane, and it had started to rain, pounding down like steel rods, blanking out visibility and isolating every fighter in a howling world of his or her own.

Ryan shook his head, dashing water from his good eye. The action was so close that he could only use the pound and a half of steel as a clumsy club, swinging it to try to buy himself a little space in the soaking, deafening maelstrom.

The ghoulies were both male, with the characteristic pallid skin of their type, displaying the strange bluish sheen that was said to glow in total darkness. They had enlarged eyes, looking like someone was trying to push them out from inside the sockets. Their mouths were open, showing the filed teeth and reptilian tongue that typified the ghoulie, creatures who dwelled in the darkest corners of city ruins, waiting to rend and chill.

Once they'd made their kill, they would stash the corpse somewhere until it had reached the right degree of stinking decay that they so loved.

This pair was armed with blades, old knives honed thin as whipcord, tied to hilts of whittled wood two feet long, making them somewhere between a dagger and a spear.

They were panting with their desire to slaughter the norm that had wandered into their demesne, pushing and jostling each other, giving Ryan a slight edge over them.

But their attack was so frenzied that the one-eyed man had no chance to level the blaster and shoot them down. It was desperate work, dodging and weaving, trying to parry the lethal weapons of the ghoulies with the four-and-a-half-inch barrel of the SIG-Sauer.

The curtain of solid rain parted for a moment and a small bedraggled figure, dressed all in black, stumbled over the edge of the sidewalk and cannoned into the taller of the ghoulies, sending him sliding into his colleague.

It was the heartbeat of space that Ryan needed.

He snapped off a shot at the shorter of the muties, the bullet exploding into the center of the skinny, rag-covered chest, killing him instantly. The second one fought for balance in the wash of mud, like a failing skater, waving his half spear at Ryan, missing by a clear yard.

The SIG-Sauer barked once more and the ghoulie went down with the full-metal jacket reaming the brains from the inside of his angular skull.

Ryan glanced at Emma to thank her for coming to his rescue, but she had vanished.

The air was filled with a deafening roar, like a hundred war wags on full-throttle.

Like a theater curtain being lifted, the rain stopped, and Ryan stood frozen for a moment, unable to believe what he was seeing. The clouds were circling above his head and the noise was staggering. To his right he saw Jak holding Emma by one hand, a short-bladed throwing knife in the other, backing away in front of a stout ghoulie armed with a cleaver tied to a broomstick.

Doc had his Le Mat drawn, his nose bleeding, trying to blink the rain out of his pale blue eyes.

Krysty was to Ryan's left, a dying ghoulie, shot through the lower abdomen, writhing bloodily at her feet. She had one arm around Dean, protecting the boy from another pair of sword-bearing muties.

J.B. had taken off his glasses, blinded by the rainstorm, and was holding the Uzi at his hip, three dead or dying muties ranged around him. Mildred was standing back-to-back with him, in a classic shootist's stance, her Czech ZKR 551 in her right hand. There were five or six of the muties still on their feet. Everyone was soaking wet.

But the fight had suddenly taken the back burner to the force of nature that was bearing down on them. Scything along the wide avenue, keeping to its center, was a tornado.

The funneled top looked to be a mile or more wide, circling like a great whirlpool, while the fifty-foot-wide tail was skipping along, sucking up small trees and chunks of debris. As Ryan stared at it, he saw the whole wall of a house sucked into oblivion, hundreds of bricks scattering out of the side of the whirlwind funnel, like mortar shells.

"Get under cover!" he roared at the very top of his voice. But he could barely hear the words echoing inside his own head, and he knew that they would have been inaudible to the others in the group.

The heart of the storm was nearly on top of them, less than a hundred yards and closing like a runaway wag.

Ryan could do nothing for the others.

He had half a dozen beats of the heart to save himself.

Glancing quickly from left to right, he saw the half-open door to a three-story building. He sprinted for it, holstering the blaster as he moved, shouldering through the door, splintering it off its hinges and crashing inside.

His feet were running on nothing, and he had only a nanosecond to realize that someone had taken out the entire floor for fires, and he was falling into the basement, landing not with a bang but with a whisper.

He slid inaudibly into deep mud, the consistency of molasses, cold and noisome. Even as he began to sink helplessly into the clinging ooze, Ryan heard the pounding thunder of the tornado, raging right on top of him.

Then came darkness and silence.

Chapter Twenty-Seven

Krysty scooped Dean under one arm, carrying the kicking boy to the right-hand side of the street, heading for a detached house that still had a third of its roof in place. There was no door and she dived in, seeing in the pulsing gloom that most of the staircase remained.

"Under there!" she yelled, throwing the boy under the cover and jumping on top of him.

J.B. and Mildred went for the building opposite, spotting Ryan crashing into the storefront next door. The noise of the rushing tornado was cataclysmic, so overwhelming that there was a temptation to give up and lie down and await the lethal embrace of the storm's heart.

There was an odd display unit near the door, and they both went for it, hugging each other tightly.

Mildred was praying, though nobody could hear her desperate words—nobody but herself and God.

Emma had looked at the raging tornado as though she saw her own death riding toward her. For a moment she resisted Jak's hand as he pulled at her to try to steer her toward safety. Then she allowed him to drag her to the same side of the street as Krysty and Dean, where they both flattened themselves against the front wall, directly beneath the broken window. There had been no time to find anywhere safer.

Doc was last and slowest of the companions to seek shelter, hindered by one of the ghoulies, its eyes and mouth stretched in a rictus of terror, who blocked him off from getting under cover in one of the buildings.

"Damn you! Get out of my buggering way!" Doc spit, pressing the Le Mat deep into the mutie's stomach and squeezing the scattergun trigger. The .63-caliber round almost cut the ghoulie in two, wrapping his pulverized intestines around the shattered remnants of his spine.

Doc pushed the dying man aside, his knees creaking as he powered himself into a laborious, clumsy sprint for safety in a doorway.

RYAN CRIED OUT IN PAIN as the pressure in his ears rose and fell sharply, while the heart of the tornado passed directly over the building where he'd run for shelter, with its still, small voice of calm.

The roaring sound stopped for a few long seconds, then resumed again, and he was aware of dozens of predark shingles, finally loosing their hold on the remnants of the roof, and whirling around like discarded playing cards.

The joists of the first floor of the building were a dozen feet above his head, stained with mold, several of them either rotted away or taken for fuel like the boards.

The cellar was roughly twenty feet square, and Ryan had landed more or less in its center, immediately sinking to midthigh in the cold slimy ooze.

Only when he looked around him did Ryan realize that one of the murderous gang of ghoulies had made the same mistake, leaping for safety from the teeth of the storm, landing in the deep lake of mud that filled the basement.

The man, barely five feet tall, had landed near one of the walls and had immediately tried to reach the furrowed brickwork and breeze blocks to steady himself. But he'd failed and had gone facedown in the stinking tentacles.

Ryan kept himself very still, remembering Trader's advice about quicksand. Throw yourself flat and don't try to struggle—you'd just drown yourself that much quicker.

It looked like the ghoulie had followed that advice which, unusually for Trader, didn't seem very sound.

The mutie was dying in front of Ryan's eye, the sucking pit of mud pulling him down, bubbling and heaving like a sentient creature as it shrouded him.

Ryan had holstered the SIG-Sauer and sheathed the panga, waiting with all the patience he could muster for his friends to come and rescue him. He had no doubt that they would have been able to see off the attacking ghoulies.

What Ryan hadn't reckoned on was the tornado, blindly erratic, revolving about its own axis and coming back along precisely the same path.

THE NOISE WAS WORSE, the buffeting shock far more powerful. Once again it brought rain racing ahead of it, like a solid wall, bursting over the derelict suburbs of the Hole, bringing down walls and roofs, filling the very air itself with a bedlam of screaming chaos.

Doc had thought it was over and was in the act of returning to the open air. When he glimpsed the sinister funnel, hissing its way toward him along a narrow corridor of total destruction, he dived into the building that he thought Jak and Emma had chosen, reaching it just as the whirlwind struck again.

AFTER THE TORNADO had finally gone raging away toward the west, the first thing that J.B. did was to remove his spectacles from one of the pockets of his coat and carefully check them over for damage or dirt. Next he gave the Uzi and the Smith & Wesson M-4000 scattergun the once-over. After that he turned to Mildred, who was lying on the floor alongside him, hands still clasped over her ears, eyes tight shut, her plaited hair soaked and filthy.

"You all right?" he said.

"What?"

He gently moved her hands. "I asked if you were feeling all right?"

"Jesus, John. If I'm still alive, then I guess I'm all right. Not something I want to go through ever again. Has it finished?"

"Yeah. Think so."

"Are the others?"

"Let's go see."

THE GHOULIE HADN'T lasted long in the mud. Ryan figured that the man had inhaled a mouthful of the watery slime as soon as he fell in, and it had been downhill from then. The movement had stopped, and only the hump of the mutie's shoulders and one arm were visible above the filth, now sinking very slowly, held up by pockets of air in the ragged clothes.

He was now waist-deep himself, with nothing below his feet to indicate the depth in the cellar. The stuff was too thick and clinging for there to be any possibility of swimming. Ryan had already decided that he would make a last effort if it got to his chest.

And if that failed he'd swallow the muzzle of the SIG-Sauer. It was as simple and final as that.

"Anyone there?" he shouted, his voice stifled by the rising gruel and by the enfolding walls of the basement.

Nobody answered, and Ryan was left alone in the stinking dimness with the corpse of the mutie.

DEAN PUSHED HIS WAY out of Krysty's protective embrace, walking out into the aftermath of the morning storm. It was still raining, but the sun had broken through, casting a rainbow to the south of the Hole.

The red-haired woman was at his heels. "Get your blaster out, Dean," she snapped. "You know better than that. Ghoulies could be around."

"Tornado sucked them up and spread them thin all over," he said. "Nobody out here."

Krysty joined him, the short-barreled Smith & Wesson 640 in her hand. She looked around, shocked at the devastation left by the receding storm.

"Doesn't seem possible," she said. "This part of the old ville was already a total wreck. How can anything happen to make it so much worse?"

Water glistened off the few remaining roofs, but the streets were covered in shingles and slates and piles of bricks. The tornado had done more damage across the narrow path of its passing than had been done to the suburb for nearly a hundred years.

The wind was still close to gale force, and Krysty steadied herself against the crumbling wall behind her, catching movement out of the corner of her eyes, from across the street. She swung the blaster around to cover J.B. and Mildred, both looking like they'd been dragged through a hedge backward.

"You two okay?" the Armorer called. "Where's Ryan?"

"Not with us."

"Doc chilled one of the ghoulies," Dean said. "Saw it just before we made safety."

The whirling funnel of the tornado was still visible, dancing away in the distance. A strange orange light seemed to glow in the depths of its black heart. The rain was easing, and the storm's noise was almost gone.

"Listen," Krysty said, turning her head to try to focus on what she'd heard.

"Dad!" Dean exclaimed.

"Wait!" J.B. snapped. "If Ryan's calling for help, then it means he's in trouble. Don't go and jump into the same trap that's caught him."

RYAN HEARD THEM and saw a shadow thrown across the wall above his head. By now he'd sunk to the middle of his chest, feeling the pressure tugging him down. The corpse of the trapped mutie had finally vanished.

"Watch out!" he yelled. "No floor."

It was the Armorer's narrow face, the spectacles glinting, staring down at him.

Mildred peered over his shoulder. "Well," she said. "Here's another fine mess you've gotten yourself into."

"I'll start laughing when you get me the fuck out of this stuff."

Dean and Krysty were also in the doorway. "You all right, Dad?"

"Sure. Sinking into a lake of cold shit is the best fun in the world. I like to spend my mornings this way. Do it whenever I get the chance."

"Sorry," the boy muttered.

"You reached the bottom yet?" the Armorer asked.

"Not so you'd notice. There's a dead ghoulie someplace around, and I don't even know if he's reached the bottom yet."

"Can we get you out, lover, and cut out all this talk?" Krysty said anxiously.

Ryan had already unslung the Steyr SSG-70, holding it clear of the surface of the mud, and he now balanced himself, ready to throw it up to J.B. The Armorer had lain down on the floor, reaching to try and grab it, but it was just out of reach.

"Take your time," J.B. said. "Don't want to drop it in the shit."

The effort of lobbing it up above his head, with the muck up to his armpits, was intensely difficult. And Ryan knew that his old friend was right. If he screwed up on it and the rifle fell back, it could easily sink beyond his reach.

He gripped the middle of the muzzle in both hands and readied himself, then threw it butt-first as hard as he could.

J.B. was crouching, with Krysty at his side in case he fumbled. But the throw was good and the catch effortless.

"I'll knot the strap to the one off the scattergun," he said. "Should give us enough length to reach you."

"Sure," Ryan replied, though he didn't have the confidence he tried to fake. He was sunk so deep that it would take an enormous effort to heave him out.

It took the agile fingers of the Armorer a couple of minutes to securely knot the straps together. "Get it around your wrists," he shouted down.

Ryan moved his feet experimentally, hoping that he might have sunk as far as the bottom. But there was still nothing below him but the thick ooze.

The strap came down slowly and he reached up and took it, looping it around his right wrist, folding the end tightly into his palm.

"Ready."

He had no worries that the strap would prove strong enough, but there wasn't all that much spare length at the top for them to use efficiently. No possibility of anchoring it around anything, or of them all getting a good grip.

J.B. was crouched down, with Krysty immediately behind him. Mildred was ready to pull at the Armorer's shoulders, and Dean was at the back, hanging on to Krysty to give what help he could.

"Here we go," J.B. said, as calmly as if he were setting off on a sunny walk through the countryside.

Ryan straightened his legs to make the pull as easy as possible, bracing himself as the strap tightened.

He felt the strain through his shoulders and back, but there was no upward progress.

After several seconds of intense pressure, the strap loosened. "Relax awhile," J.B. called. "You feel any movement down there, Ryan?"

"No." He thought for a moment. " 'Least I'm not going down any farther."

"Best I use the power," Krysty called.

"No! Not yet, lover."

The Earth Mother power that Krysty had been taught by her mother back in Harmony ville gave her, for a brief few moments, almost supernatural strength. Ryan had seen her use it only a limited number of times, and it was a truly fearsome sight. The downside was that it devastated the woman, sending her unconscious immediately after its use, gravely weakening her for up to a couple of days.

"Might be the only way," J.B. warned. "This isn't the easiest way of doing a lift."

"I know it. If we have to use Krysty's power, then we will. Not until it's the only option. Try again. This time brace the strap and I'll try and haul myself against it."

"We'll pull as well," Mildred said. "Give more chance."

"Yeah." Dean's worried face appeared above Ryan. "All go for it, Dad."

"You got it, son."

The strap became as taut as steel. Ryan drew on all of his strength, gaining additional force from his free left hand. Muscles creaked in his shoulders and across his broad back. With a convulsive effort he kicked both feet together, feeling the suction break for a heartbeat.

"Pull," he gasped through gritted teeth. "Coming."

He heard groaning from above him as the four friends gave it everything.

"More!" Ryan panted out the syllable, aware that the mud was reluctantly relaxing its hold on him.

"Moving," J.B. yelled triumphantly. "One more good one'll do it, Ryan."

Now he was free to his belt, the middle of his thighs.

"Hold it there." J.B. called down. "Can you hang on a second while we reorganize it up here? Angle's wrong now. Just hold on."

"Sure. Not much farther."

As they changed positions above him, there was a heart-stopping moment when the straps loosened and he slipped down a few inches. But they managed to hold the grip and started the upward haul again.

There was a sullen plopping sound as his combat boots broke free of the sticky mud.

From then on it was easy, pulling him free until he could reach the jagged edge of the broken flooring and roll himself up and over to safety.

All five of them lay back, panting with the effort. Dean was beating the dirt with his fist, whooping breathlessly. "Hot pipe, we did it!"

"Thanks, friends," Ryan said, shaking his head in relief. "Close call. Best try and find myself some fresh water and get cleaned up."

"Strip that SIG-Sauer, as well," J.B. warned.

As Ryan sat up, a thought occurred to him. "Hey, where're the others? Doc, Jak and the woman?"

Chapter Twenty-Eight

It took only a few minutes to be sure that Jak, Doc and Emma had vanished from the suburb as totally as if the tornado had sucked them up and spread their atoms into the dark sky.

"Could the whirlwind have snatched them?" Dean asked. "The ghoulies are all gone."

"More likely the ghoulies took them," Ryan said. "Probably got a maze of their tunnels dug under the ville. Often the way they play the game."

"We going after them?" Mildred asked.

Ryan nodded. "Sure. One thing first. No, two things. Got to clean myself up."

"I'll do the blaster," J.B. said. "Save time."

"Sure. Then we take a good look for some sign of where they've gone."

THE STORM HAD LEFT PLENTY of fresh water around the devastated suburb of Washington Hole, though a lot of it had simply raised the levels of the quagmire that underlaid the place.

Ryan found a shopping plaza where the central fountain now overflowed with clean rainwater, stripping off and scrubbing away as much of the filth as he could. By the time he'd finished, J.B. returned the

SIG-Sauer to him, looking in immaculate showroom condition.

"Greased and ready to kick ass," Mildred announced.

"Now let's take a look for the others," Ryan said, using his sleeve to wipe a few drops of water from the puckered socket of his left eye.

It was less than half an hour since the attack of the ghoulies and the appearance of the tornado.

Even to experienced trackers like Ryan and J.B. the recent cataclysmic storm had destroyed any marks that might have been left by their friends.

After three-quarters of an hour of careful scouting, Ryan called the others together. "Wasting time," he said. "No chance of seeing where they've been taken."

Dean coughed into his hand, gently attracting his father's attention.

"What is it, son?"

"All the basements are flooded, like the one where you nearly drowned."

"Yeah?" Ryan's mouth dropped open. "Right, Dean! Ghoulies can't have taken them under the ground."

J.B. banged himself on the forehead, nearly dislodging his fedora. "Stupe! Well done, Dean." The boy turned pink with pleasure at the rare praise from the Armorer. "Means we got to look farther afield for tracks. They'll have moved after the rain eased, so if we spread out we can find the trail quicker."

Krysty had looked away, turning toward the direction that they'd come in from. "Unless..." she said.

"Unless what?" Ryan followed her eyes. "Joaquin and his sec men?"

"Haven't seen them since the tornado."

"And it probably wouldn't have reached them, the way it veered around on itself."

Krysty nodded. "They'd have gotten wet, but that's all. And we all know the warnings about the baron."

Dean spit in the mud. "That double-sick bastard was interested in Emma because he thought she might've been a doomie, one that he could pluck and put in his zoo."

Ryan sighed. "Joaquin obviously saw the tornado. Ace on the line that Emma had predicted. Blew her cover in a big way. Yeah, it fits together like a knife and sheath. They came in behind the storm. Caught them hiding somewhere close by here. Lifted them and away while I was being rescued. Easy as taking sugared candy from a sleeping baby."

"Wind covered any shouting," J.B. said.

"Let's go check for tracks on the road back toward the ville," Ryan said. "But fifty gets you one that we know what we'll find out there." As he looked around, the arrow wound tweaked at the small of his back, exacerbated by the strain of heaving himself out of the basement.

EMMA HAD FAINTED.

The roaring of the tornado had drowned out all the senses. Jak had picked up the young woman in his arms, intending to carry her to safety out of the creaking building, when Doc had stumbled in, looking for all the world like a demented scarecrow, hair blowing, eyes open wide, waving his arms in the air, shouting something inaudible. He was holding the sword stick in his right hand, the massive Le Mat in the other.

When Doc was close, Jak could just hear his screamed words. "Coming back! Tornado's coming back."

A chunk of the roof whirled loose, scattering its shingles around the empty staircase, some of them flying down to the first floor, narrowly missing Jak.

"Out back!" the albino yelled. "Shelter there!"

He'd spotted that the roof was slightly more solid at the rear of the building, and he staggered the few steps along the hallway, nearly falling over the piled masonry, heels crunching through piles of broken glass.

The next half minute was blinding madness for all three of them.

As the tornado finally raged away, Doc was first on his feet, brushing dirt and mud from his frock coat, running his fingers through his silvery hair to try to restore it to some sort of order.

"By the Three Kennedys!" he exclaimed, aware that there was still too much noise from the storm and the pounding rain outside for the others to hear him properly. "An old friend once told me that all experience is good experience, but I think I might pass if that one came around again."

Jak blinked open his ruby eyes, finding that he was still holding Emma in his arms. When he looked up he saw that the gable wall of the house where they were sheltering had been damaged, supporting beams snapped like straws. It would only take a small blow of wind to bring the whole wall down, fetching the entire roof with it.

"Out back," he shouted, clutching at the tails of the old man's coat to draw his attention, pointing at the roof.

"Oh, my goodness! Yes! May I offer my assistance with the young lady?"

But the teenager was on his feet, using all of his wiry strength to lift Emma, stumbling out through what had been the kitchen into the overgrown, muddy rear garden.

Doc was at his heels, pushing aside an overgrown currant bush that held globular fruit, the size of tennis balls, but colored a leprous yellowy white.

All three of them were soaked, and Jak laid Emma down again, her golden eyes flicking open, looking around her in bewilderment and horror. "Where?" she muttered.

"Safe," Jak replied.

"Upon my sempiternal soul!" Doc exclaimed. "But your prediction came as true as true can be, my dear. A tornado. But it has not whirled us away from Kansas, on the run from the wicked baron of the west, and the yellow brick road is somewhat beslobbered with mud, I fear."

Emma tried to sit up, staring at the ruins all about her with eyes wide in horror. "My fault. All of this is. And there's worse to come."

Jak smiled at her, his voice close to her ear so that she would hear him above the sound of the storm. "No worse. What can be worse than this?"

The cold voice drifted down from above. "Plenty, Whitey, plenty."

The three friends looked up to find themselves covered at short range by Joaquin and his trio of sec men, each of them holding a cocked musket.

ONCE THE REALIZATION had dawned on Ryan and the others what might have happened to Jak, Doc and Emma, it didn't take long to find the tracks of the four horsemen from the ville.

"They waited for the heart of the tornado to pass," J.B. observed. "Knew we'd hide out. Came in around the back, along that alley. Rain makes it hard to see, but they probably picked them out of the garden of the house where the wall was falling down. Tied them and stuck them double-up on the horses. See how the hoof marks on three of the animals are markedly deeper heading out than they were riding in."

Krysty was distraught. "That sorry girl! Sharpe'll stick her in his bloody collection for the rest of her life, like a little toy. And probably butcher Jak and poor old Doc."

Ryan patted her on the arm, managing a smile. "Not if we stop him, lover. And we will."

Chapter Twenty-Nine

"Baron Sharpe is in need of getting himself chilled," J.B. stated.

"A man who breeds tigers shouldn't weep if his children are devoured," Mildred said.

Krysty nodded. "Right on, sister. Won't catch me shedding tears for him."

"Not the easiest ville in the world to break into." Ryan looked at the others. "Got a goodish sec force."

"Undergunned," the Armorer said.

"Agreed." Ryan dug his index finger into his ears, scraping out the residue of mud. "But well trained. And Sharpe looks like the sort of man who might expect us to try and stage some sort of a rescue of Jak, Doc and Emma."

"We got to try, Dad."

Ryan grinned at the worried expression on his son's face. "Sure we do."

JAK LAY on the single bed in the room where he, Doc and Emma had been taken by Joaquin and the sec men. Closely guarded, they had been searched and their weapons taken from them.

The woman hadn't been carrying any sort of blaster or blade.

Doc's Le Mat had been removed, but he had clung stubbornly to the sword stick, claiming that it was only an ebony cane to help him walk.

"Ligament trouble in the old days. Stealing second at the top of the forth in a big college game," he said. "Unfortunately the damage proved to be inoperable and I am forced to rely on my trusty walking stick." He paused and favored Joaquin with a toothy smile. "The saddest thing of all was that the squint-eyed umpire called me out."

Jak's Colt Python was also taken from him, and one of the guards gave him a cursory pat-down, so cursory that it failed to find any of his hidden throwing knives.

The leader of the sec team had paused in the doorway. "Should be safe here. Men in the corridor and all around. Wait here until Sharpie decides that he wants to see you. Probably won't be until supper. Likes to do some of his thinking and talking over food, does the baron."

The heavy oak door had been firmly shut, and the three friends had heard the sound of heavy bolts being slid across and a key grating in the brass lock.

Now they were alone.

Emma sat down in a large brocaded armchair beneath the barred and shuttered window. She put her head in her hands and began to cry.

Jak stared across her, his ruby eyes drilling into her face. "Waste time weeping," he said. "Dish's broke. Can't be repaired. Crying doesn't do shit."

"My fault."

Doc laid a gnarled hand on the young woman's shoulder. "Jak's right, my dear," he said. "Once the milk is spilled, and the wine drunk and the cane raised back up when it's in the field . . . No, that's not quite what I had in mind to say. But the point is, assuming blame does none of us any good. Our sole intent now must be to seek a remedy. A remedy a day keeps the doctor away, I always say."

"But I couldn't help saying that I saw the tornado. Because I did!"

"And was right," Jak said.

"Not the point, Jak, dear."

"Point is, Doc's right. Escape is number one."

"I won't escape from here."

Her voice had gone flat and distant, making Doc look worriedly at her.

"The others will put their best feet forward, my dear lady. Ryan's shoulder to the wheel. John Barrymore Dix's chin out. Mildred with her fist clenched. They are not folk who would allow any harm to come to their companions. I know them a deal better than you do, Miss Emma."

"And I know what's going to happen, Doc."

"Ah, do you now? Do you, indeed?"

Emma stood, her golden eyes moving from the old man to the albino teenager. "I know the most likely future for us all. See it clear as I see this room."

Jak swung his legs off the bed, uncoiling with the easy grace of a panther, laying his hands on her arms, shaking her gently. "Said not always right. Not always clear. Said that!"

She nodded, tears clustering in her eyes, trickling down her cheeks. "Times I think I know. Other times I know that I know. I see my death, Jak."

"We all die some time," Doc offered. "Just a matter of where and when."

"I shall die within the next two days."

"No," Jak said, almost shouting.

"Yes, dear friend," Emma stated gently. "I see you alive and safe. And Doc the same."

"Do you see whether we manage to escape from this durance vile?" Doc asked. "And what of Ryan and the others? Do you see their fate?"

Emma shook her head. "No. I think that you and Jak will escape safely, but I can't make out any details. I see the death of Baron Sharpe."

Jak let go of her. "What?"

"Oh, yes. My death is linked with his. We go together into the blackness. Almost hand in hand. Perhaps an hour will pass, but not longer."

Jak suddenly opened his arms and took the young woman, embracing her tightly, his mane of stark white hair mingling with her short black locks.

"Won't let it happen," he said.

"I die and then the baron," she insisted.

"So, I'll chill him first. Then you won't die at all." Jak's voice was cracked with the tension.

"It doesn't happen that way, my dear. Oh, Jak, I want to live. I've met you and I think I'm falling in love with you. And there could have been some happiness. But it won't happen."

Nobody said anything.

"WE WAITING until it's full dark, lover?" Krysty asked.

Ryan was crouched in deep undergrowth, a hundred paces from the main entrance to the ville. "Mebbe. I know I said it looked like an easy egg to crack, but having been inside, I'm not sure. Might be worth a look around the back."

J.B. was lying flat on his stomach, glasses pushed up on his forehead, peering through the leafy cover. "That zoo collection sort of place is around the rear. Could be there's another door for supplies and stuff like that."

"We all going in, Dad?"

Ryan shook his head. "Probably not, Dean. And don't pull that miserable face at me."

"Sorry."

"Just me and J.B. is all. Best chance of moving fast and quiet. Rest of you wait here and get ready to give us cover when we all come out."

"If you come out," Mildred said quietly.

"We'll do it."

"Sure, Ryan. Just like you did last time and the time before. But there's going to be a day coming when you won't do it. If Emma was here, she'd probably be able to tell you if that day's coming now."

"She isn't and she can't, love," J.B. said, turning to Ryan. "Let's go recce."

"YES." THE WORD HISSED out from Ryan. "That's what we need."

It was a rear entrance to the ville, a double door, made from wood, about ten feet high, topped with rusting barbed wire. A dirt track wound away from it, toward the north. A single sec man paced slowly up and down in front of the doors, a musket on his shoulder. There was no sign of any other sentry anywhere around.

It was late afternoon, the copper bowl of the sun sinking slowly out of sight toward the far west. A few high, thin clouds streaked across it, tinted purple and pink.

"We'll go back tell the others," J.B. said. "Then get ready to go in after full dark."

SHARPE WAS WEARING a dark suit with narrow pinstripes of lighter gray. Beneath it he had on a T-shirt with a picture of a revolver, and a message that said New York—Kansas It Ain't. His own satin-finish Ruger GP-160 double-action revolver was jammed casually into his belt.

"Pretty vest, Baron," Doc said. "Guess that must be a predark replica."

"Why?" The voice sounded tired.

"Because it's a sort of reference to *The Wizard of Oz* and there haven't been any yellow brick roads since the nukecaust, have there, Baron?"

"I have no idea what you're droning about, old man. The shirt was brought to me by Joaquin a month ago from some newly discovered ruins. What you say might be true. I don't know. And I don't care."

"I always said that conversation was killing the art of eating," Doc muttered.

Not that the food was any better than the rest of the meals they'd been offered in the ville. The meat in an overcooked stew had disintegrated into a dark sludge, and most of the vegetables had melted into the liquid. It was utterly impossible to try to guess what sort of animal had provided the base for the stew.

There was a side dish of chopped greens that had barely been shown the steam from a cooking pot and were inedibly raw.

Doc had sliced into his blackened roll to find that the inside of it was a runny, watery dough that trickled out onto his plate.

For dessert the women servants brought in platters of fruit: waxen apples that looked wonderful and tasted like cotton; plums whose interiors revealed tiny mealy grubs, white with crimson eyes.

The beer in pitchers was warm and sour.

During the meal, with Joaquin seated at one end of the long table opposite his master, and the others placed along the sides, there had been no conversation at all. Jak had chosen to sit next to Emma and held her hand throughout the dire supper.

Each door to the dining hall had a pair of armed guards, and four more had escorted the trio down from their locked room to the first floor.

Sharpe suddenly threw his goblet across the room, where it smashed in the vaulted fireplace.

"I had thought that the redhead woman was possibly a mutie. There was something about her that whispered to me of a power lying close beneath the skin."

His meltwater eyes turned to Jak. "An albino. Rare as unmined gold. White hair and skin, and eyes like rubies. Surely someone that would grace my collection. And perhaps you still will, boy."

"Don't call, 'boy,'" Jak said quietly.

"Call you what I like, boy. Call you 'mine,' if I want, so shut that white-lipped mouth. I'll decide soon enough what I want of you."

Emma stood, the legs of the carved beechwood chair scraping on the stone flags of the floor.

"I won't tell you," she whispered.

Sharpe smiled, his brutally handsome face relaxing for a moment. "Very good, my dear," he said. "Oh, that is so good. You knew what I was about to ask you?"

"Yes."

"Joaquin?"

"Baron?"

"It was a tornado?"

"Biggest twister I ever seen, Baron. We were lucky to avoid it. Came swooping down like the wrath of God."

Sharpe smiled at Emma. "The wrath of God. The seventh seal was opened. A darkness upon the face of the earth... The horsemen bringing pillage and pox and plague and... Destroyers of worlds... And you, little lady, saw it all."

Emma had hardly touched any of the food. Now she sat slumped, not looking up, seeming unaware that Baron Sharpe was talking to her.

Joaquin called a warning down the table. "Baron's speaking to you, Emma."

Sharpe glowered at his sec man. "I expect that visitors prefer to listen to the organ-grinder and not to his monkey, Joaquin. No need for interruptions."

"Sorry, Baron."

Jak stood, confronting Sharpe. "Emma doesn't care speak you. Nor me. Not Doc. Let us go or be chilling. Ryan be around soon as knows you holding us. Bad move, Baron."

"Cheeky whelp. Good flogging for the white-hair, Joaquin. Next time he speaks without being spoken to. Strip the pallid flesh from his white ribs. Set the white blood flowing."

"Leave him alone." Emma was standing, still holding Jak's hand in hers.

Sharpe's milky blue eyes locked with her golden stare. "Ah, yes, well... A true doomie and seer. I have seen men and women and puling children who claimed to be doomies. They saw through a glass darkly. You are pure, Emma."

"Let Doc and Jak go and I'll do what you want. Stay with you and tell you what you want to know."

"What do I want to know, little lady?"

"Same thing everyone wants to know."

"And that is..."

"The manner of your death, Baron."

"Don't talk to him, child," Doc warned. "Your gift is from the Almighty and shouldn't be brought into town and peddled cheap off the back of a wagon."

Sharpe stood and pointed an accusing finger at the old man. "Your life rests on a steel blade, Dr. Tanner. The only way to save yourself is to close your mouth and keep it closed." He turned to Emma. "If I release these two, then you'll be content to stay with me?"

"It is for such a short time." Her voice had gone flat and toneless, and her eyes seemed to be looking within herself. "Such a short time."

"But you'll tell me anything I want to know? Anything at all? Will you?"

"No," Jak whispered.

But Emma smiled at the baron, a smile of empty menace. "Yes," she said. "Yes, I will."

Chapter Thirty

By the time the uncomfortable supper had dragged its way to an ending, the torches were burning and the water-powered generator was thumping rhythmically, bringing electric light to the corridors of the large mansion.

Beyond the reflecting windows, Jak could see that it was already full dark. His guess was that Ryan and the others, assuming that they had survived the murderous twister, would probably make their play during the hours of night.

He had briefly entertained the small hope that he might see a sliver of a chance to try to escape, taking Doc and Emma along with him, at least getting away into the farther rooms of the house to try to draw some of the guards away and make it easier for Ryan to break in.

But Joaquin and his men were too well trained, too alert. And there was only Doc's rapier and his own hidden knives against the array of firearms.

After the meal, Sharpe had walked to the main door from the dining room without a backward glance, paused and looked across at Joaquin.

"Time has come to show them the rest of my collection. Don't you think? Well?"

"Sure, Baron. All three of them?"

"Why not? Why should be knotted? Cut the knot is best. All of them. Yes, all. Jak for his hair. In place of my son and heir. Doc for his mutie way of talk. And the prize in my collection. Ace on line. The diamond in my crown. Emma, the finest doomie in all of Deathlands."

Oddly, after his intense interest in the question of his own death, Sharpe had totally dropped the subject. He had sat down, head to one side, as though he were listening to a small voice talking into his ear.

As they walked out after him, Joaquin bringing up the rear with three sec guards, it occurred to Jak that they were soon going to run out of time.

"COULD EASY RUN OUT of time real double quick," J.B. whispered.

They were crouched close together, flattened against the back wall of the ville. The darkness had covered them so far, but there was still the pacing sentry and the locked door.

Ryan had drawn the panga from its soft leather sheath and gripped it in his right hand. If there was silent chilling, then he would do it. J.B. had the Smith & Wesson scattergun unslung and cocked. If there was any close-contact noisy chilling to do, then it was an ideal weapon with its twenty-inch-long Remington fléchettes in each of the eight rounds.

"Don't know what's inside the door." They had been waiting patiently, watching the change of guard, seeing that there was an exchange of words with someone within the ville. But if it was a password, they had no way of learning it.

"Go like we said." The Armorer straightened, pulling down his fedora to shadow the whiteness of his face.

Ryan was at his side. "Yeah."

He led the way along the wall, keeping close to it, dropping to hands and knees every time the sec man reached the far end of his beat and turned toward them.

Luckily the moon was only a fingernail of fresh-minted silver, partly shrouded by a bank of cloud, covering the ville in an impenetrable veil of darkness.

The sentry was a young man, married only three days earlier to one of the maids who worked in the big kitchens of the ville. He wasn't due off the night shift until three in the morning, which seemed an eternity away. Knowing that his Molly was sleeping in a warm bed, less than fifty yards from where he was on patrol, only made it worse.

The walk—fifteen paces out and fifteen paces back again—had become a mindless routine. His attention had drifted away to the warm body in the warm bed.

He was so locked into the thoughts of his young wife that he was totally confused by the dark figure that rose from the undergrowth near his feet. There was only one person that he could think it might be.

"Molly?" he whispered.

Within a heartbeat he knew that he'd made a lethally stupe mistake.

The figure was a tall and powerful man, who was holding a long, bladed knife to his throat, the needle point pricking the skin so that a small worm of warm blood inched down his neck, under the collar.

"Not a sound," the voice whispered.

There were two of them, one shorter, with the watery moonlight glinting off a pair of spectacles.

Then he knew who they were—the one-eyed leader of the outlanders and his heavily armed companion. There had been talk in the ville that Joaquin had brought in three of the gang as prisoners—the old man, the white-haired boy and the young woman, the one they said was a true doomie.

"Is there a password?" The man's mouth was so close that the guard could feel it tickle the hairs in his ears. "Tell me quiet as a mouse fart."

"Just have to say my name."

"What is it?"

"Jerry McCaffrey. Only been married three days... Please don't—" The words were cut off by a gasp as the steel was pushed a little deeper into his flesh, turning the worm of blood into a steady trickle.

"Don't talk less we ask you. How many behind the door? Truth!"

"One. Just one." He was trying to get up onto the tips of his toes to stretch away from the questing knife.

"We're going in," Ryan said.

"Sure. Sure."

BARON SHARPE STOOD about ten feet away from Ryan and J.B., on his way back from showing his "guests" around the more private part of his collection.

It hadn't been a very successful visit.

They had gone through the mutie animals, fish and reptiles, pausing in front of the large glass window opening onto the expanse of desert where the hidden monster called Rupert lived in its own mysterious seclusion.

Sharpe had tapped on the glass, but nothing stirred. "One day I'll find out what Rupert is really like," he said.

Emma's fingers had tightened on Jak's hand, but she had remained silent.

The door through to the rear of the private zoo was opened by Joaquin, who left it unbolted as they passed through.

"By the Three Kennedys! But that's a foul and noisome stench," Doc muttered, gripping the lion's-head hilt of his sword stick.

It was a sorry and dismal place, smaller than they had expected.

The dozen or so iron cages held only four occupants. Once the visitors were inside the section, the baron seemed to slide off into one of his withdrawn depressions, hardly bothering to talk about his prizes.

A small woman, less than four feet in height, showed all the classic characteristics of the stickies. Sharpe poked at the bars with a broom handle, making her show her hands with the circles of suckers on palms and fingers. But the mutie hardly stirred, returning to a pile of straw in a corner where she lay and coughed.

"Seen stickies all over Deathlands," Jak said. "That one triple sick."

The next occupant of the collection was in even worse physical condition. He was elderly and squatted in a corner of his cell, his head shaking back and forth in a rhythmic swaying. As the baron reached his cage the man rose and started to pace up and down, brushing his shoulders on the stone walls at either end, leaving a smear of blood at every turn.

His body was covered in suppurating sores.

"What they call a scabbie," the baron said. "Prime specimen of the type."

"Why don't you let it die like it wants?" Emma asked, near to tears.

"Perfectly happy, you know. Oh, yes. Oh, yes. Nothing wrong with it. Fed and watered and kept dry. Seems fine to me. Oh, yes, fine."

Doc's face had become suffused with anger. "This is a disgrace, Baron Sharpe! I have read of zoos during the twentieth century where captured beasts showed a similar pattern of grossly disturbed behavior. Pacing and mutilating themselves. Just as that poor wretch does."

Joaquin touched a warning finger to his lips behind the baron's back, trying to warn the old man to be quiet, who wouldn't be quieted.

"No! This is a sickly and debased commentary on you, Baron Sharpe. In the ancient days of ignorance and barbarism, decent men and women would pay a handful of coppers to go along into the lunatic asylums and bedlams and laugh at the antics of the poor demented devils held prisoner within those dank walls. It was a fine sport for a Sunday afternoon! But those times are long gone. I *thought* that they were long gone. I see now that I was wrong. Can we leave this foul place?''

The baron turned his cold eyes on the old man. ''I decide when we leave. I might leave. Joaquin might leave. But it could depend on the lady whether the rest of you ever leaves. Let her think on that and on what she decides to do.''

The third occupied cage contained a pair of children, looking to be aged about twelve and wearing stained cotton shifts. The girls were identical twins and clung to each other as the baron appeared in front of them.

''They are mysterious,'' he said, showing a brief flicker of interest. ''They speak a language so rare that no man can understand it.''

The twins looked terrified, big eyes turned to face their tormentor, who glanced at Joaquin. ''Make them speak their mystic tongue.''

The sec man was carrying a musket and he thumped the butt against the iron bars, making them ring. ''Come on, speak up!'' he shouted.

The girls began to talk at the same moment, making, as far as anyone could tell, an unbroken string of identical sounds in perfect unison.

''There,'' Sharpe said proudly. ''If I could get that translated, who knows what mysteries it might reveal.

The secret of how to transmogrify lead into gold. The fountain of youth. The Grail itself.''

As quickly as they'd started, the twin girls fell again into silence.

Doc looked at Sharpe and shook his head. "Those poor waifs are demented. Can you not see that in your own blindness? They speak only gibberish."

"Nonsense, Doctor." A smile crossed the baron's brutal features. "I have just conceived a solution that will solve two of my problems in a single shot. You can pass the remainder of your days in the cage with them, and you will translate for me."

"It won't happen, Doc," Emma said with a complete confidence. "Don't worry."

"If I say it will, then it will," Sharpe thundered, his hand dropping to the butt of his Ruger.

"You can say all you like, but if it won't happen, then it won't," the young woman replied, facing him down.

"This is a doomie," the baron said, losing interest in the argument. "Of a sort. He makes prophecies but none of them can yet be understood. Perhaps another task for you, Doctor?"

The occupant of the last cage was a tall, slender man in his thirties, with a long, trailing beard that almost covered his nakedness. He seemed in both better physical and mental health than the others.

"Afternoon to y'all," he said in a Southern drawl. "Y'all come to hear the latest news from God and his Holy Apostles? I can tell y'that the bear will rise from his sleeping and his claws will strangle the lion in the west.''

''There,'' Sharpe said loudly. ''A true doomie, isn't he?''

''And the crescent moon's goin' t'cast its shadow over the sleeping two-headed eagle. Result'll be piles of corpses that'll block the river of silver.''

''Second-rate Nostradamus!'' Doc snorted. ''Been fools making up mock prophecies since the dawn of time. Means anything you want it to mean.''

The man ignored the comment. ''An' I have heard true gospel word that the crooked cross will lie broke in the snow while the thorned crow burns on the mountaintop.''

Sharpe suddenly drew his blaster and aimed it at the prating naked man, his hand trembling. ''Shut him up, Joaquin, or by sweet Jesus, I will!''

RYAN HELD THE GUARD by the shoulder, the panga at his throat. J.B. was close behind him, the scattergun drilling into McCaffrey's stomach.

''We're going in,'' Ryan breathed in the darkness. ''Just say your name and nothing else. If the man inside asks what you want, say you feel sick. Understand?''

''Yeah, mister. Please don't kill me. Baron'll likely do that when he finds out I let him down.''

''Right. Sec man inside does what's sensible, then you both carry on living. What's his name?''

''It's Robbie Ford tonight.''

THE SEC MAN STANDING by the bolted back door that led to the open night snapped smartly to attention as the baron and his party approached.

"Everything all right, Ford?" asked Joaquin.

"Quiet as a grave."

"Who's outside?"

"McCaffrey, sir."

"Didn't he just get married?" Sharpe asked. "Man should be with his wife, not out in the cold and dark."

"Not long on his spell, Baron," the sec chief said. "Then he can get in to his Molly."

"Well…well… Good enough. Then we'll go back inside, Joaquin."

"Good enough, Baron."

"And I shall ask questions from the doomie woman." Sharpe looked at Emma. "And you will tell me the truth, or it's the ending for your friends."

She smiled at him with an oddly gentle expression on her face. "I've already decided, Baron. And I'll answer all your questions for you. Though the answers might not be what you want to hear in your heart."

"Matters nothing. Good, good. Come on, quickly, then."

MCCAFFREY KNOCKED on the door, giving his name to Ford, explaining he felt sick. There was no delay or suspicion, and the door began to swing open.

"Had the baron here with the outlanders only five minutes past," Ford said through the widening crack.

The mention of the fearful name pushed the prisoner over the edge, stepping instantly from sanity to blind panic. Taking Ryan by surprise, he pushed at him and started to yell a warning.

Chapter Thirty-One

"Fireblast! Get the door!"

The reaction from the terrified sentry had been so sudden and unexpected that he nearly pulled it off. Ryan was unbalanced, the panga moving from McCaffrey's throat. And J.B. had stepped away to one side so that he wouldn't be visible to the guard opening the door to the ville.

The sec man was in a blind panic, flailing at Ryan with both hands, his musket still dangling from his shoulder. They were at such close quarters that it was difficult to use the panga, though Ryan was trying to back off a half step to buy himself the room for a clear swing.

Out of the corner of his eye he saw that J.B. hadn't hesitated, kicking at the partly open door with his steel-tipped combat boots, knocking it wide, golden light streaming out into the night, vanishing inside.

"Don't kill me...don't kill me...don't kill..." the young guard panted, his face as a white blur, his mouth wide open in terror. There was the sudden acrid smell of urine as he lost control of his bladder.

It was a potentially disastrous situation. If any other guards heard the outcry, they could easily gun down

Ryan and J.B. Or, at best, simply drive them off into the night with the opportunity of a rescue bid gone forever.

"Please..."

As Ryan backed off, the sentry came toward him, but he was slower, crucially slower.

Ryan saw his chance and didn't hesitate.

Swinging the eighteen-inch steel blade with all of his strength, he aimed at the sec man's midriff. The panga was so sharp that there was almost no sensation of it cutting through the green jacket, deep into McCaffrey's belly, before the eruption of steaming blood splashed over Ryan's hand and wrist.

McCaffrey gasped in shock and clamped his hands to the wound, trying to tuck the tumbling lengths of slippery intestine back inside himself. But the loops uncoiled, ghostly pale in the light from the door, dripping in a wash of dark blood, tangling around the dying man's feet.

"Shouldn't have... Molly won't..." he muttered, falling to his knees in front of Ryan, who quickly and economically slit his throat.

"Stupe," Ryan said.

There was the noise of a scuffling fight from inside the door, the movement stopped by the flat explosion of the Smith & Wesson M-4000 and the familiar sound of a man passing from life into the endless mystery of death.

Ryan left McCaffrey's corpse where it had dropped in the dirt, stepping quickly through the heavy sec door, pushing it shut behind him.

He saw a dying man on the floor, heels drumming, fingers clawing at the stone floor, the scratching nails the only sound in the stillness. There was a massive wound in his chest where one of the 12-gauge rounds had torn him apart. Blood still flowed, slowly, bubbling pink over the ruined lungs. The guard's eyes were open, staring blindly up at the scarlet-splashed ceiling. A little blood was trickling from the open mouth.

"Anyone else?" Ryan asked.

J.B. was thumbing in a replacement round. "Not so you'd notice."

"Shot sounded loud outside."

The Armorer nodded. "Best bolt that door. Though I don't reckon there'll be anyone walking around outside."

Ryan slid the bar across, taking a moment to look around him. The room was more of a space off a passage, with two doors, both closed. His automatic sense of location told Ryan that one door would open into the rear part of the baron's collection of mutie creatures. The other one would lead them back toward the heart of the big house.

The dying man was finally still, and the ville was totally silent.

"So far so good," Ryan said.

"I HAVE NO WISH TO ENTER into the more sordid and intimate details of why I wish to go along the corridor to the bathroom. Suffice it to say that I have a pressing need. Now, will you... It's Morgan, isn't it?

Joshua Morgan? The sec man that we saved from the..."

Morgan nodded, half smiling, showing his prominent teeth. "Me, all right, Doc. Just about recovered from the run-in with the stickies. Thanks to you and your friends."

"So, why can I not go to the bathroom?"

"You got a bowl in the room."

The conversation was being carried out through a gap in the partly open door. Morgan stood guard there with two of his companions.

"I have no intention of... of doing what I need to do while in the company of two friends, one of them a young woman. You have my revolver and you are armed."

"Baron's orders, Doc. If he or Joaquin came by and found one of you out of the room, it'd be my back being bared on the triangle. Can't do it."

Doc glanced behind him, seeing Jak, hidden from the sight of the sec man, gesturing for him to persist in attempting to get out. They had talked it over and agreed that Doc would try to make a break for it. Whatever it took. The albino teenager had pointed out, with more accuracy than tact, that they likely wouldn't bother too much with an old man like Doc.

Emma had taken no notice, lying on the bed in a restless sleep, waiting for the promised summons to visit the baron.

"I have to go, there's a good chap."

Morgan sighed. "All right. But the others don't try to pull this one on me. Understood?"

"Of course."

The door opened, slowly and cautiously, and Doc slipped into the passage. The other two sec men ostentatiously looked the other way, making sure they didn't have anything to do with the flagrant breach of orders.

Morgan led the way along the shadowy corridor, past the flickering lights, beckoning for Doc to follow him. His musket remained on his shoulder, and there was a cap-and-ball pistol in his belt.

"Hurry up, Doc," he whispered.

"I'm making the best pace I can, my dear fellow. I trust it is not too much farther."

"Third door around the corner."

They passed barred windows, shadowing only the blackness of the middle of the night. Doc didn't have a chron on his wrist, but he guessed it was close to twelve.

He and Jak had discussed this escape plan, and it hadn't seemed too difficult then. Just words.

Now the words were going to become action, and Doc was beginning to feel deeply uneasy about what he had agreed to do.

"In here, Doc."

Carrying his ebony cane, Doc followed the sec man into a bathroom. He saw that there was only a single low-quality light overhead, a row of six stalls to the right and a single compartment with a door to the left.

"I am most grateful, Master Morgan."

"All I can do. Like to help." Doc went in and closed the door, making fumbling noises to indicate he was lowering his breeches. "Out of my hands. You know that the baron'll keep the woman in his zoo, don't you?"

"We had reached that supposition." To try to gather himself, Doc sat down for a moment on the polished mahogany seat, wiping sweat from his forehead with his dark blue kerchief.

"Mebbe he'll let you and the white-head kid go free."

"Do you believe that, Master Morgan? Open your heart to me and tell the truth. We are all doomed, are we not?"

There was a long pause and he could hear the sec man's boots shuffling on the tiled floor.

"Well, I might be wrong."

"But..."

"But it doesn't look good."

"Why can't you help us to escape? You seem a decent enough fellow."

There was a long pause.

"Your blaster and the kid's big .357 Magnum are both on a table at the end of the dining room. There's guards all over the place, though."

"Is that truly the best you can do to aid us?"

"Yeah, afraid so. I don't want to die, Doc. Know what I mean?"

"None of us do," the old man said, slowly and silently drawing the steel rapier from its hiding place.

"You coming out, Doc?"

"Oh, yes. I shall be out very shortly."

JAK LAY ON THE BED with Emma. The young woman was dozing, seeming to be hardly aware of his presence.

"Doc's gone," he whispered.

"Who?"

"Doc. Gone."

"Where?"

"Pretend for shit. Going try escape."

She opened her strange golden eyes. "Doesn't need to do that. You'll all be safe."

"You see that, Emma?"

"I do. Not totally sharp. But enough. Shapes and colors and things."

He leaned over and kissed her very gently on the lips, his tumbling mane of stark white hair falling like a cascade of frost crystals across her face.

After a moment she responded, her arms going around him, holding painfully tight.

"Oh, Jak," she said quietly. "You're such a good person, and I did glimpse happiness with . . . a sort of prospect of happiness with you."

"Can still be," he said.

She eased him away, holding his head between her hands, staring intently into his eyes. "No, my love. There is no chance of our going on together. And you have to believe this. You *have* to. It'll make it a lot easier to cope with, when it happens. And it won't be long now."

RYAN AND J.B. HAD MADE their way through the animal part of the baron's collection, not bothering to check out what lay behind the other door.

The inner door had a simple handle. Ryan turned it, SIG-Sauer ready in his right hand, with J.B. and the Uzi close at his heels.

A corridor stretched ahead of them, with a long tapestry along one wall. There were three doors on the opposite side, all of them closed. The passage ended in a single oak door with a rounded top to it.

Ryan catfooted toward it, started to open it and then froze.

"Someone coming this way," he said.

"Take him with the panga," J.B. whispered "Can't risk noise now. Unless we're trapped and have to blast our way out of the ville."

Ryan nodded, holstering the SIG-Sauer and unsheathing the panga.

DOC TOOK a long slow breath, let it out and took another.

"Come on," Morgan whispered. "Get a move on, Doc, or we're both in it head-deep."

There was the faint sound of the bolt sliding back. "Ready or not, here I come," Doc called.

The door was flung open, and the sec man had a moment to glimpse the old man holding the ornamental hilt of a slender sword, the point aimed at his chest.

"What the..." he began.

And didn't finish.

The Toledo steel pierced him below the breastbone, a little to the right, sliding between the guarding ribs, puncturing his heart and beginning to kill him.

The thrust had been perfectly directed, and Doc twisted his wrist as he withdrew the point, increasing the lethal effect of the wound.

Morgan took three faltering steps back, his eyes wide in disbelief. "You done me with a fuckin' little sword, Doc."

"I'm really most awfully sorry, Master Morgan," Doc said, his face paler than usual. "Not the way of a gentleman, but I have learned during my eternity in the hell called Deathlands that the way of a gentleman means very little."

The strings went down and Morgan fell heavily, banging his head against a washbasin, rolling on his back. He coughed, and blood flecked his beard. His right hand reached for the butt of his pistol, but with no great urgency, as though to remind himself that it was still there.

Doc watched him carefully, not wanting to lunge again at a dying man.

"Done for me," Morgan whispered.

"Indeed, I rather fear that I have. Did you say that the two handguns were on the table in the dining room?"

Morgan struggled to speak, then laid his head down and became still.

"Touché," Doc said, starting to giggle with nerves.

THERE WAS A LOUD KNOCK on the door of the bedroom. Jak let go of Emma and stood, hand going for one of the concealed knives. "What?" he said.

"Where's that lazy fucker Morgan? Went off with the old man?"

"Don't know," Jak said.

"Better get back quick. Baron's just sent the order to fetch the doomie woman."

"Come in and get her," Jak said, his fingers gripping the taped haft of one of the slender blades.

"Not stupe, son. I open the door and we keep you covered. Woman walks out. Now."

"It's all right," Emma whispered. "I'll go. It's written that I have to go and see him."

"But we won't—"

She kissed him on the cheek. "Yes, we will. We will see each other one more time, my love. Very soon."

J.B. WAS FLATTENED against the wall, the Uzi braced at his hip.

Ryan waited until the door began to open, then he hefted the panga and started to swing it down in a murderous arc—at the silvery head of Dr. Theophilus Tanner.

Chapter Thirty-Two

Baron Sharpe sat sprawled in a deep chair in his own bedroom, hardly looking up as the slender black-haired woman was shown in, waving a hand to dismiss the escorting sec men.

"Morgan's gone and . . ." one of them began.

"Out of my sight," Sharpe snapped. "You can tell me later, but not now. Oh, no. Not now."

Emma stood silent, hands folded in front of her, her face as pale as an enclosed nun.

The baron wore a long white robe, made from harsh toweling material, roughly knotted at his waist. His feet were bare, his blond hair unbrushed and damp, as though he'd just finished having a shower.

"So," he said, nodding as if he'd just come out with some unbelievably wise saying. "So, you are here."

"The deal was that you let Doc and Jak go if I tell you what you want to know. Does that still hold?"

He stood. "Perhaps we should go and view the quarters where you will be living from now on. With the rest of my pets. You and the old fool and the bloodless boy."

Emma realized that he wasn't listening to her and tried again. "Let the others go, Baron."

The cold milky blue eyes turned toward her as if he'd just seen her for the first time. "Perhaps I will. I can't believe that among my other creatures, I will have access to a true, living, breathing doomie. In my struggles against other barons and other villes, your foreseeing will give me total power. I can make no mistake with you to guide me."

"And Doc and Jak?"

"Later, woman, later. The question that all men seek to know. This first."

"How will you die?"

He smiled eagerly, like a child about to open an expected present. "Yes. But I am also puzzled. Do you see your own death, Emma? See it clear?"

"I see it in symbols, which I will understand only in the moments before death touches me."

"What are they?" He moved closer, and she could see that he was naked beneath the robe.

"For me?" She closed the golden eyes and her face went slack. "For me it will be to drown in a sea of brightest crimson."

"What's that mean, woman?"

She shook her head, rubbing her hand across her face. "I don't know, Baron. I'm so tired I don't—"

He grabbed her and shook her, surprising her with his anger and his strength. "Don't snow me, woman! I know what you are and what you know. And—" he smiled at his own cunning "—*you* know that *I* know it!"

"True. But why do you want to know how you'll die? Can't you imagine what a bleak secret that is?

One that you will carry, in every sense, with you to the edge of the grave. And then—only then—will you understand it.''

He smiled gently, and Emma realized with a frisson of fear what she had already suspected. That Baron Sean Sharpe was as crazy as a shithouse rat.

''I love knowing secrets, woman. Love them. My friends whisper them to me during the long hours of the night. I hear them, now. They're precious to me. So precious. And this is the biggest secret of them all, isn't it?''

''Yes, I suppose so.''

He still held her with fingers like steel. ''So, tell me of my death.''

Emma had hoped in her inmost heart to be able to barter with Sharpe, but it was impossible. Only her certainty that Jak, Doc and the others would be able to escape to safety kept her from collapse.

Her eyes closed, and she allowed the power to enclose her in its dark veil.

''Your tongue will turn to silver and you...you will pass through the mirror into the desert. And from there you will become nothing.''

The room was quiet. A small fire was burning in the hearth, and a log crumbled in on itself in a whisper of gray ash.

Sharpe let go of her and took a step backward.

''Tell me it again.''

''Your tongue will turn to silver and you will pass through the mirror into the desert. And from there you will become nothing.''

"Nothing?" His brow wrinkled. "How can I become nothing? That's impossible, woman."

"That is what I see."

"Then see something else. Something better that makes some sort of sense!"

"You want me to lie? Is that it, Baron? I'll lie if you want. You'll die on your hundred and fiftieth birthday in bed with your six teenage slut mistresses. That better? More the sort of crap you want to hear?"

He ignored her outburst. "A tongue of silver. A broken mirror. A desert. And . . . nothing."

"That's the truth. I don't know what it means, but that's all I see."

He nodded. "Well, and why not? Now we were going back to my collection of precious muties. Find you a home. And you shall be the sun in that system."

"Jak and Doc?"

"They can come or go, be drunk or sober, dead or alive for all I care."

"You swear they'll go free?"

"I promise you, Emma my doomie princess, that within the hour they will no longer be my prisoners."

And Sean Sharpe began to laugh.

Chapter Thirty-Three

Ryan just managed to divert the murderous blow with the panga, though the hissing blade brushed against Doc's left shoulder, making the old man jump sideways, starting to cut at Ryan with his drawn rapier.

"By the—!" he began, stopping himself at the instant realization that silence was vital in the middle of the sec patrolled ville.

"Sorry, Doc," Ryan whispered, turning to J.B. and adding the unnecessary comment, "It's Doc."

"So I see," the Armorer replied. "You nearly gave him a new close haircut there, friend."

"Said I was sorry. Didn't expect to find you wandering around free, Doc. We thought that the baron must've made you and Jak and Emma prisoners."

"Indeed he has. I should say that he did. No, that fails to meet the requirements of accuracy, as well."

"Doc..." Ryan said warningly.

"Of course, Ryan, my tried and trusty comrade. Let me be as concise as I can. Joaquin appeared from the whirling center of the tornado and took the three of us prisoner. He had his men with him or we—"

"Sure you would, Doc," J.B. said quietly. "Just get on with it, will you?"

"We were removed to a locked room, our guns taken from us. But they left me my sword and Jak his throwing knives. We agreed that we would—"

"Blood," Ryan said.

"What? Where?"

"On the blade of your rapier, Doc." He pointed to the drying smear of crimson. "Kind of fresh, too."

The old man sniffed, shaking his head. "I fear that your sight is all too good. But I put the cart before the horse. We agreed that as the oldest and most foolish they would guard me least. That was how Jak put it. The baron was all too interested in Emma's mutie skills."

"Where are they now?" J.B. asked.

"I have not yet reached the engorging of my reeking falchion. Though, if we are to be a trifle pedantic, my rapier can hardly be described as falcate since its blade is quite straight and true and shows not a curve. Anyway, I begged to be excused, and it was Joshua Morgan, the poor fellow, who finally agreed to accompany me to the jakes."

"Jakes?" Ryan queried.

"Bathroom. There I am afraid that I killed him with a single thrust of my sword. Not something I shall ever look back upon with any pride. Only the shame of being struck a coward's blow. It came with no warning, Ryan."

"Did the right thing, Doc." Ryan saw that the old man was genuinely distressed at what he saw as an act of willful murder. He put his arm across Doc's shoulders. "I swear you did right. This isn't the courts of King Edwin."

"Arthur, was his name, Ryan."

"Oh, you sure?"

"But, of course. Arthur Pendragon and the knights of the round table. Chivalry. A very parfait gentil knyght, as the poet Chaucer put it. You know that he wrote—"

"Dark night, Doc!"

"My apologies. Anyway, I have escaped after butchering poor Joshua Morgan. I have since been hiding and skulking around dark corners. There is no arras that has not enfolded me in its embrace. I attempted to return to our room. I was nearly caught on the way as I saw Mistress Tyler being escorted by Joaquin down to see the baron. I haven't been able to get to the Le Mat and Jak's cannon. They are by the dining room. If we can find those we could rescue Jak, could we not?"

Ryan nodded. "Sounds good to me. Get to the kid and then go after Emma."

The Armorer shook his head slowly. "Don't like the idea of leaving the young woman, but if we can spring Jak and all get out of here, I wonder if that might be enough. Let the rest lie where it falls."

Doc swung around and pointed at J.B. with the blood-slick point of his rapier. "Shame on you, John Barrymore Dix," he said loudly.

"Keep the noise down, Doc," Ryan hissed.

"Sorry. But I cannot just 'let it lie' as our bespectacled companion puts it. The young woman is traveling the highway with us, and it would be grossly unchivalrous of us to desert her. The spirit of King Arthur would spin in his tomb if he heard you, John Dix.''

''Yeah, I guess you're right. Don't tell Mildred I even suggested it. She'll just give me hard time number one. But I agree about going up to get Jak first. How many sec guards on the door, Doc?''

''I fear that I don't know for certain. There were four or five of them. I think one or two went with Joaquin. But by now there must be some alarm over my disappearance and the nonreturn of poor Master Morgan.''

''Cross that one when we reach it, Doc.'' Ryan glanced through the door. ''Jak's on the second or third floor?''

''Third floor back.''

''Then let's go.''

IN A GROVE OF SLENDER POPLARS, two hundred paces from the rear entrance to the ville, Krysty waited with Mildred and Dean, both women working hard to reassure the boy that everything was going well.

''You saw them go inside,'' the black woman said, running her fingers through her beaded plaits. ''And they were both pretty up and walking good then.''

''But there was a fight. The corpse of the sec man's still out there. I went and looked.''

''You shouldn't have gone without checking with me or with Mildred,'' Krysty chided.

''And I reckon I heard a shotgun.''

"We didn't hear it." Krysty stood to stretch her legs, taking a deep breath of the night air. "You know what your father said?"

"Sure. Wait until dawn. No word, we move back to the redoubt. Wait there for twenty-four hours until the next dawning. Then we jump out."

Krysty nodded, the moonglow catching the fiery radiance of her hair. "And that's what we do."

Dean grinned, his teeth white in the darkness. "Sorry, Krysty. I can just see you and Mildred walking away from Dad and from J.B. Sure you will."

THE SERVING WOMAN would have lived if she hadn't tried to scream a warning when she saw the three outlanders picking their way through the sleeping ville.

Her job was to rake the ashes from all of the fires, so that another servant could come around the house in a couple of hours and lay them fresh and light them, ready for a new day in Washington Hole.

J.B. was closest when she came walking sleepily around the corner of the second-floor corridor and he took a lightning-fast step in, the moment he saw her mouth open and the muscles of her throat become taut, ready to deliver the yell of warning. He brought the butt of the Uzi up under her chin.

There was a loud crunching sound and her head snapped back, eyes rolling white in their sockets. As she began to fall, Ryan stepped in and caught the iron bucket she'd been carrying. Her head hit the flags with a sickening sound, like an apple under a man's heel.

Doc gasped. "Did you have to strike her that hard? It looks as though the poor woman is no longer with us."

"She's chilled if that's what you mean, Doc," the Armorer said. "Didn't mean her to get to be dead. If she'd gotten off a scream, then we could all have wound up dead. It's the way it goes, Doc."

The old man said nothing, but his lips moved silently as though he were muttering a prayer for the departed spirit of the unlucky woman.

IN THE HEART of the darkness the ville was quiet, almost deserted.

Twice the three friends had to withdraw into the shadows as a patrol of two or three sec men went by. One of the groups stopped for a minute or so, within hearing.

"Joaquin's fit to be tied."

"Josh was a friend from years back."

"Right. Looks like it was the old bastard who did him with a hidden knife. Chilled him with a single blow, I heard."

"Joaquin came close to losing it all. Went after the baron."

"And old Sharpie didn't give a flyin' fuck about poor ol' Josh, did he?"

"No. Too locked up with that doomie slut."

"Where's he takin' her?"

"Down the zoo."

"Joaquin was pissing steam when he came back up the stairs. Said Sharpie was off on his mental wanderings. Couldn't get no sense from him. Just shooed Joaquin away like he was some beggar."

"Yeah. Told him to come back after breakfast. He was too busy until then."

"Didn't Joaquin say he was ramblin'? Sharpie?"

"Sure. Told Joaquin that he was speakin' to him with a tongue of silver. Somethin' about a mirror and goin' off to get himself lost in the desert."

The sec man laughed harshly. "Sooner that happens the better for this ville."

There was a mutter of agreement, then the three sec men wandered off along the corridor, leaving the main hallway of the house unguarded.

Ryan moved from the black space beneath the staircase, followed by J.B. and Doc. "Sharpe's got Emma and he's taking her to his zoo," he said.

"And I fear that they have found the body of poor Master Morgan." Doc bit his lip. "We should hasten to release Jak from his imprisonment. He was becoming markedly fond of the young lady. If anything were to happen to her..."

"You said that the blasters were being kept in there," J.B. said, pointing through the curtained archway toward the dining room.

"What I heard them say. I confess that I would feel more comfortable with my Le Mat holstered once more on my hip."

To Ryan's considerable surprise, the two guns lay unguarded on the table, exactly where Doc had been told. The old man picked up the gold-plated and engraved Le Mat, checked the action, watched by J.B.

Ryan tucked Jak's satin-finish Colt Python into his own belt.

"Didn't expect to find them unguarded," the Armorer said. "Getting sloppy."

"Sounds like Sharpe's losing control." Ryan glanced around. "When things start folding, they can run away like a brakeless war wag."

"How true is the saying that the center does not hold," Doc said in a sonorous voice.

"Yeah." Ryan rubbed a finger down his stubbled chin. "Let's go see about springing Jak."

EMMA STUMBLED ALONG like someone in a drugged, waking dream. She was vaguely aware from the acrid smell that Sean Sharpe had dragged her with him into the first part of his mutie collection. He sent his guards away, shouting angrily at them that he wanted to be left totally alone.

The door to the rest of the ville was closed, though Emma registered that the baron hadn't bothered to lock it. Once they were alone together in the relative stillness, Sharpe seemed to become a little more calm.

"There, now we can listen to the whispering voices, my own little doomie. We can find you a cage. Crude, I know, but it'll have to do for a while. We can add comforts as you tell me more of your secrets."

The young woman was feeling sick, her head spinning, prey to a vicious attack of vertigo. The rooms, with their cages and display cases, seemed to spin around her.

Sharpe stopped in front of the large sheet of plate glass that contained the sandy waste with the mysterious creature lying hidden within it, deep in the dry, barren earth. The overhead lamps turned the glass into a kind of mirror, reflecting the tall figure of the baron in his snowy robe, holding on to the black-clad woman, her face as white as parchment under the stark lighting.

Sharpe pressed his face against the cold glass, tapping softly on it with his fingers. The surface of the pale sand rippled for a moment, so quickly that you could almost think that you'd imagined it.

"This was my favorite pet. Oh, yes, it was. Yes, it was. It was!" His voice became louder. Once again the sand trembled, but there was nothing to be seen.

"Death," Emma whispered, but the baron was so busy with his ranting that he didn't hear her.

"Let's go on, shall we, doomie? Yes, we shall. Shall go on. All the way to the end."

"ALONG THERE," Doc whispered, gripping the huge Le Mat in the right hand, his walking stick in the other. "Hear the guards talking."

Ryan and J.B. were three-quarters of the way up the rear set of stairs that led to the room on the third floor where Jak was still, as far as they knew, being held prisoner.

The Armorer crawled up to the top and squinted around, returning to Ryan and Doc. "Four of them, holding pistols. Seem kind of alert."

"No way of making this quiet," Ryan said. "Fireblast! Then we might as well go in and open up. Have to let them know we're loose and running some time. Ready? Then we'll do it!"

Chapter Thirty-Four

The breaking glass and burst of automatic gunfire brought Mildred, Krysty and Dean to their feet.

"That was the Uzi," the boy crowed. "And I think it was Dad's SIG-Sauer. Sounded like they're in there and giving them some double-hot tar."

"On the top floor," Mildred said, peering out from the bushes toward the ville.

There was a yell that could have been either pain or anger. Krysty reckoned that it sounded like pain.

"Can't we try and find a way in, Krysty, please? Could be they need help."

She nodded. "Yeah, Dean. Mebbe they do. But the doors are going to be bolted and guarded. I know it's not what you want, but we still do what Ryan told us to do."

"Wait and watch!" His voice was sullen, and he kicked out at a loose pebble.

They all looked up as a single gunshot sounded into the night. But it wasn't repeated.

IT WASN'T MUCH of a firefight, closer to a massacre.

Ryan went up the final half flight of stairs, as swift and silent as a striking cobra, opening fire on the unsuspecting group of sec men as soon as they were in sight.

J.B. was right behind him, the Uzi snapping out a chain of death along the corridor.

Only one shot was fired in retaliation, and that was merely a postmortem reflex from one of the men as he went down, his finger going into spasm, pulling the trigger of his blaster, the hand-cast bullet breaking a window toward the rear of the house.

Apart from the sudden burst of gunfire, the attack was almost soundless. Only one of the guards even cried out, a single high-pitched scream of agony as a 9 mm round ripped into his groin.

The rest tumbled together, arms flailing, blood fountaining over the floor and the walls and dappling the white-plastered ceiling.

As Ryan and J.B. looked down at the charnel-house scene of writhing corpses and puddled crimson and splintered bones, Doc lumbered up behind them, knees creaking noisily.

"Upon my soul! I have my trusty Le Mat primed and ready and find that the skirmish is over and done."

"Open the door for Jak," Ryan said. "Key's already in the lock there."

One of the sec men was still alive, trying to get up on hands and knees, carrying three bullet wounds. Ryan leveled the SIG-Sauer at the base of his skull at close range and squeezed the trigger one more time.

"That's it."

"Likely to bring us some company," said J.B. "Looks like a staircase along the end there. Should bring us down somewhere close to the entrance to the baron's zoo."

Doc fumbled with the key, before he worked out that it was quicker to holster the Le Mat and lay the sword stick on the carpet, away from the spreading pool of blood, leaving both his hands free to open the door.

As soon as it swung back, Jak was in the doorway, hair tumbling about his shoulders like the spray from a winter fountain. His red eyes turned to Ryan, ignoring the tangled pile of corpses that lay at this feet.

"Emma? Baron?"

"Seems that he's taken her down to his collection, Jak. Anything happened we should know about?"

"Saw her own death. Drown in scarlet sea. Before she went down to see Sharpe, told me saw his death. Tongue's turned silver and broke mirror and vanished in desert."

Ryan shook his head. "Run that past me again, will you, Jak? I didn't—"

"No time."

"Wait. I got your Colt here."

But the teenager was already on the move, running through the dimly lighted corridor, hair blazing like a flare, calling back to Ryan over his shoulder.

"See you in zoo!"

Doc coughed, stooping to pick up his sword stick. "Should we not follow the young fellow?"

"Yeah," Ryan said. "We will. Right now."

IN HIS ANXIETY, Jak took a wrong turn at the bottom of the first flight of stairs, going to the left instead of right, finding himself in a series of abandoned rooms. There was no sign of stairs down to the first floor that would have brought him closer to the mutie collection.

And closer to the baron and Emma.

There was no sign of life in any of the rooms, except for the last of them.

Jak had thrown open a tall door, sending it crashing back onto its hinges. He coughed as the movement sent up a cloud of fine gray dust.

The room was much bigger than the others, with a high vaulted roof in black and white. It was filled with dozens of wooden carvings, all brightly painted, looking like parts of roots or branches that had been cut and polished and then covered in layers of startling colors.

A hammock was suspended between two of the taller sculptures, and the noise of Jak's entrance woke the occupant, an unbelievably ancient man in filthy clothes, with a ragged beard and a mane of long, matted hair.

"Who in the name of the imps of Beelzebub are you?" squawked a high, cracked, angry voice.

"How get to ground and baron's zoo?" Jak asked.

"Why do..." Venomous little eyes focused on the teenager. "You're a poxy mutie runt!"

Jak suddenly noticed a narrow iron staircase that spiraled down from the far corner of the room. Without any hesitation he ran through the room, leaving footprints in the dust, past the hammock, to the top of the stairs.

"You've not seen my collection, you snow-top bastard! First visitor in a year or more and you don't wait to—"

The vituperative anger drifted into silence behind Jak as he raced around the dizzy staircase, emerging through a creaking door at the bottom to find himself behind a huge moth-eaten tapestry. The light was poor, but Jak's night sight was preternaturally sharp, and he could see that the wall-hanging showed a handsome youth swooning away as he was attacked by a pack of hunting dogs, while an elegant woman with a bow looked down at his distress with an expression of vicious sensuality.

Jak cautiously looked around the corner of the tapestry, seeing that he was in a wide passage with torches flickering in all sconces.

He recognized it from his previous visit to the mutie collection, knowing that only one door now separated him from Emma and the baron.

RYAN HAD LED Doc and J.B. back down the flight of stairs that had brought them up to the third floor of the mansion. He turned to his right and headed for the main stairs that would bring them to the first floor and give them access to the part of the ville that housed the mutie collection.

A tall plump sec man appeared at the far end of the corridor, hastily pulling on his green jacket. As soon as he saw the three outlanders moving fast toward him, he yelped and bolted back around the corner like a startled rabbit. There wasn't much time for a clear shot at him, but there was no longer any point in needlessly killing anyone.

They'd sprung Jak, and Ryan had the strong feeling that events were now moving inexorably toward their ending, going faster and faster, like the progress of a lethal rad cancer. He doubted that the race would still be being run by dawn.

There was nobody around the stairs to the dining room, and Ryan paused a moment, halfway down, the short hairs prickling at his nape.

"We got someone . . ." he began warningly, when a musket fired from above and behind them.

The ball thudded into the rounded oak balustrade, eight inches from his left hand, stripping away a long splinter of white wood. Ryan spun, seeing the give-away cloud of black powder smoke hanging in the air, a yard from the top of the wide staircase. He had the SIG-Sauer already drawn, and he aimed and fired as part of the same lightning reflex.

He heard a yell of pain and a body falling to the floor, and a musket clattered down the stairs, sliding all the way to the bottom.

As Ryan turned back, moving toward the dining room, Joaquin appeared by the door that led through to the rear of the ville. He was holding a machine pistol in his right hand and had two men with him, both armed with the old cap-and-ball revolvers.

"Far enough, outlander," he said.

Ryan paused on the bottom step. J.B. was just behind him, Doc about halfway down.

"Ville's tighter than a duck's ass, Cawdor." The torchlight shone on the sec chief's grizzled hair. "You got nowhere to go from here. Men above you. Doors secure."

"We got in."

Joaquin nodded. He was tense, every nerve strained and alert. "Like to know how. My guess is around back, but there hasn't been time to check it. Also, Sharpie told us to keep out of his zoo. He's in there with the doomie slut." He smiled mirthlessly at them. "Guess he's real busy and don't want no onlookers right now."

"You going to face this one down?" J.B. asked. "Three against three. But we got the better blasters."

"Stuck halfway up the stairs. Doesn't leave you room to jump, does it? And it ain't three against three. There's half a dozen more in the hallway above you. More scattered around the ville. They don't like the fact that Josh Morgan got butchered." He stared accusingly at Doc. "We know you did that, old man. Be a reckoning soon."

Doc coughed. "I had no wish to take his life. But he would not accede to reason."

Joaquin sniffed. "Reasons aren't worth puma shit in a thunderstorm!"

"Time's running, Ryan," J.B. whispered. "Better we get to the baron soon as we can. Jak might be there by now."

Ryan nodded. "Yeah."

Joaquin gestured with the machine pistol, which looked to Ryan like a hacked-down, altered version of the old M-3 submachine gun. "Cut the muttering. You putting the blasters down, or do we take you all out?"

Ryan's combat mind was racing, considering all the various possibilities, rejecting most of them, setting other ideas to one side.

Trader used to say that talk beat shooting. But if talking didn't work, then that only left shooting.

"All we want is Emma."

Joaquin sniffed. "Doomie slut?"

Ryan nodded. "Yeah. We find the baron. Take her from him. We all leave. Easy as that."

The sec boss laughed. "Easy as that?" he mocked. "I don't think so. Baron pays us. Feeds us. You got to have some sort of respect for that, Cawdor. Not counting the blood debt for Josh Morgan and the others." He shook his head. "No, I don't think so."

The range was around twenty yards. If the sec man had been armed with a revolver like the others, there would have been no need to waste time on talking. But the machine pistol could be lethal at that distance.

J.B. had exchanged the Uzi for the eight-round scattergun, feeling it might be better suited if they ran into a close-combat situation.

"Me, Ryan," he breathed.

The one-eyed man didn't say anything to his old friend, just nodded once.

J.B. had been holding the shotgun down low, against his thigh, hidden from the sight of the sec men by Ryan's body. Now he eased it forward. Ryan knew what was going to happen and moved his right arm a little away from his side, leaving a narrow gap for J.B. to push the Smith & Wesson M-4000 through.

"Not goin' to change your mind, outlander? Sure?" the sec chief asked.

"Do it," Ryan said.

He felt the shock of the explosion between his ribs and arm, and moved sideways, opening fire with the SIG-Sauer at the group of men, seeing them going down. He spun to put a burst of full-metal jackets into the dark at the top of the stairs.

J.B. fired a second round into the wounded sec men, while Doc stood half up the staircase, hesitating.

Each of the shotgun's 12-gauge rounds held twenty of the murderous Remington fléchettes, inch-long steel darts that scythed through the still air of the hall, spreading out a little by the time they reached Joaquin and his two henchmen. They cut into and through flesh, muscle and soft tissue, scraping off bones, distorting as they angled sideways, causing terrible injuries.

Ryan put Joaquin and one of the sec men out of their misery with bullets to chest and throat, while the second charge from the Armorer's Smith & Wesson chilled the last man, who had already sunk screaming to hands and knees, fingers groping at the bloody mask of his face, where the tiny arrows had jellied his eyes.

There was a shout of pain from the landing above them and the sound of running feet, fading into the distance.

J.B. had pumped another round under the hammer, and he stood still, eyes raking the dining room ahead of him, turning to peer into the dim light of the stairs above.

"Think that's it," he said.

"Looks that way," Ryan agreed, his good eye turning from side to side as he carefully reloaded the five spent rounds into the big automatic. "Scared the rest off."

"By the Three Kennedys! I had no idea that you were about to release those miniature arrows, John Barrymore! My beloved Le Mat remains unfired."

"If you'd been a little closer you could have taken them all out with a single round, Doc," the little man said. "But you weren't, so you didn't."

"That way." Ryan pointed across the dining room toward the rear of the building. "Can't take any more time."

DESPITE KRYSTY'S and Mildred's efforts, Dean had insisted on moving closer to the back door of the ville. The new burst of firing and shouts had driven him close to panic.

"Dad's getting chilled in there, and we sit out here with our thumbs up our asses!" he hissed at Krysty.

"Give it another ten minutes. Nothing happens, then we'll go in. All right?"

The boy nodded. "Sure hope we won't be too bastard late, Krysty. There's some bad things going down in there!"

Chapter Thirty-Five

"I think this would do well for you. Oh, yes, I think it will."

Emma's arms were bruised from Sharpe's steely grip, and there was a dark swelling on her right cheek where he'd casually backhanded her for refusing to come with him into the dank, dark rear part of the building.

She had briefly seen the occupants of the four cages: the pathetic stickie and the poor mad old scabbie, the crazed twins and the tall young man. Only the last of them had taken any notice of the baron and his hapless victim. He had moved slowly to the front of his foul-smelling cage, bare feet brushing through the urine-soaked straw, skinny fingers grasping at the rusting iron bars, eyes staring wildly.

"The stone will lie deep in the water, and the water shall become dry dust," he said loudly.

Emma's golden eyes opened wide, staring at the man. "You have something of the power," she said quietly.

"Power is knowledge and I have little of that. I know that the nuke walls will crumble and the wind carry sightless death around the world to blight the pasture and the animals and people.''

Sharpe had pulled her away with a snort of disgust. ''His life is measured in hours. Yes, it is. Why feed a midget when you can have a giant chained to your table?''

Now they stood in front of the last cage in line.

It stood in almost total darkness, its stained concrete floor swept bare, the heavy metal door hanging open.

''At least let me die in the light,'' she begged.

''No, here is where you'll stay. If you give me what I need, then I might allow you to be imprisoned within the house. But not yet. The iron fist comes first and then the glove of velvet, my dear little Emma.''

''There is so much death here.'' She shuddered in his hands. ''Dear God, so much death.''

Sharpe smiled at her, the torchlight dancing off his cold milky eyes. ''So right, doomie. Think of being imprisoned here. At the end of the world. Sentenced to endless misery. Perhaps I might die in some accident and then you would be forgotten. Oh, yes, such neglect. It has happened before. I have sometimes quite forgotten about my pets through listening to my own private voices, and they have not been fed or watered. One wretch bit off his own hand and drank his own blood to sustain life.'' He threw back his head and laughed loudly, the echoes quickly fading, muffled by the oppressive weight of the thick walls and ceiling.

The baron gazed proudly at the empty cage, nodding to himself as he anticipated the pleasure of seeing Emma locked away inside it.

"I've already told you what I see of our deaths. That shows you can trust me."

"You to drown in an ocean of red. Me to speak with a tongue of silver and vanish through a mirror into a desert where I shall cease to be. Oh, yes. Yes, I heard all that." He lowered his face close to her. "But you don't think I'd be fooled by your carny medicine show gabble? Oh, no! Lies all lies, woman!"

He slapped her again, making her nose bleed.

"It's truth," she protested, swaying in his grip.

"Lies, lies, lies, lies, lies." He smiled at her. "Let us open up your new home, doomie slut."

"No!" She screamed loud enough to shatter crystal at fifty paces, then dropped her head and sank her teeth into his wrist, making him curse and let her go.

Emma turned and started to run away, back toward the main part of the collection, toward the half-open door into the rest of the ville. And a last chance of life.

Jak, less than a hundred yards away, darting through a maze of narrow passages, heard the scream and began to run even faster toward its source.

Sharpe caught up with Emma in the main room of the mutie animals and reptiles, just past the doorway that led into the chamber where the vast glass case held the mysterious hidden monster in the warm sand.

"Stupe bitch," he said, laughing delightedly. "Oh, yes, what a stupe bitch." He paused, posing as he caught sight of his reflection in the mirrored glass."

"Please," she whispered.

"No."

He began a swift, brutal beating, holding her against the wall by one hand, while he punched and slapped at her with the other. Both eyes closed and her mouth split, blood trickling down her chin and over the front of her black dress.

"Doomies...do...what...they're told." Each word was punctuated by savage punches, knocking her head from side to side like a disjointed doll.

Emma slipped quickly into merciful unconsciousness, but the baron didn't seem aware of it. Grinning mirthlessly, nodding as if he were agreeing to some whispered instructions from an invisible presence, he continued the beating.

Teeth splintered and sliced her tongue open, releasing a flood of scarlet.

"Lie there until you learn sense, doomie!" Sharpe snarled, suddenly throwing her to the floor.

Emma lay where he dropped her, half in the doorway between the rooms. She was on her back, mouth open, the flow of blood trickling steadily down her throat and into the air passages to her lungs, beginning to drown her.

RYAN, J.B. AND DOC had suffered another brief delay in their pursuit of Jak, and the baron and Emma.

Someone had loosed a pack of hunting dogs into the rear of the ville, and they came snarling toward the three outlanders.

At last Doc had the chance to use the Le Mat, aiming into the middle of the animals, pulling down on the trigger.

The .63-caliber shotgun round, fired at thirty feet, tore into the dogs with a devastating effect, killing three and injuring half of the rest of the pack.

The survivors, including the wounded, turned tail and scampered, howling, down a side passage and vanished behind a length of tapestry that concealed a small door.

"Ace on the line, Doc," Ryan called as they hurried on.

JAK HAD HESITATED a moment as he heard the thunderous boom of Doc's blaster and the barking of the dogs. But after the shot the noise faded quickly into stillness, and he ran on.

He was only a few paces now from the half-open door into the collection.

SHARPE HAD DRAGGED Emma into the middle of the room, beside the big glass case with its strange desert landscape. A trail of blood smeared along the floor, as he pulled her by the feet, head scraping along the concrete, most of it seeming to spill from her sagging, open mouth.

"Playing dead on me, doomie? We know how to deal with that, don't we? Oh, yes, my precious."

He let go of her feet and knelt astride Emma, hands gripping her throat, tightening.

"Wake up, little doomie. Wake up. Don't play sound asleep." He started to giggle, squeezing tighter. "Can't see your silver tongue. Looks big and purple to me, doomie. Oh, no. Oh, no. It was my tongue that went silver. You sank... What was it?"

The golden eyes were wide open, protruding from the dark, swollen sockets, staring sightlessly over Sharpe's shoulder. Blood still poured between her purpled lips.

The body shuddered as though possessed by a violent ague, then went completely limp.

The baron continued to squeeze at the slender neck for several seconds, then he stopped and sat back on the body, his face puzzled. "Doomie's can't die," he whispered.

He stood and kicked at the corpse, shaking his head when there was no resistance, wiping his hands down the front of his white robe, staring at the crimson smears. He looked at the dead woman, a small ocean of blood around her head, matting her black hair.

"Dead?" he said in a loud conversational voice. "Drowned in an ocean of crimson?"

JAK HAD OPENED THE DOOR silently, hearing strange grunting sounds from one of the farther rooms, then a silence.

"Dead? Drowned in an ocean of crimson?" The voice was unmistakably that of Baron Sean Sharpe.

Jak tiptoed onward, seeing a single shadow, motionless, thrown on the wall of the room that he was in, coming through the door of the chamber that he remembered held the bizarre mutie creature that lived deep beneath the surface of the pale sand in its cage.

"So? What the fuck do I care?" It was Baron Sharpe, but who was he talking to? "Plenty of doomies on the beach. And fish in the ocean. Ocean of crimson. Scarlet. Red. Bloodred ocean. Oh, yes, red is the color of my true love's blood. Go down, you bloodred roses. The old song." A peal of wild laughter chilled the heart of the albino teenager.

He stepped through the door and saw Sharpe standing there, his back to him, wearing a white robe that was streaked with blood. And lying on the floor at his feet was . . .

"Emma," Jak said.

The baron swung around, his right hand falling to the butt of the satin-finish .357 Magnum Ruger GP-160 in his belt. And Jak saw that the crumpled front of his robe was totally sodden with blood.

Emma was lying still, on her back, arms spread wide, her golden eyes already fading in death. She was surrounded by a lake of blood.

"Ah, white-hair! See that your friend here is in a trance. She has been telling me such truths about living and . . . Living and partly living."

"You sick bastard!"

For a moment Jak wished that he had taken back his own blaster from Ryan when he'd had the chance.

Regret was for roads not taken, and it was point-less.

"Sick murderous bastard!" he spit, feeling grief battling with a bloody rage.

Baron Sharpe was backing toward the glass wall of the container behind him, with its simulated desert landscape. Jak watched the two images of the man, one facing him, the other retreating in the mirrored glass.

The hand still rested on the butt of the Ruger, but the baron hadn't drawn it. His milky blue eyes were looking at Jak, as though he were someone that Sharpe recognized from some previous incarnation. "Oh, yes, I think... Your name is Jak, isn't it? I know you well, I think."

"You killed Emma." The voice was flat.

"No. She was dead when I found her."

"Liar." The accusation was no louder than a whis-per.

"I am the baron of this ville. I am Sean Sharpe. No outlander child comes in here and calls me a liar."

"Liar," Jak repeated.

They were about fifteen feet apart.

Now, very slowly, like a lover's caress, Sharpe had begun to draw the Ruger.

"Yes, I hear what... He will be. I will punish him myself. Yes, I will."

The Ruger was halfway out.

"She was innocent and meant no harm. No reason chill her. Shouldn't."

"Hear my silver tongue, boy." A crackle of loud laughter rang out, so loud that Ryan heard it as he approached the door to the mutie collection.

The Ruger was full-out, barrel questing toward the heart of the albino teenager.

"Die, mutie." Baron Sharpe's mouth was wide open in a smile of purest pleasure.

Jak's fingers closed on the taped hilt of one of his delicate throwing knives, whipping it from behind his back with a snap of the wrist, sending the leaf-shaped, polished steel blade hissing to its target.

It struck home with inexorable perfection.

Jak had aimed at the laughing center of the baron's face, the gaping, grinning mouth.

The spinning knife pinned Sharpe's tongue to the roof of his mouth, shining silver between the teeth, the point driving upward.

There was a hideous gurgling sound from the wounded man, and he staggered sideways. The blaster swung aimlessly around the room, and his finger tightened spasmodically on the trigger, firing one of the .357 rounds. The bullet struck a roof pillar and ricocheted back down and behind Sharpe, smashing the center of the thick glass wall of the container at his back, which collapsed in a tumbling river of shards of mirrored glass.

The blaster dropped, clattering to the floor, and Baron Sharpe stumbled three paces away from Jak. His hips were just above the level of the bottom of the broken cage and he simply fell backward, slumping into the dry heated desert sand.

As he fell back, his hands went to his mouth and he tried to remove the knife that had made him dumb. But it was driven home too hard. His eyes were wide with horror as he realized where he was, and he kicked his legs helplessly in the air, the bloodied robe riding up to expose his bare flesh.

Jak thought he was trying to say something.

It could have been "He tore it," or "She saw it."

Yes, that was it.

The sand erupted in a spray as the man flailed and thrashed, trying to recover his balance and get out of the container that held the mysterious mutie beast.

Ryan appeared behind Jak in the doorway, with J.B. close at his heels, Doc a few paces farther back.

All four of them stood frozen to watch the last dreadful scene of the life of Baron Sean Sharpe.

The sand seemed to be alive, writhing and churning into tiny funnels that seemed to be slowly sucking the helpless man deep into its embrace. Sharpe was still trying to scream, his face contorted in a rictus of fear and agony.

One arm plunged below the surface of the sand and, when the doomed baron pulled it clear again, the hand was missing. The stump was matted with tiny grains of sand, now crimson, but the jetting wound showed clean and smooth, as though it had been cut off with a surgeon's saw.

"Lord have mercy on him," Doc breathed, "whatever his sins."

None of the others spoke.

Sharpe was sinking deeper, and the eruptions of sand were all flecked with blood and occasional glistening white splinters that might have been bone. But at no time did the terrifying mutie creature show itself, though Ryan thought for a moment that he saw, beneath the flying dust, a number of mouths, as large as a man's palm, each with rows of serrated teeth that seemed to be revolving at high speed, surrounded by sinewy layers of sucking lips.

But he couldn't be certain.

Sharpe had almost disappeared, only his head showing, thrown back in straining agony.

The room was almost soundless, except for a muffled, munching kind of noise, with an occasional crunching snap to it, like a bone splintering.

A brace of heartbeats later and the broken-fronted case was clear and empty, except for the ruffled surface of pale sand. Even the blood had gone, and it looked again like a stretch of untouched desert.

"Dark night! I never saw anything . . . anything like that before," J.B. said, having first noisily cleared his throat, taking off his glasses and wiping them on his sleeve. "And I don't think I ever want to again."

"He beat up and chilled Emma," Ryan said, stooping to check that she was truly dead.

"Yeah." Jak looked balefully at the cage. "And I lost knife, too."

"Why not go in after it?" J.B. asked. "If it matters that much."

Jak shook his head. "No. Nothing matters now."

"I am truly sorry." Doc laid a hand on the teenager's shoulder. "She was a good person whom God had given a dreadful burden to carry through life."

"Best get out of here." Ryan looked around. "Want to take her body along with us, Jak? We can probably give her a decent burying someplace."

"No. Thanks, Ryan. Emma's gone. What's left is...like suit of clothes."

"Come on, then."

They went quickly to the back door and left the ville without encountering any kind of threat. Though there were lights blazing everywhere, not a single shot was fired.

Dean, Krysty and Mildred were waiting to greet them as they came out into the cool air of Washington Hole.

"What happened, Dad?"

"Long story, son. Have to wait the telling. Best we get back to the redoubt right away."

THE SOLITARY ROOM, inside the stinking depths of the late baron's mutie collection, was quiet again, except for a single odd incident. About a quarter of an hour after the four men had left, the sand belched open and there, on top of it, lay Jak's throwing knife, the polished silver of the steel covered in great scratches and gouges.

Chapter Thirty-Six

They traveled quickly and safely back to the corpse-filled redoubt, skirting a nameless pesthole as well as the shantytown called Green Hill, reaching the ancient complex near dawn.

The air was unusually clear and they stood grouped together, looking across at the gigantic crater of fused black glass that was all that remained of the old predark capital of the United States of America.

"Rad count's still high, up in the yellow band," J.B. observed.

"Mine shows close to orange." Ryan laughed. "Mebbe the next jump'll take us someplace away from a high rad count."

"Be good if it took us clear out of Deathlands," Mildred said. "Sometimes I find the shooting and the dying gets me down some."

"The only time that happened was when we became transported to Russia," Doc said, "and I can't say that was one of the happiest experiences of my life."

"Least we all got away safe from the big Hole." Dean realized immediately what he'd said and he looked quickly across to Jak. "Hey, I'm real sorry about saying somethin' that was so triple stupe. I didn't..."

The albino shrugged his shoulders. "Guess losing's something you sort of get used to. Wasn't like with Christina and Jenny. Deep. Heart-deep. But still sorry. Emma was... Could have... You know."

THE SENSE OF DAMAGE was more clear-cut within the redoubt. The cracks seemed wider, the dust thicker. The scent of old, old death lay more heavily in the nostrils and on the senses, an awareness of the futility that had been life in the last years before the nuke-caust.

Doc pointed with his sword stick at a slashed piece of graffiti, carved into the plaster on the wall. "Living is mistakes not made."

"I wonder whether our dear old companion Trader might not have passed this way at some time," he pondered.

"Could be," Ryan agreed. "Sounds like him."

"You think that we'll ever meet up with Trader again?" Dean asked.

Ryan flicked dust from his son's hair. "Who knows? All things are possible, aren't they?"

AS THEY DREW CLOSER to the entrance to the gate-way, Jak called for them to stop. "Blood on floor," he said, pointing to a small cluster of black spots, touching them with his forefinger. "Not fresh. But only days old. Not years."

"None of us had any injuries." Ryan stooped and examined the marks. "Yeah. Agree with what you say, Jak."

The albino crouched down, examining them very carefully. "From shape you can tell which way moving." He pointed ahead of them, along the corridor, toward the mat-trans unit itself. "Person bleeding was walking that way. Dust's too messed up to tell more. Mostly our old tracks."

As they rounded the bend, J.B., who was leading, held up his hand in warning. "Sec door's open. We closed it."

"You sure, John?" Mildred looked at the Armorer, who simply nodded. "Yeah, guess we did. We always do."

"Condition red," Ryan said unnecessarily, as everyone had already drawn their blasters.

There was more blood on the green handle, smeared in a blurred handprint on the concrete wall at the side.

"Woman or child," Jak said. "Small."

The fact that the bloodstain was days old meant it was probably safe, but Ryan hadn't lived as long as he had by taking foolish chances.

"I'll go in with J.B. and Jak," he said. "Rest of you wait here. Won't take long."

It took less than five minutes.

The control room and the small anteroom were all empty, and they could see through the sky blue armaglass that the gateway chamber itself was clearly devoid of life.

But they found something.

J.B. spotted it, rolled under one of the desks near the entrance through to the chamber.

"Look at this," he called.

They all gathered around him as he bent and picked the object up, laying it on the control console.

It was a helmet of archaic design, mounted with a carved bronze moon.

"Samurai," Doc breathed. "That was the one worn by the fellow who had the bow and arrow. I recognize that lunar design on top of it."

Ryan nodded. "Seems like the shot found its target, Doc. There's more blood around the side of it, and the throat strap's been cut. See the ragged ends. One of the pieces of buckshot from the Le Mat must've done that."

"He was wounded and managed to get this far back. Then he must've jumped, Dad."

"Right, Dean. I spotted more congealed blood on the handle of the mat-trans chamber."

They stood in a silent circle, staring at the intricate workmanship on the helmet, engravings of big birds like storks, and flowers with frilled petals, an ornamental bridge between two little temples.

"Beautiful," said Krysty. "Sort of thing you'd only see in a... What were those places called, Mildred?"

"Museums."

"That's it. Really lovely."

Dean picked it up and tried it on, finding that it was a little too small for him. "Hey, the guy has a real double-shrunk head."

"Take it off and leave it there," Ryan said.

"Can't I keep it, Dad?"

"No."

"Why?"

Ryan looked at his son, feeling a sudden welling of anger at the repeated questions, but controlling it. "Because the man who owns it might come back for it. Good enough reason?"

"But he tried to chill Doc. Why can't I take a dump in it, Dad?"

"Because we aren't animals, and I don't think that the man who owns the helmet is, either. Now leave it lie and let's get on with the jump."

When he opened the door of the chamber, Ryan consciously tried to avoid touching the patch of clotted blood.

"More inside," Mildred said.

"Can you tell anything from it?" Ryan asked. "Kind of how bad it might be?"

"No. Clusters on the floor where he sat down. I guess Doc's shot must have taken him high up. Face or neck and shoulders. At that range it would've probably starred out a lot. Not enough to show how serious the wound is, but it looks like it was getting worse. Might be the effort of returning here made the bleeding worse. That often happens."

"Where in Hades did a Japanese samurai warrior come from?" Doc said. "Seems like they know how the gateways work. They come and go. And we've heard these strange rumors of gangs of them raiding around, all over Deathlands."

"Guess we'll never know." J.B. was picking his spot to sit down on the floor, avoiding the metal disks. "Unless we accidentally jump right on top of them, one of these fine days."

"I can't hardly wait," Ryan said. "Come on, people. Let's get out of here. I'm sure I can feel that rad hot spot eating into my bones."

The Armorer sat himself first, taking off his fedora and brushing dust from it, laying it on the floor on his left. He folded his glasses for safety and put them in a pocket of his jacket. The Uzi stayed in his lap, the big Smith & Wesson scattergun on the floor on his right, ready for his hand.

Mildred sat next to him, the beads in her plaited hair rattling against the sky blue armaglass walls of the chamber, folding her hands in her lap and waiting patiently for the next jump to begin.

Dean was next in line, wriggling to his left to miss the speckled spots of blood.

"May I join you?" Doc asked with a small bow, smiling at the boy's nod. "Well, thank 'ee, Master. Thank 'ee. I shall attempt to avoid puking all of my last miserable meal up all over you, but don't blame me if—"

Krysty pulled a disgusted face. "Do you have to, Doc? It's up to the elderly to show a good example to the young. Not teach them bad manners."

"I stand reproached, ma'am," Doc said. "Or, to be more accurate, I sit reproached."

Krysty was next to him, leaving a space for Ryan to join her once he'd safely locked the door.

"Make sure you do it properly this time, lover. Don't fancy another jump like the last one. I'm sure a good part of my brain cells are floating around somewhere in the deep black heart of cold space."

Jak sat next to J.B., completing the circle. His white face was set like stone, and he kept his ruby eyes downward, staring at the floor.

"You all right?" Mildred asked.

"Been better. Thinking of Emma. Never had chance. Mutie power like that can only chill you."

"Guess that's right," Krysty agreed. "Might be she's better off, resting easy now."

Doc laid his hand on his chest, a sure sign he was about to declaim. "It is a far, far better rest that I go to, than I ever known." He smiled gravely. "The excellent Mr. Dickens said that."

"Nice," Jak said.

Ryan looked around, handing the Steyr rifle to Krysty to put on the floor. "We all ready? Good. Then here we go."

He closed the door, making sure that the lock had clicked securely into place, triggering the mat-trans system, beginning the jump.

After sitting quickly next to Krysty, he stretched out his legs and leaned back against the wall, reaching his right hand to take her left hand tightly in it.

There was the usual faint humming noise, and the disks in the floor and ceiling started to glow brightly.

Ryan felt his brains beginning to blur and his vision grew dim. The familiar mist gathered high above him.

He closed his eye.

Chapter Thirty-Seven

The sick darkness was passing.

Ryan steadied his breathing, conscious that the jump had been one of the easiest that he could remember. There had been none of the hideous gibbering dreams that sometimes swam out of the black horror of a bad jump.

He felt slightly sick, there was a throbbing pressure behind his eye and his stomach felt as though it had gone ten rounds with a rabid mule.

"Fireblast," he whispered to himself, still not risking opening his eye.

Ryan was conscious that his hand was still being gripped by Krysty. That in itself was a sign that the mat-trans unit had functioned well.

All he needed to know now was whether everyone was all right, and where the jump had taken them.

He breathed in slowly, aware that the air felt very hot and moist.

And *green*.

Ryan opened his eye.

The wheels of retribution are turning in Somalia

STONY MAN™ 17
VORTEX

Sanctioned to take lethal action to stop the brutal slaughter of innocents, the Stony Man team challenges the campaign of terror waged by two Somali warlords. But in the killing grounds the Stony Man warriors are plunged into a full-blown war fueled by foreign powers with a vested interest in the outcome of this struggle.

In September, don't miss
the exciting conclusion to

D.A. HODGMAN

STAKEOUT SQUAD

THE COLOR
OF BLOOD

The law is the first target in a tide of killings engulfing Miami
in the not-to-be-missed conclusion of this urban police
action series. Stakeout Squad becomes shock troops in a
desperate attempt to pull Miami back from hell, but here
even force of arms may not be enough to halt the hate and
bloodshed....

Don't miss THE COLOR OF BLOOD, the final installment of
STAKEOUT SQUAD!

Look for it in September, wherever Gold Eagle books are sold.

**Don't miss out on the action in these titles featuring
THE EXECUTIONER®, ABLE TEAM® and PHOENIX FORCE®!**

SuperBolan

#61436	HELLGROUND In this business, you get what you pay for. Iberra's tab is running high—and the Executioner has come to collect.	$4.99	☐
#61438	AMBUSH Bolan delivers his scorched-earth remedy—the only answer for those who deal in blood and terror.	$4.99 U.S. $5.50 CAN.	☐ ☐

Stony Man™

#61894	STONY MAN #10 SECRET ARSENAL A biochemical weapons conspiracy puts America in the hot seat.	$4.99	☐
#61896	STONY MAN #12 BLIND EAGLE Sabotaged U.S. satellite defenses leave the Mideast prey to a hungry predator.	$4.99 U.S. $5.50 CAN.	☐ ☐

(limited quantities available on certain titles)

TOTAL AMOUNT	$
POSTAGE & HANDLING	$
($1.00 for one book, 50¢ for each additional)	
APPLICABLE TAXES*	$_____
TOTAL PAYABLE	$_____
(check or money order—please do not send cash)	

To order, complete this form and send it, along with a check or money order for the total above, payable to Gold Eagle Books, to: **In the U.S.:** 3010 Walden Avenue, P.O. Box 9077, Buffalo, NY 14269-9077; **In Canada:** P.O. Box 636, Fort Erie, Ontario, L2A 5X3.

Name:_____

Address:_____ City:_____

State/Prov.:_____ Zip/Postal Code:_____

*New York residents remit applicable sales taxes.
 Canadian residents remit applicable GST and provincial taxes.

GEBACK10A